Other Books
by Rae D. Magdon and Michelle Magly

All the Pretty Things

Dark Horizons Series
Dark Horizons – Book 1

Rae D. Magdon
Amendyr Series
The Second Sister - Book 1
Wolf's Eyes - Book 2
The Witch's Daughter - Book 3

Michelle Magly
Chronicles of Osota - Warrior

D1713304

Starless Night

By
Rae D. Magdon
&
Michelle Magly

Desert Palm Press

Starless Nights
(Dark Horizons - Book 2)

By **Rae D. Magdon and Michelle Magly**

©2015 **Rae D. Magdon and Michelle Magly**

ISBN: 9781517503666

Editor: Kellie Doherty (http://editreviseperfect.weebly.com)
Cover Design: Rachel George (http://www.rachelgeorgeillustration.com/)

Printed in the United States of America
First Edition October 2015

Acknowledgments

There are a few people we need to thank for this book. Without them, we would have never finished it, and we appreciate the support they have provided us through this project. We would first like to thank our respective partners. Both provided support and insight into the writing process when we struggled. Thanks to our editor, Kellie, and to our cover designer, Rachel. Both were instrumental in making this book everything it could be. Finally, thank you, Lee, for keeping us moving forward.

.

Dedication

To our fans.

Chapter One

LIGHT STUNG RACHEL HARRIS' eyes as soon as she stepped through the door. She winced and raised a hand to her forehead, shielding her eyes to get a better view of the room. She couldn't see much with the floodlights aimed at her face, but if she squinted, she could just make out a long row of shadowed figures seated in high-backed chairs. Her stomach dropped. Every person of rank near San Diego Base had to be here, though she could not see who they were. They would hide from her even at her own trial. The door shut behind her with a loud clang, and her shoulders suddenly felt heavier. It took effort to keep them straight.

"Rachel Harris," a deep voice said, coming from the middle of the group. She recognized it immediately. General Hunt was usually fair, but as the commanding officer of the base, he was ultimately responsible for the recent events that had brought her here. "You are charged with treason against the Coalition. According to reports, you aided Lieutenant Taylor Morgan's escape from Earth with a valuable prisoner of war. How do you plead?"

Rachel locked her hands behind her back and chose a spot on the wall to stare at. She was the scapegoat. That had been clear since they first accused her. They needed someone to pin their mistakes on, and she was the lowest-ranking soldier involved. Of course she had to take the fall. "Not guilty, Sir."

"So you've stated before." Hunt glanced down at the datasheet in his hand, scrolling down the glowing screen. "Your statement says that you followed Chairman Bouchard's orders in an attempt to capture the fugitives when they tried to escape."

Fugitives. The word made her stomach clench. Even though it was technically true, it felt like a mask. Taylor was a traitor, an outlaw. Yet only a few weeks ago, they had been close friends. Before that damn ikthian's arrival, this situation would have been unthinkable for both of them. She pushed the thought aside and nodded. "That's correct, Sir."

1

Hunt set the sheet back on the table and stared directly at her. Rachel kept her shoulders squared, refusing to cower under his gaze. Even though she was already guilty in his eyes, she didn't want to look it. "Chairman Bouchard is neither a military official nor your commanding officer. He is only a liaison between the Coalition and the military. Why did you defer to his orders instead of approaching your commanding officer with your concerns?"

Rachel had heard it all before. This might be her official sentencing, but she had already been found guilty a month ago, the night Taylor had escaped with Maia Kalanis. "Sir, I approached Chairman Bouchard because I also suspected Commander Michael Roberts of treason. He was close with Lieutenant Morgan, and—"

"You failed to follow the appropriate chain of command," someone else interrupted, although she couldn't tell who was speaking. "Your disregard for protocol came with too high a price."

"I know I failed. I'm not denying it." She had done worse than fail. She had kept quiet when Taylor had been assigned to guard the ikthian prisoner. She had done nothing when her friend started to show signs of being bewitched by the alien's powers. She had waited too long, and during her last chance to make things right, she let Taylor get away. She'd had a gun pointed at Taylor, but she hadn't been able to use it.

"We've also taken a statement from Chairman Bouchard," the voice continued. This time, she recognized General Lee's face through the glare. He was another of the Coalition's five generals, and if the number of seats in front of her was any indication, the rest of them were in attendance as well. She swallowed back a rising lump in her throat. "He claims the traitor, Lieutenant Morgan, was responsible for the death of Commander Roberts. Your statement claims otherwise. Would you care to elaborate?"

Rachel flinched. She had hoped it wouldn't come up. She was just a grunt with a couple of bars on her chest. Even though he had shot Roberts, Bouchard was untouchable. He was an elected representative, outside the military, and he didn't have to follow the chain of command. They would take his word over hers no matter what she told them.

"No, Sir," she said, struggling to keep her voice steady. "Everything I need to say is in my statement." Roberts was a traitor like Taylor, but watching him die had been ugly, in some ways uglier than watching ikthians slaughter their troops. With most of the galaxy against them, humans couldn't afford to start murdering each other, too.

The dark figures in front of her moved. A few turned to whisper at each other. Rachel's heart sank. They would never clear her of these charges. She would be stripped of her rank and sent away in shame. If she was lucky, they'd ship her off to an asteroid mine where she could work herself to death for the war effort. She would never see her family again.

At last, General Hunt spoke up. "We have one last question. Do you know anything about Lieutenant Morgan's whereabouts?"

Rachel tried to conceal her surprise. She knew the brass hadn't caught up with Taylor yet, or they wouldn't have called her here to take the blame. But if they were desperate enough to ask her, they had to be completely out of leads. "Taylor...Lieutenant Morgan is probably headed for Nakonum or maybe one of the other planets in that system. She escaped on a naledai ship with Akton. She's got this delusion about helping the rebels on their homeworld."

"A delusion indeed." Hunt peered down at the report again and furrowed his brow. "If we're to believe your assessment of the situation, you would have us accept the possibility that the ikthians are rebelling against their own kind and are in league with the naledai, our allies."

Rachel blinked against the bright lights. She had to choose her next words carefully. "I didn't want to rule out any possibilities in my report, Sir, but it's what Taylor told me. Whether it's true or not, she believes it."

"It's what Taylor told you while under the influence of a dangerous war criminal."

"Where else would you prefer to look, Sir?" Rachel asked.

None of the generals responded at first. Hunt stood and walked around the table, approaching her slowly. She stood at sharp attention, waiting without hope. "We are done looking," he said, staring at her with a stern expression. "Rachel Harris, as punishment for your act of treason, this tribunal court sentences you to exile from the planet Earth."

Rachel knew there was more. There had to be more.

"You are to seek out the fugitives Taylor Morgan and Maia Kalanis and bring them back to Earth if possible. This assignment is strictly off the records, and as such, you will receive minimal aid from military personnel. You will reveal to no one the nature of your assignment, and you will not enlist the help of the Coalition of Humanity. Should you fail to apprehend Morgan, you will execute her. Until you succeed in your task, you are not to return to Earth."

Rachel could see the pity in Hunt's face. This was not a special assignment. It was a death sentence. Hunt could no longer meet her gaze, but Rachel stared at him. She wanted to remember the guilt in his eyes so she would remember to kill Bouchard the next time she saw him. She had messed up, yes, but the slimy politician had left her to the wolves. Despite his rank, Hunt had no power in this matter.

Finally, Rachel took a step back. Her path was clear. There really was only one choice from this point. "I'll leave immediately."

"I suggest you do. You're dismissed, soldier." Hunt nodded, and Rachel threw one last salute before turning and exiting through the door. More whispers came from behind her, but whatever the generals thought of her fate didn't matter. On paper, their decision would look generous. They were offering her a chance to fix her mistakes and redeem herself. But in reality, they had sent her on a suicide mission. Even though Taylor had been bewitched by the ikthian, she was still a very dangerous fighter, and she would not be alone. Rachel would be outnumbered and outgunned, assuming she even managed to track her quarry down.

Once she stepped into the hallway, Rachel headed for the nearest wall and leaned against it. The two guards posted by the door stared, but she ignored them. She needed a moment to ground herself. She closed her eyes and sighed, trying to decide what to do. Despite everything, Taylor was still her friend. It wasn't her fault the ikthian prisoner had warped her mind. She didn't deserve to die, but she couldn't stay with the ikthians either. Not if she was going to help them.

Rachel opened her eyes again and pushed off the wall, striding down the hallway with new purpose. She would follow the brass's orders. She would find and stop Taylor, kill her if she needed to. She would make sure Kalanis never turned another human again. Then, if she survived, she would come back to Earth and take care of Bouchard. He was to blame for all of this. Now that she was exiled, there was nothing stopping her from taking justice into her own hands. The military couldn't touch him, but she wasn't part of the military anymore. If Taylor was going to die and Roberts was already dead, Bouchard deserved the same.

She stopped in front of the elevator and hit the pressure pad, waiting for it to carry her to the lower levels of the building. She needed to go to her room, grab her kit, and take one of the shuttles. If the brass really did want to keep this quiet, they wouldn't get in her way. If the look on Hunt's face meant anything, maybe he would feel guilty enough give her a little money for food and ammo.

Once the elevator reached the bottom floor, she headed outside. The sky was clear, and she stopped to look up as a soft wind blew past her face. A brilliant blue flooded her vision. This would be the last time she ever got to see Earth's sky, the sun, or anything else familiar. She hadn't been born here, but Earth was her home and had been ever since she enlisted. She didn't want to leave.

"I'm not going to let them take Earth from me," she whispered. The ikthians, the brass, Bouchard. They had ruined her life, forcing her to abandon her home in the middle of a war. And they were all going to regret it.

Chapter Two

TARKOHT ORBITAL STATION APPEARED on the ship's navigation screen before it was visible through the viewport. Taylor had to stop herself from gasping when they flew close enough to see its outline. She had visited many stations on her tours of duty, but the behemoth looming in orbit around the small planet dwarfed everything else.

"This is the heart of the rebellion?" she asked Akton, breathless with disbelief. "It's huge! How could they miss it?"

The naledai shrugged and leaned further back in the pilot's chair. It was hard to tell with his wolfish face, but even he looked impressed. "Oh, they know exactly where we are. Officially, Tarkoht is a naledai trading port under Dominion control. Most of the population here is ikthian, with a few naledai and other 'assimilated' races thrown in to keep the place running."

"Well, that explains why they haven't blown it out of the sky yet."

Taylor paused when the communications light blinked on to signal an incoming transmission. Akton hit the "accept" button, and an automated voice filtered through the speakers. "This is Tarkoht Station. Please give us your authorization code." He rattled off a series of numbers, and the voice confirmed they were clear for landing before listing a docking bay for their use.

"Security here is tight," he said as they drifted closer. "If those landing codes weren't on their list, they would have dispatched a sentry to gun us down."

"That seems a little hostile for a trading port, doesn't it?" Maia asked from the navigator's seat. Taylor smiled and turned to look at her. She had chosen to remain further back instead of gawking through the viewport. Her blue eyes were bright with curiosity, and she had the same look that crept across her face whenever she discussed her research.

Akton laughed, and Taylor cringed. Although she had grown used to the tall, fierce aliens, naledai vocals still sounded harsh. "Tarkoht isn't any old trading port. It's the largest, busiest space station on this side of the galaxy. They have to be hostile to survive." Taylor glanced over and watched him engage the docking protocol. His massive claws worked the naledai controls with a deftness she could scarcely believe. "And Sorra always makes sure Tarkoht survives."

Maia's curious look disappeared. Instead, she groaned in exasperation and rolled her head back against the seat. "Oh no. Sorra is in charge here? I should have guessed."

Akton glanced over at Maia, and they shared a look that Taylor didn't understand. "So, you're...familiar with her?"

"Familiar enough to know she has a flair for dramatics," Maia muttered.

"Good. Then you won't be surprised by whatever welcoming committee she's arranged."

Taylor grew curious enough to turn away from the viewport as they pulled toward the docking bay. "Who is Sorra? How do you know her?" she asked Maia. "And what kind of welcoming committee are we talking about here?"

"Every ikthian knows Sorra's name, even though most won't admit it." A wrinkle formed in the middle of Maia's forehead, and Taylor had to resist the impulse to smooth it away. "I know her a bit more personally. Back when my research was still funded by the Dominion, my files would often go missing. It didn't matter how many times I backed them up or what kind of protection I used. She always found a way to corrupt the data, usually right before I was due to present. Some of her agents even stole my physical hard drives once, along with a great deal of expensive lab equipment."

Taylor shifted, resting some of her weight on the armrest of Maia's seat. "Didn't the Dominion just corrupt your research for their own goals anyway? It's probably a good thing she destroyed it. Well..." She hurried to backtrack when she saw the irritated look on Maia's face. "I didn't mean it quite like that."

Maia sighed. "No, you're right. I don't want to think about what the Dominion would have done with some of the genetic research Sorra stole. It was just frustrating. You put in months of work, stay up for several days straight to write a presentation, and right before you're finally finished, everything falls to pieces. It was like I was back at school all over again, without any homework to give the professor."

Taylor grinned. She rested one of her hands on Maia's shoulder. The muscles beneath her fingers were tense, and she gave a soft

Maia tensed at the comment. "I'm sure you have."

"You should be grateful that Maia decided to share her research. She risked her life to bring it here." Taylor knew she probably shouldn't have spoken, but she needed to come to Maia's defense. She didn't like the idea of Sorra mocking Maia, or anyone for that matter, no matter what her role in the rebellion was.

Sorra's gaze snapped in her direction. "And you brought the human." Her smile faltered, but only for a moment. "How intriguing."

Taylor bristled, but did not retaliate. Instead, she pressed her lips together and met Sorra's stare. This was clearly someone who was not used to being crossed or challenged. Something about Sorra grated on her nerves, but now was not the time to test limits.

"We thank you for your hospitality," Maia said. She was outwardly polite, but Taylor detected a note of annoyance in her voice. "There are few safe places in the galaxy left for us anymore. The Dominion has declared me a subversive individual, and the humanity's Coalition considers us fugitives."

Sorra's eyes narrowed. "Hmm. I wouldn't go so far as to call Tarkoht 'safe.' I have eyes and ears everywhere on this station, but subterfuge won't do any good if the Dominion brings their entire fleet here. The two of you will have to keep a low profile, especially your new pet. A human is bound to draw unwanted attention."

So I'm a pet, then. Taylor's fingers clenched, and she opened her mouth to protest, but Akton spoke up before she could get the words out. "I was thinking about that on the way here. She needs some kind of cover story, something no officials visiting the station will question."

"The Dominion will consider her presence on this station to be a hostile gesture," Sorra said. "Humans aren't welcome anywhere in Dominion-controlled space. Just because the naledai rebels are friendly with the Coalition doesn't mean she can waltz over to any star system she likes."

Taylor narrowed her eyes. "Personally, I'm thinking of running naked down the station halls, but if you're so worried I'll blow your cover, I'll take suggestions."

Sorra's lips curled into a smirk. "Well, I do have one suggestion, although I suspect you'll find it distasteful..." She let her voice trail off, and something in her tone made Taylor distinctly uncomfortable. "Due to the nature of my profession, I've developed several aliases over the years to protect myself. The one I use on this station is Dalia Talamakis, and I'm known for being particularly rich and eccentric. I've even got a private menagerie, with unique life-forms from all across the galaxy."

Taylor shook her head and crossed her arms. She took a deliberate step away from Sorra, ignoring the way Maia, Akton, and the soldiers stared at her. "No way. I don't know what you're trying to pull, but there's not a chance in hell I'm going to be part of your weird collection. Can't you just hide me if someone from the Dominion visits the station?"

"I thought that was what I was suggesting," Sorra replied. "Dalla doesn't add sentient species to her menagerie, but the average ikthian from Korithia won't know the difference. Thanks to the Dominion's leaders, most of them think the other races are savage anyway. You'll be hidden in plain sight."

Before she could continue to object, warm fingers circled her hand. The touch was enough to keep her silent while Maia turned toward Sorra. Although her polite smile was still present, the edges remained forced. "Taylor will only need to go to the menagerie for official Dominion inspections, correct? I won't allow you to lock her away for our entire visit."

"Of course," Sorra drawled. "I'll leave it to you to keep your human on a leash when there aren't any Seekers or Dominion officials sniffing around. I've got local law enforcement on my payroll, and the people who live on Tarkoht are smart enough to keep their mouths shut. She'll be safe as long as she sticks to the lower ring with the naledai and the other aliens. Most of the ikthian civilians are too elitist to go down there anyway."

"I still don't like this," Taylor grumbled, speaking to Maia instead of Sorra.

"If it helps, I'll split the profits on any ticket fees," Sorra said.

Maia's thumb grazed the top of her knuckles in a soft gesture of reassurance. "Don't worry, Taylor. I won't allow you become a part of anyone's collection." She leaned forward and kissed Taylor on the lips. "We did not leave Earth just so we could reverse roles. Sorra's plan is distasteful, but it is only for dire situations."

"I know." Taylor sighed and glanced over at Sorra. "So, do I have to do or wear anything to be part of the zoo?"

Sorra waved a dismissive hand. "Oh, no. You can wear whatever awful human clothes you want, and I won't even code you like the rest of the pets. You're free to wander around the station so long as no ikthian government loyalists are aboard." She gave Taylor a confident smile. "Fortunately, I always know about their inspections well in advance."

Taylor scowled at Sorra, but Akton nudged her. "Play along with her. She's much friendlier if she doesn't think she can goad you."

"The three of you must have had a long and interesting journey here," said Sorra. She offered her arm to Akton. "Allow me to show you to your quarters. I'll give you some time to freshen up first, but I want to hear about the events that brought you here afterward."

"Would I ever rob you of a good story?" Akton asked.

"I dare say if you ever did I'd jettison you off the station myself." She laughed, and so did Akton. Taylor frowned as she felt even more out of place.

Sorra led them out of the hangar and into the corridor. The walls were metallic, sparse, with no windows to the outside of the station. Viewfinders were available to activate, with large panels hooked up to cameras outside the station. Taylor saw one of the station residents standing at one, cycling through the different views available. She could not tell if the ikthian was a sentry or merely bored, but he seemed to take notice as she passed. His stare followed her all the way to the next turn, and she suddenly understood why Sorra had instructed her to remain in the lower wards.

As Taylor followed alongside Maia, she could not help thinking Akton and Sorra looked like something out of a horror movie. Akton's large fangs and snout lent him a wolfish appearance, and Sorra looked more like a siren with every passing second. As they walked through the corridors, she realized just how out of her depth she was. Aliens surrounded her, all of them staring at her wide-eyed as if she was the oddity. Eventually, she just looked at the floor and allowed Maia to guide them the rest of the way.

***

Maia had not had a room with proper humidity controls in a long time, and the large pool built into their bathing quarters afforded her a luxury she had not enjoyed since her captivity. Her heart leapt when she saw it was already filled, and she shed her clothes and submerged herself completely, relaxing as the cool water rolled over her skin. At last, she emerged from the depths and drew in a deep breath.

"Why don't you join me?" she asked, turning to look at Taylor. She sat on the edge, trailing her fingers through the water. "It's almost room temperature."

Taylor offered a small, apologetic smile. "No thanks. I prefer it hot."

Maia shrugged and dove under again, floating beneath the surface. The water felt like home, and she sighed, letting bubbles of air stream up behind her. But even in the silence of the water, her thoughts of Taylor refused to quiet. Her lover had been agitated ever since their arrival on the station, and the change in behavior worried her. She resurfaced and crossed her arms over the edge. Taylor stared at the opposite wall, her expression vacant. "Are you doing all right?"

Taylor blinked and looked down at her. "I'm fine," she answered, though her voice sounded unconvincing.

"You cannot allow Sorra to aggravate you," Maia said, resting her chin on top of her folded arms. "I know she is...difficult to deal with, but her influence runs deep, even in ikthian-controlled space. We need her if we're going to have any chance of distributing my research."

"I know," Taylor said. "She isn't the first asshole I've dealt with. I'm military, remember? Or, at least, I was..."

Maia's heart sank as Taylor's smile flickered and faded away. She knew that Taylor had grown homesick for Earth over the last few weeks, and it became more apparent with each passing day. When they had first escaped, both of them had been full of hope, but Taylor seemed to be feeling the weight of her sacrifice. She hoped that Taylor would not come to regret her choice.

"I'm sorry for what you had to leave behind," Maia whispered, sinking a little further into the water. She wanted to reach out and touch Taylor, but she was not sure if the gesture would be welcome. They were lovers, but their relationship was still new, and it had formed under very trying circumstances. Their future still looked uncertain. "I know it was hard for you to leave Earth, especially after what Chairman Bouchard did to Roberts."

Taylor pulled her hand out of the water and rested her elbows on her knees, slumping forward. "It isn't only about Roberts. The two of us had to get away from the Coalition, and we couldn't have done it without him. I just..."

"You miss Earth," Maia finished for her. "You miss your old life. I cannot blame you. You sacrificed a great deal to save me." She left the rest of her thoughts unspoken—the silent worry her presence in Taylor's life was not enough to make up for what she had lost.

Taylor did not answer. Instead, she wrapped her fingers around the hem of her shirt and tugged it off. Maia bit her lip as Taylor revealed the hard plane of her stomach. She itched to reach out, but remained still as Taylor pulled the shirt over her head, careless of the way it ruffled her black hair. The pants came next, and within a few moments, Taylor stood naked before her. It was a sight she had grown familiar with over the past few weeks, but it still made her pulse with want.

Kicking aside her clothes, Taylor swung her legs over the edge of the tub and eased herself in. Maia noticed the small bumps that erupted along Taylor's skin and the shiver that coursed through her body. The human reactions always fascinated her.

"I thought you said the water was too cold," she murmured, unsure whether to push away from the side of the tub and give Taylor more room, or shift closer to provide her with some warmth.

Taylor shrugged. "Changed my mind. It's not so bad. Not what I'm used to, but..." Her smile returned, and this time, it was genuine. "I can adjust."

Maia gave in to temptation and reached out resting her fingertips on Taylor's bare arm. She gave it a light squeeze. "In the short time I have spent interacting with your species, I have learned that adjusting is something you do surprisingly well. Perhaps ikthians could learn something from you."

"You seem quite gifted at adapting." Taylor covered Maia's hand with hers. "Are other ikthians not as flexible?"

Maia struggled with the human word. Her translator suggested that Taylor assumed her to possess more physical dexterity than other ikthians, but that was not what the sentence implied. "Some are more resistant to change than others." Human colloquialisms had always been difficult for her to understand, even with a fully programmed translation chip. Now that she was aboard a proper station, she could modify the parameters to suit Taylor's figurative language.

Taylor drew Maia out of her musings by pulling her close, and Maia shifted so that they sat next to one another in the pool. "You'd be surprised how many humans are just as resistant. I bet the rebel naledai have tried for ages to get us to cooperate with this organization."

"And you truly believe the Coalition would refuse simply because of a few ikthians?"

"Ikthians and other species." Taylor sank deeper into the water until it covered her chest. "Before there were aliens to fight, we were just as divisive with our own kind."

Taylor's sullen tone suggested experience to Maia. She knew Taylor looked different from quite a few of the humans back at San Diego base, but had not thought much of it. "Do you wish to talk about it?"

"There's not much to talk about. I was just a little isolated growing up. I've told you my mom was Japanese. My dad was a westerner. The kids from my dad's home country made fun of me for being different, and when I went to visit my mom's home country, I was told I belonged back in the West. Thankfully, the teasing stopped as I grew up." She let out a small laugh. "In hindsight, it wasn't all that bad, just weird for a little girl to process."

"You were isolated, because your parents were from two different regions?" The behavior made little sense to Maia. When Taylor nodded, she shook her head. "How strange." She leaned up against Taylor, offering closeness as a comfort.

"Ikthians don't do stuff like that? They don't make fun of the people from the ninth planet, or whatever, and call them names?"

"Why would an ikthian from another planet automatically be a degenerate?" Maia asked, still trying to understand what Taylor was getting at. "Is this behavior similar to ikthian dominance over other species?"

"I guess that would be the best way to explain it." Taylor leaned over and kissed her on the cheek. "Anyway, the point is that humans have never played well with others, including their own kind."

"How unfortunate." Maia felt bad for digging up obviously painful memories. "I have been thinking about something," she said, already regretting the awkward transition.

Taylor grinned. "Oh, what could that be?"

"We will be on this station a while, and it's customary for new ikthian partners—well, and old I guess—to spend time with one another outside of their private homes." Taylor laughed and Maia felt her face heat. "What? Did I say something wrong?"

"No," Taylor grinned. "Is this your way of asking me out on a date?"

"We have not set a date or time for an outing yet, but I'm assuming that was another human colloquialism."

"You're catching on."

Maia cupped Taylor's face in her hands and leaned forward, stealing a quick kiss. A spark lit in her chest as their lips brushed, and she shuddered at the warm glow. When she finally pulled away, it was only far enough to whisper. "I am a scientist. We specialize in logical deductions."

"But you did just ask me out on a date," Taylor said, her grin spreading.

Maia brushed the tip of her thumb over the soft dimple in Taylor's cheek. "It is nice to see you smile again. You have not seemed very happy since we left Earth, except when we are..." She felt the start of another blush heat her face. "I mean, I know it was difficult to leave your home behind, but I hope you can find at least some happiness here."

"If you're going to take me on a date, I'm sure I will," Taylor said. Maia's breath hitched as Taylor's fingers wrapped around hers. "I might not have much to look forward to here, but at least I can spend some time getting to know you better. What we did back on Earth was a little bit..."

"Rushed?" Maia had grown attached to Taylor very quickly during her imprisonment on Earth, and the rapid pace of their relationship frightened her, even though it was also exhilarating. "I do not regret anything we have shared, but I think our start was unorthodox, to say the least. Perhaps this is purely scientific reasoning, but I want to...discover you. I want to learn more about you. I want to understand why I am so drawn to you."

Taylor smirked, letting her thumb trace the underside of Maia's wrist. "Well, that's what dates are for, right?"

Maia looked to their joined hands. Their bodies were blurred by the rippling surface of the water, but she could feel the warmth of Taylor's thigh pressed against hers. "I have not been on many dates. I told you how isolated I used to be. My work kept me too busy to worry about things like..." The word "love" hovered on the tip of her tongue, but she was too unsure of herself to say it. "Like this."

"Don't worry. I haven't been on many, either. The military doesn't give you a lot of leisure time for things like that. Let's just spend some time together and see what happens. No pressure, no expectations."

Maia drew closer to Taylor's side, resting her head against the human's shoulder. "That sounds wonderful. I am already looking forward to it."

Chapter Three

RACHEL STOOD BACK AS the doors to the civilian shuttle hissed open. The green surface of Signus looked just the same as it always did. The planet had been terraformed to support huge forests, and the lumber harvested made up most of Earth's imports. A faint breeze blew through the trees, causing the rustling of leaves to echo around her.

"Home sweet home."

She stepped out onto the walkway and inhaled the familiar scent of her home planet. She had not known planets could smell so different until she arrived on Earth for the first time as a fresh recruit. It had been nothing like Signus, salty, earthy, and polluted at the same time. In contrast, Signus smelled of crisp leaves and pine needles. The large trees were the first to be part of the terraforming initiative.

Rachel picked up her supply pack at the off-load bay and waited in the various lines at customs. For a moment she worried her ID card would be flagged and the security system would deny her access, but the machine blinked green and let her through the final access point and out of the shuttle quarantine zone. The military had not passed any restrictions on her stay at Signus. She would have some flexibility.

After taking another moment to get her bearings, she activated her comm. "Call home."

A few seconds passed before a familiar voice filtered in. "Hello?"

"Mom, it's Rachel." She braced herself for the onslaught of questions.

Her mother squealed. "Rachel! How are you? It's been weeks. You know how I feel about you taking so long to call. Are you on assignment, honey? Is everything okay?"

"I'm fine, Mom. Everything's okay for the moment. I'm actually at the Signus drop-off just out of town if you or Dad wants to swing by for me."

Nothing had ended a conversation with her mother faster. "We're on our way." The line went dead, and Rachel sighed. She had five minutes before they arrived, and she was forced to explain she had been exiled from Earth and all but discharged from the military. Not exactly a pleasant conversation.

She perched on the edge of a nearby bench and spent the remaining time checking her kit. Everything was accounted for: money, weapons, ammo, clothes, and some basic toiletries. Aside from her guns, none of the items were particularly valuable, but since the Coalition had abandoned her, she wasn't likely to get replacements any time soon.

"I'm surprised they let me take anything at all," she muttered. "It's not like they really want me to succeed."

It was a half-truth. The Coalition wanted Taylor brought to justice for her crimes, but they definitely weren't going to give Rachel any help along the way. The lack of resources was supposed to be part of her punishment, and if she died because she didn't have the supplies or the information she needed, it would be a win-win for them. In truth, Rachel knew the Coalition didn't have any resources to spare and that her manhunt was a show.

"Succeed at what?" her father said.

The familiar voice made Rachel look up and she smiled when she saw her mother and father waiting for her a few yards away. They dressed in the same worn-down, practical clothes and muddy boots, but more lines etched into her mother's face then she remembered and grey streaked her father's temples. She climbed off the bench and slung her pack over her shoulders, tucking her pistol into its holster at her hip.

"Hey, Dad. Hey, Mom. Never mind, I was talking to myself…"

"Sounded like a pretty serious conversation," her father said.

Rachel shrugged, hoping he wouldn't press the issue. She had no idea how she was going to tell them about what happened, but here wasn't the place, and now definitely wasn't the time. She needed to wait until they were home at the very least. Fortunately, her mother stepped forward and opened her arms for a hug before the silence became too awkward.

"Welcome home, sweetheart. It's been too long since you visited."

"Well, the military isn't big on granting vacation time in the middle of a war." The arms around her tightened, and Rachel revised her statement. "But I missed you too, Mom. I'm glad to be back."

"How long did they give you?" Her father moved in for his own hug as soon as her mother stepped back. Her father gave her a brief hug, but it felt good to relax into his grip, if only for a moment, just like she had as a little girl.

"A few days, give or take. For once, I'm not on a strict schedule." They walked over to her parents' car and hopped in. Designed to navigate the large forest, the vehicle had big tires and a high ground clearance for rolling over uplifted tree roots.

"Your siblings are preparing dinner," her father said from the driver's seat as they pulled away from the shuttle port.

Rachel nodded and stared out the window. The trees flashed by as they drove the distance back to town. Memories from her childhood flooded back as she spotted the secluded areas she and her friends had played in. She had left for the war as soon as she was of age to serve. Four years was a long time to stay away.

"So, why the sudden visit?" her mother asked.

Rachel's stomach clenched up, but her dad intervened. "I'm sure it doesn't matter, Helen."

"It's okay. I'll tell you guys about it later. I just want to enjoy being home for a little while." Her parents didn't probe her any further for the rest of the drive. When they pulled in front of Rachel's old home, she took a deep breath. Her two brothers and younger sister would be far more perceptive than her parents, and even though she could deflect their questions, she would rather not.

"I'll head on in and tell your siblings to hold off on the interrogation," her mother said, giving her a knowing smile and jumping out of the car first.

Rachel groaned and slid out of her seat, glancing at the exterior of the house. They had made a few improvements since she left, like new shutters on the windows, but it was still run down by military standards. Rachel glanced at her father. "She's just going to make things worse if she tells them to leave me alone."

He laughed and walked around the car to stand next to her. He gave Rachel a hard look, and his smile faded. "You're not putting anyone in danger by being here, are you?"

Rachel shook her head, brushing a lock of stray hair away from her face. She usually kept it up, but she hadn't bothered since leaving San Diego base. "No, it's nothing like that. I'd never put you guys in that position."

He frowned. "I know. I had to ask all the same."

"Things are just complicated right now." She knew it wasn't a satisfying explanation, but it was the most she could offer until she had some time to get her thoughts in order. If she knew her siblings, they'd be furious when they found out about her new mission, and her parents would worry.

"Well, should we head in?" her father asked.

Rachel handed him her bag. "Let's do it."

The moment she stepped inside, a blur flew toward her, and her younger brother had her trapped in a vice grip. "Rach, welcome back," he yelled, hugging tightly.

"Nice to see you, too, Marcus." She tried to pry her way out of his arms, but she had to wait until her father came over and tugged him away.

"Let her breathe. She just jumped a shuttle straight from Earth."

Marcus raised an eyebrow. "So quick? What's the rush?" Their mother reached over and pinched his arm. "Ow! Fine, I'll lay off."

"We'll talk about it later." *Is it too much to want one comfortable evening with the family first?*

Ben stepped in from the next room. Her older brother was tall, taller even than their father, and had muscles stretching across his broad shoulders, filling out a light shirt. He didn't rush to hug her, and although he was smiling, she could see traces of worry in the tight lines of his face.

"Hey, Ben. I'm glad I caught you this time. I was worried you might be out on a haul." While she had sought her fortune offworld and earned her Earth citizenship by enlisting in the army, Ben had chosen to remain on Signus. Gathering and treating the lumber that served as the planet's main export meant spending long stretches of time away from home.

"It was pure luck. None of us knew you were coming. We didn't think you'd get shore leave again so soon. Not much news comes through here, but we know things are getting hotter with the ikthians. Most of the families haven't seen their kids in at least a year." Ben reached back and rubbed the base of his neck. "I mean, I'm glad to see you. It's been a long time. We just weren't expecting it."

Rachel sighed and accepted her duffle back from her father, dropping it on the ground. She could settle into her room later. "Neither was I, but I'm grateful." She was even more grateful than they knew. Once she started on her mission, there was no guarantee she would ever come back. The Coalition, the ikthians, Taylor, they were all her enemies. More enemies meant more chances to die.

"Is it as bad as they say?" Marcus asked. "You know, with the ikthians?" He said the word "ikthian" in a whisper as though he was afraid speaking their name would summon them.

Rachel frowned. "I haven't been in a combat zone lately..." She had been in combat, if the insane night of Taylor's escape counted, though not actually in a war zone. "But yeah, it's bad."

"I could have told you that." Ben looked at Marcus. "They're talking about bringing a mining drill to the edge of the forest. They want to shell us out."

"What?" Rachel's eyes widened. She had never expected the planet to be forced into abandoning the forests. "Shell out Signus? That would mean giving up the lumber."

"Not to mention us." Ben shrugged. "The Coalition doesn't have much need for millions of lumber mill workers. Those of us who can't transfer our skills will end up jobless."

Ellie, Rachel's younger sister, walked into the front entrance and gave her sister a hug. "Not to mention the mineral quality is low to begin with. Something must have shaken them." She pulled away and smiled. Ellie, who had just entered adulthood while Rachel was away, looked well settled in her loose shirt and shorts. She had tanned dark, suggesting she spent long days out in the forests. "But of course, it's nice to see you, regardless of what happened."

"Yeah, wonder what it could be," Rachel said, trying to hide her sarcasm. She knew all too well why the Coalition was making poor choices. They were desperate without Maia, their only bargaining chip, and the thought of more traitors like Taylor in their ranks had them terrified.

Her father stepped up beside her and gave her shoulder a brief squeeze. Rachel hung her head. Apparently, she hadn't done a good job at hiding her emotions. "Why don't the four of you sit down while your mother and I serve up the food?" he said, heading toward the kitchen. "That is, if it's ready."

"We would never leave a job unfinished," said Marcus.

"Oh, sure," their mother called, waving a hand as her and their father left to collect plates and utensils.

Rachel stared at her hands, but she could feel the three of them watching her.

"We know you're not on shore leave," Ellie said, breaking the silence.

Rachel nodded. She ran her fingers together testing the callouses. "What gave it away? Aside from my weird behavior, I mean."

Ellie gestured toward the dining room, and they all filed in, pulling out seats and settling down around the table. Ellie stopped at a cabinet and grabbed a datasheet. She pushed it over, and Rachel glanced at it. Taylor's face flickered on the screen. A warning flashed beneath it, and a number to call if the "dangerous fugitive" was seen. "Taylor's gone missing."

Rachel sighed and picked up the datasheet. Of course the Coalition would send out warnings. And of course her family would see them and recognize Taylor from the base. "Yeah, Taylor's gone. She ran off with the fishface."

"So it's true?" Marcus leaned forward. "She left with one of them on her own?"

"I'm sure it's manipulating her," Rachel said. She hoped the hurt did not come through in her voice. She pushed her chair back and stood. "If you'll excuse me." She left the room, grabbed her duffle, and walked upstairs to her room. Her parents had left it mostly untouched, but dust had not begun to gather, so her mother must clean it regularly. The sentiment made Rachel's heart wrench even more. She wouldn't see these people again once she left. The bed was made like the morning she had deployed. She sat down on it and tested the weight. Her bunk on base had never been quite as comfortable.

"So, what's the mission?"

Rachel looked up and saw Ben leaning against the doorframe. He stared down at her with a hard look, one warning her against lying. "I shouldn't talk about it."

Ben shrugged. "The others are downstairs. If you really can't, don't say anything, but you've been looking at this house like it's a dream ever since you set foot inside."

Rachel shrugged and looked around her room again. "It's just crazy when you don't know the next time you'll see this place."

"So you're going to the warfront?"

"Something like that." She kicked the bed with the heel of her boots. For some reason, she was nervous about telling Ben what had happened. The things Taylor had done weren't her fault—or, at least, that was the way he would see it—but they were her responsibility. If she had stepped in sooner, or even if she had gone to someone other than Bouchard with her concerns, things might have been different. "You know about Taylor, so you might as well know the rest. She brought an ikthian prisoner on base after her last mission. The brass put her in charge of it..."

Unwanted memories pushed themselves to the front of Rachel's mind: Taylor, popping a fresh clip of ammo into her gun and shaking her head in disapproval. *'She's not an it.'* At least, she thought that was what Taylor had said. Rachel remembered the hurt in Taylor's voice more than the phrasing. That was the first moment she had started to suspect there was something strange about Taylor's defensiveness. It wasn't just coming from a place of sympathy for the alien.

"And then what happened?"

Rachel blinked. Ben was still staring at her from the doorway. She shook herself, trying to cover up the awkward pause. "And it was a huge mistake. The ikthian started controlling her. She wasn't acting like herself. I brought up my concerns, but it turns out the person I approached had his own goals. One night, Taylor and the ikthian made a break for freedom, and things didn't go the way he planned. It ended with a dead officer."

Understanding dawned on her brother's face. "You're taking the fall, aren't you? They stripped you of your post."

"Not quite. The Coalition kindly offered me a chance to redeem myself, but I'll probably die trying. I think that's what they want. They're sending me after her."

Ben's frown deepened into a snarl. "What? They're sending you after a fugitive all alone? Are they even allowed to do that?"

"This is war. They can do whatever they want. Taylor's dangerous and I'm expendable. Why not send me after her to see if we end up killing each other? Then, two of their biggest problems would go away. They'd still have the entire ikthian armada to deal with, but..."

"But nothing." Ben stepped into the room, narrowing his eyes. "Why are you really doing this, Rach? You could stay here, quit the army, and work with us on Signus. It sounds like they were a breath away from dishonorably discharging you anyway."

Rachel shook her head. "Don't you get it? This was Taylor's fault, but I'm the one who let her go! I didn't tell the brass soon enough. The night she escaped I had a gun pointed at her, and even though I knew the ikthian was controlling her, I couldn't fucking shoot. Now, she's out there, doing God knows what under that thing's power. I can't just leave her like that. I have to try and fix this."

"And if you die trying to fix it?" Ben asked. She looked away. "What about us? What about your family?"

"You'll manage," she said, pushing herself up off the bed. "This isn't about me. I'm not doing this to prove my innocence to the brass, and they don't want me to do that either." She clenched her fists and her jaw tightened. "Taylor's out there somewhere, and if I can't save her, I'll kill that ikthian for ruining her. And then I'll kill Bouchard for using me."

It felt good to say the words aloud, she realized, and Ben didn't look terrified by her admission. If anything, his frown had softened. He nodded. "You'll need more than what you brought with you."

Rachel snorted. "Well, fuck. Some battle armor and a truckload of ammunition would be great. My own private starship might be nice at this point, too."

Ben grinned and leaned back against the doorframe. "I'm willing to offer what I can, idiot. You want help or not?"

"How much help can a lumberjack give?"

"More than you might think." He glanced over his shoulder and down the hall. "We'll talk about it after dinner, though. Ellie will need to come along, too. But don't say anything to Mom or Dad."

"What, you an illegal arms dealer or something?"

Ben shushed her. "Not so loud. Wait until tonight, all right? Just let your big bro take care of this."

Rachel punched him on the arm. He flinched and pushed her away, laughing. "What? Not gonna say I hit like a girl anymore?"

He massaged his shoulder. "If all military girls hit that hard, I'm kind of scared."

Before Ben could grab her and lock her into a hold, their father's voice floated in from the other room. "Rachel? Ben? Get down here. Everyone is waiting."

"Lucky break," Rachel teased as they walked down the hall. "I'll just have to beat you up later."

"This is the thanks I get for helping you?"

Rachel shrugged. "I haven't seen your version of help, yet. If you're doing something stupid, I might have to beat you up on principle."

Chapter Four

TAYLOR STARED AT THE tray in front of her, narrowing her eyes at the slab of seared meat in the center of her plate. The texture and smell reminded her of beef, but the color was a strange, pale grey. "What is this?" she asked, nudging it with her fork. "I mean, I know it's some kind of dead animal, but..."

"It's a cut of meat from a Baledon," Maia said. She sliced off a large piece with the side of her fork, but paused as she brought it up to her mouth. "They're an aquatic species native to my home planet."

Taylor had to suppress a shudder as Maia shoved the grey lump into her mouth. As appetizing as the meat smelled, she couldn't get over its appearance. She had been hungry when Akton first showed them to the cafeteria, but the Baledon had taken the edge off her appetite. Now she sat in the common area, staring sullenly at her plate. Their small table was tucked toward the edge of the large, domed room. This way, Taylor attracted as few stares as possible from the wide array of different species that occupied the station. "Are you sure it's okay to eat? It's supposed to be that color, isn't it?"

Maia swallowed and looked over at her, eyes wide. "What color?"

"You know...this-meat-went-bad-a-week-ago grey?" She gave the cut another doubtful look.

"I'm still not sure what you're talking about. This is how Baledon looks."

Taylor sat back in her chair, shifting away from the edge of the table. "If this is how it usually looks, I'm not sure I want to put it in my mouth." Maia took another bite of her lunch and Taylor's stomach growled. "Hmm, maybe it will help if you tell me what it tastes like. You said it's aquatic, right? So, fish?"

"My brief time on Earth wasn't spent sampling the local food. I'm afraid any comparisons I make won't be of much help." Maia looked pointedly at the untouched slab of meat on Taylor's plate. "Perhaps you should try it for yourself."

"Well, I guess I'm not on Earth anymore. I can't expect the same food, and I've got to eat something." Taylor sliced off a chunk of the meat and stabbed it with her fork, trying to ignore the way it quivered on the end of the prongs. "Here goes nothing." She screwed up her face and tried not to breathe as she slipped the Baledon into her mouth. Fortunately, the flavor was relatively bland, not like most fish. A little slimy, but it didn't taste spoiled. She gulped it down and reached for her water on reflex.

"So? How was It?"

Taylor looked over to see Maia staring at her with a curious, hopeful expression. She shrugged. "Well, I didn't spit it out, and I'm still alive for now. I guess it's a success."

"What's a success?" Akton approached them with his own tray. Unlike the modest spread on her plate, his was piled high with several kinds of food. A few looked somewhat familiar, but most were decidedly alien.

"Taylor just tried Baledon for the first time," Maia said, somewhere between teasing and proud. "Apparently, it meets with her approval."

Akton's wolfish features pulled into a look of surprise. "What, you've never tried Baledon? Well, I guess you wouldn't have had the opportunity. The ikthians haven't taken over your planet yet."

"Let's not talk about Earth right now." Taylor sliced off another bite of meat and speared it with her fork. The Baledon looked more palatable now that she had proven she could stomach it, but it still didn't have anything on burgers. Her shoulders sagged a little as she thought back to the mess hall at San Diego base. The food there wasn't great either, but at least she'd been in good company. Andrew's outrageous flirting cheered everyone up, and Rachel was always good for a laugh. *Rachel.* She set her fork back down as what remained of her appetite vanished. Thinking about Rachel hurt, and she remembered the last time they had seen each other more often than she wanted to admit. She still wasn't sure whether she was angry at her best friend for pointing a gun at her, or relieved she hadn't fired. Despite their differences, Rachel's choice was the only reason she and Maia had escaped Earth with their lives.

"Taylor?" Akton said from beside her. She blinked and turned to see the naledai staring at her. It was hard to tell, but his face seemed concerned. "You all right there? You seemed lost in thought."

She picked her fork back up and forced a smile, cutting off another chunk of her meat. At least she wasn't completely on her own here. She had Maia, and Akton had proven himself to be a very loyal friend. "Sorry. I'm fine. I was just feeling a little homesick. What were you saying?"

"I was thinking we'd visit the hangar this afternoon. It's near the back of the station, but it's where we keep all our ships."

Taylor smiled. Hopefully, the hangar would prove to be more comforting and familiar than the cafeteria. Even the general layout of space was so different than what she was used to. The high ceilings felt odd for a space station, and the low, small tables made little sense as a surface to eat off of. Just the little ways the room was arranged and the furniture constructed threw her off. She had spent plenty of time in all sorts of hangars during her tours of duty, however, despite never piloting much herself. Maybe it would feel more familiar to her. "That sounds like fun. So, you're finally going to show us those famous naledai fighters you keep bragging about?"

"He isn't exaggerating," Maia said, turning in her seat. "Properly trained naledai pilots are extremely dangerous. Even the ikthian armada gives them a healthy amount of respect. Of all the alien homeworlds the Dominion has conquered, Nakonum cost them the most lives."

"Oh," Taylor said. She decided to try some of the steamed vegetables, most of them a brilliant violet shade, heaped up next to the fish. At least, Maia had assured her they were vegetables. "What the hell do the humans have that's keeping the ikthians at bay, then?" It seemed humanity hardly compared to the rest of the galaxy.

"You have a certain element of surprise," Maia said thoughtfully. "Most ikthians underestimate humans from the start. And then there's the issue of you being so spread out, and that you choose to fight groundside whenever possible. It makes things difficult for the ikthians. They're trying to conquer for the resources and labor. That means they cannot simply destroy the resisting planets."

As Taylor ate the rest of her food, she felt Akton nudge her. "And you've got the naledai rebels at your backs."

His confident tone made her smile. "Yup. So, when do I get to see these starships? And when are you going to teach me to pilot one?"

Akton barked out a laugh. "Not today, if that was what you're hoping. We don't have clearance for that kind of thing. You'll have to wait until Sorra is ready to let you climb aboard. She's protective of the fleet." He stood up and stretched. "If you're ready, I'll take you down there now."

Taylor and Maia joined him in a tour of the rest of the station. The hangar was larger than any of the others she had seen, and the fighters looked much different than any other ship. She could not help glancing over at the small fighters every time she got a chance. They were oddly shaped, round instead of narrow and tapered, with rings around the sides. "These look more like small planets than fighters," she said.

"Wait until you fly one," Akton said. "They turn better than any other ship in the galaxy. You'll understand once you go for a spin."

Taylor studied the guns mounted on either side of the round hull. The laser blasts alone could rip through any human craft. As Akton led her down the line, her fingers itched to get behind the controls. "So, how much ass kissing will I have to do to get on Sorra's good side?" Taylor stepped up beside one of the fighters. Despite its odd shape, the ship looked sleek up close, and she rested her palm against its cool metal body. "I don't think I can die happy until I've tested one of the famous naledai fighters."

Maia's eyes widened. "I have never heard that term 'ass kissing' before, but I assume it's an idiom and not a literal offer. If you want to convince Sorra to let you fly one of the ships, I would start by apologizing for your earlier behavior."

Taylor turned away from the fighter and casually leaned against the frame. "Apologize? She was the one who wanted to keep me in a zoo."

"During emergency situations, and for your own protection," Maia replied. "You will need a place to hide when the Dominion inevitably comes to inspect the station."

"I still don't see why I need to apologize. Even if she's right, she didn't have to be so damn smug about it."

"Perhaps she took a little more pleasure in the suggestion than necessary..." Maia admitted. Taylor rolled her eyes at the obvious understatement. "Very well, a lot more pleasure than necessary. Still, I would do everything possible to gain her approval. She is a powerful ally and an even more dangerous enemy."

Taylor glanced over her shoulder and eyed the naledai fighter. "Well, if she gets me in the pilot's seat and keeps my ass alive to sit there, I guess I can put up with her bullshit."

"Good plan," Akton said, stepping forward and pulling her away from the hull. "Let's get out of here and finish the tour before you dent the ship."

They left the hangar to explore the labs and research facilities, which Maia was much more excited about than Taylor. She even insisted on investigating the various conference rooms. "I need to select an appropriate place to present my research to the rebel leadership," she said when Taylor gave her a small sigh and glanced pointedly down the hallway. "The right setting is crucial."

Taylor wanted to say Maia's research was far more crucial than the location but was too polite to do so. "It's okay. You look cute when you're excited. Go and find the right setting if it's that important to you. We can wait." Maia gave her a brilliant smile and squeezed her hand before hurrying over to the next door.

While Maia poked through the rooms, Taylor stood in the hall with Akton. She watched several unfamiliar species walk by, most of them too busy to give her more than a passing glance. It was a welcome change from the stares she had attracted in the cafeteria. Most of the naledai were friendly, and the ikthians avoided the lower mess to dine in the fancy restaurants of the upper wards, but even they were surprised to see a human walking openly in their midst.

The naledai weren't the only ones on the station. Taylor stared at a large, eight-eyed fuzzy red alien at the other end of the hallway, and Akton nudged her arm. "Don't let your eyes wander too much. The vordak hate direct eye contact. Makes it tricky, since they have so many."

"I'm sorry," Taylor muttered, glancing away from the giant, hairy beast. It looked more intimidating than the naledai, although at least it didn't seem to have fangs. "I've just never seen these different species. In fact, the naledai and the ikthians are the only two I've seen since my first deployment."

"You'll get used to it." Akton attempted to smile. "You got used to my face, didn't you?"

"You also possess an uncanny ability to adopt human mannerisms," Taylor said. Akton was a rare person. He blended in easily with whomever he spoke to.

"Survival," Akton said. "Most people think war is about killing, but that's a mistake. It's about connections. You've got to form alliances, big ones and small ones, if you're going to have a chance. It's always better to look at the things we have in common instead of zeroing in on the differences."

"I'm okay with some differences, although I don't think I'm ever going to get used to the way Baledon looks before I put it in my mouth."

"You're more open-minded than the average human...or the average naledai, if I'm being honest. We're designed to find people like

31

us and stick with them. Leaving Earth to come here with Maia must have been difficult."

"Yeah," Taylor sighed. "Don't get me wrong, I really want to be here, but it's harder than I thought. I didn't realize how weird it would be walking through a station without seeing another face like mine." Before she could continue, Akton nodded toward the opposite end of the hall, and Taylor glanced over to see Maia returning. "Hey there. Find the perfect space?"

Maia nodded. "Yes. The second conference room from the end has everything I need to present my research." Her brow knit together in concern. "Are you ready to head back for the day? You look a little overwhelmed."

Taylor shrugged, trying to downplay the stress she felt. It had only recently struck her that everything about this station was different from what she knew. "Yeah, if you don't mind. It might be nice to go relax for a while."

Akton led them to the living quarters and then, after promising to fetch them for dinner, parted ways. Taylor waited patiently while Maia entered in the code to their rooms. The keypad was in a different numerical system that Taylor did not recognize, though Maia explained every time that ikthians used a 'nearly identical integer system to humans, only from base twelve.'

Once inside, Taylor slumped down onto the low-backed couch and groaned. She felt exhausted. She had no way to keep up with her exercise regimen from Earth. That lack of stress relief and all the recent changes left her on edge.

Maia sat down next to her and took her hand. "Are you all right?"

Taylor forced a smile. "I'll be fine. Just a little tired."

Maia shifted closer to Taylor, raising a hand to cup her face. "You've been tired frequently. Do you think the food might not be providing enough nutrition for your species?"

Taylor laughed and shook her head. Maia's concern for her was adorable. "No. I think it's just that I'm not staying in shape like I used to." She turned into Maia's touch and reached up to clasp her hand. "I haven't been getting a lot of physical activity lately." She drew out the words before placing a kiss on Maia's wrist.

After a moment of hesitation, Maia pulled her hand away. "Which are you implying, Taylor? That you don't have access to an exercise facility or that you want sex?"

Taylor's face heated at the blunt statement. She was not used to Maia being so direct with her. "Well, I guess I meant both, but I think I was...I suppose I was teasing, mostly." She lowered her gaze to her lap. Part of her had hoped she and Maia could reconnect once they were alone. It certainly would have made a nice change.

"I thought we agreed to slow down? I want to get to know you. All of you, not just the physical parts." Maia's hand reached out to take hers, but this time, Taylor did not return the gesture. She stared down at the slender fingers resting on top of hers, focusing on the soft, shimmering silver of Maia's skin.

"Are you sure this is really what you want? I mean, we've been, um..." She searched for a delicate way to put it but came up with nothing. "We've been having sex for weeks now. I want to know more about you, too, and I get that there was a lot we couldn't learn about each other while you were my prisoner, but..." She sighed and let her head fall back against the top of the couch, staring at the ceiling. Anything was better than looking into Maia's eyes. She was terrified of what she would find there. "There have just been a lot of changes lately."

Soft fingertips brushed the side of her face, and Taylor reluctantly allowed Maia to turn her head. Her stomach flipped as Maia's thumb stroked her cheekbone. After a long moment, she lifted her gaze. Maia's eyes were just as sad as she had feared, and she could see hints of her own pain reflected in them. A few months ago, she never would have believed that she could see such familiar emotions on an ikthian's face. "You haven't lost me, Taylor. I just need some time. I've faced a lot of changes, too. You are one of the only good things I have left, but I need to make sure this is real before I..."

Taylor reached out and touched the ikthian's shoulder, letting her hand rest there, just over the soft ridges on her neck. "Before you what?" she whispered.

"Do you really need me to say it?"

Taylor swallowed. Part of her wanted to say something, to affirm her feelings were there, but she knew Maia was not ready to hear it. Those three little words hung in the room, acknowledged but not spoken until she tore her eyes away with a disappointed sigh.

"Maybe you're right. We should probably slow this down. We've only known each other for a few months. It makes sense that you want to make sure this is real."

Maia's hand fell away from her face. "I do think it is real, Taylor. I think you are the kindest, bravest person I have ever met, human or ikthian. Please, be patient with me. I'm only being cautious because my feelings are already so strong."

"Would it be okay if I kissed you?" Taylor let her hand trail down from Maia's shoulder, stroking the line of her arm. The fabric of her shirt was soft, but it could not compare to the warmth of her skin. After a moment, she let it fall back onto the cushion of the couch in disappointment. "I'm sorry. I didn't mean...I just..." Before she could finish the sentence, Maia's lips covered hers. The sudden warmth and pressure sent a jolt right through her chest, and a little of the pain there vanished. Her kiss was firm, with none of the hesitation she had expressed before, and a shudder rippled down Taylor's spine. She reached out to grip Maia's forearms, desperate for something to hold on to.

As quickly as the tension built, it dissipated as Maia pulled away. She climbed off Taylor and stood a few feet away, smoothing her clothes back into place. A blush rose on her cheeks. Taylor felt hot all over. "Do not think this is easy for me, either." Maia looked at the floor as if she were embarrassed. Finally, she managed to clear her throat and meet Taylor's gaze. "This is so new to me. All of it. Humans are not the only species I've had limited contact with. I barely know how to interact with my own people."

Taylor smiled and leaned forward, taking hold of Maia's hand. "So we're both out of our depth is what you're saying?"

Maia took a step closer, interlocking their fingers. "I think that's a rather appropriate saying. In my culture, we..." She hesitated for a moment, but Taylor nodded for her to continue. Maia rarely spoke about ikthian culture. "We talk about always making sure you know how deep the water is where you swim. Our ancestors were aquatic, but many young swimmers will push themselves too far when diving. Rarely, someone will go too far down and cannot resurface for air in time." Maia settled back down on the couch next to Taylor. "Being with you feels like I have dived into an ocean, and I have no idea how deep the water is."

It sometimes struck Taylor how eloquent Maia could sound, even through a translator. Maia had tweaked the chip already to compensate for certain colloquialisms, but Taylor did not need the adjustment to know Maia was a brilliant person. "You say such wonderful things.

Sometimes, I wish I could understand it all without the stupid chip in my head."

"You could if you wanted to."

Taylor laughed at the unexpected offer. She could not even begin to imagine how learning an alien language might go.

Maia tilted her head. "What?"

"I'm not the most linguistically gifted person. I barely manage to keep up with Japanese."

"Another language, I'm guessing?"

"Yeah. My mother always wanted me to be fluent, but I had no one to practice with aside from her. I was awful at writing in it. Speaking wasn't too hard."

Maia wrapped an arm around her, and Taylor felt some of her hurt go away as the comforting weight of the ikthian's head rested on her shoulder. "Well, perhaps you did not have the right instructor. I can teach you to speak my language, if you want. I doubt we will have very many social opportunities while the rebellion decides what to do with us."

"I bet you would make a good teacher."

"We can find out tomorrow." Maia pulled them back until they were both lying down on the couch. Taylor's face heated as Maia crawled on top of her and nestled her face against her neck. "Right now, I want to rest, and you are far more comfortable than the bed."

Taylor released a small chuckle and stroked Maia's back as she settled into a comfortable position. With their bodies pressed so close, she felt a familiar ache, but she tried her best to distract herself with a joke. "It was hunting for a lecture room, wasn't it? That's what wore you out."

Maia yawned. "Science is exhausting."

A few moments later, Maia's breathing settled into a long, regular rhythm Taylor had come to recognize as sleep. She stroked Maia's back and thought about what they had seen on the station. It was nothing like anything on Earth, and yet the thrum of people working, walking, and living there still pulsed with a familiar rhythm. Perhaps the rebel base was more like San Diego than she had thought. Still, it felt odd to be so separate from that rhythm. She did not fit in like Maia did. Part of her feared she would dissolve into the background. Beyond being human, what made her remarkable on a station full of freedom fighters?

Maia. Her connection with Maia made her different. It had already opened her eyes and changed her as a person. Taylor sighed and looked down at the top of Maia's head. It looked different than hers, than any human's, but the sight was still comfortable and familiar. She had hoped Maia would be her anchor in this strange place, but now, even that felt uncertain.

"She does want to be with me," Taylor whispered. And even though she believed the words, she could not dismiss her doubts completely. The fact that Maia wanted to put their physical relationship on hold while they continued getting to know each other made sense in her head, but it still felt like a rejection.

Taylor sighed and forced herself to remember the kiss, the connection she had felt as Maia's lips covered hers. Her skin suddenly felt warm, and not just where Maia's body was pressed against hers. Surely that kiss had been real. Maia still felt something for her, something strong, even though she wasn't ready to voice it yet. She just needed to be patient.

"You know, I think I'll take you up on those lessons," she murmured. She tilted her head down and placed one last kiss on top of Maia's head before settling back down against the arm of the couch and closing her eyes. She knew it wouldn't be long before Akton came to take them to dinner, but she couldn't bring herself to move. She wanted to stay as close to Maia as possible.

Chapter Five

THE NOTICES NEVER STOPPED pouring in. Odelle Lastra acknowledged this, but on some days, she wanted nothing more than to snap the nearest datasheet in half and fling it into an incinerator. She watched the messages scroll by on the flickering screen, a constant reminder she needed more help than the Dominion would provide.

She highlighted the last 500 notices, running them through a scanner that deleted 378 of them for being completely irrelevant. Her position provided more opportunities than life would have afforded her otherwise, but it came with a high cost. Suddenly, the screen flashed blue: a warning that an encrypted file had come through. "Voice activation required," the communicator chirped. She wondered, not for the first time, which of the Dominion's designers had come up with the bright idea to make the office equipment talk.

She sighed. "Odelle Lastra, Executive Media Coordinator."

The datasheet opened up the message, a basic text document. Odelle read over it quickly and frowned. She pulled up her communicator to place a call to Tarkoht Orbital Station but paused mid-dial. Instead, she rose from her chair and went to the door, peeking outside her office. The sun had set long ago, and she was the last one in the building. Still, she shut and locked the door before connecting the datasheet to a private link. If Sorra thought she could bait her with dramatics, she was wrong. Odelle would sidestep the whole dance with a call.

In a matter of seconds, the screen flashed with the words "request accepted." Sorra's pale and angular face filled the screen of the datasheet. The dark makeup she usually wore was missing, and her gaze lacked its usual piercing glare.

Odelle shook her head. "Don't tell me I woke you up. You sent the notice seconds ago."

"It was the last item on my agenda for the night." Sorra paused, letting her lips spread in a flirtatious smile. "All the best things are."

"The orbital station is on the same sleep cycle as Korithia's?" Odelle asked, purposefully ignoring Sorra's sultry tone.

"Close enough. Did you read the full message, or did you get too...impatient?"

Odelle swallowed. Sorra's deliberate pauses and intense eye contact still made her heart race just as much as it had the first day they met. "I did read it, actually. I'm curious to hear how this 'dangerous information' you have involves me. I don't have otherworldly powers, you know."

"You have enough power." Sorra's smile disappeared, and she shifted as she leaned back into her chair. Already, she looked much more relaxed. Odelle preferred talking to Sorra when her guard was down. She was a much more relatable person without the frills she put on for the public. "We'll have to find a time to meet in person and discuss this further. I don't feel comfortable saying anything more right now."

Odelle nodded and pulled up her schedule on yet another screen. "I have a party at the Foundation Institute in four Korithian days. Maybe after that? It would be an excuse to travel, at least."

"It sounds wonderful. I look forward to...we'll finish this conversation later," Sorra said in a hushed voice, her eyes narrowing suddenly. "Your connection will be compromised soon." Before Odelle could say goodbye, the call terminated, leaving her with nothing but more unanswered notices. She blinked in surprise and set the datasheet aside. She could call back, but it was unlikely that Sorra would answer.

"Sometimes I think she does it just for dramatic effect," she muttered as she looked for her keychip. "'Your connection will be compromised soon?' She probably just wanted to make me—"

Another flashing light appeared on the datasheet. This time, it blinked a brilliant red. Her eyes widened, and she hurried to answer it. She didn't have to take orders from many people in the Dominion's hierarchy, but seeing red was never good. She hit the accept button, only spending a second to collect herself.

A stern face appeared on the screen, one she had no trouble recognizing, Chancellor Corvis. Even the soft pink shading beneath her hollow silver cheeks did little to soften her appearance. "Odelle? Good, you're still awake. We have a situation."

Fear sliced into Odelle's chest. It was a familiar feeling, but it never got easier. *Is this it? Have I been compromised?* She put on her best smile. "A situation, Madam Chancellor? I might remind you that it's..."

She paused to glance over at the nearest clock. "Several minutes past twelve already. Everyone else went home hours ago. Does it need to be resolved now?"

The chancellor's eyes narrowed. "Would I have called you if it was not?"

"Of course not," Odelle murmured. Talking to Chancellor Corvis was always a dangerous game. Most other subjects would have received more than a biting comment for questioning her. People who displeased her frequently disappeared soon after. "Please, let me know what I can do for you."

"Maia Kalanis is still missing. None of our scouts can locate her. Even the Seekers are chasing each other in circles. And since she is nowhere to be found, Irana is getting restless."

Odelle's stomach dropped. She knew where this conversation was leading. She had always found Irana to be the most pleasant and reasonable member of the Dominion's council. "Restless? How restless?"

"Restless enough to forget herself," the chancellor said. "Because of her rank, I've given her several chances to control her tongue, but the loss of her daughter has frightened her. She wants us to continue negotiating with the humans, and she hasn't been subtle about asking. Her demands are making us look weak."

"And you want me to take care of it." Odelle averted her eyes from the screen. She didn't like it, but until the right moment came, this was her job, selling the Dominion's citizens whatever lies the chancellor gave her. "I'll start small at first. Whisper a few rumors in the right ears. Perhaps it will convince her to see things from your point of view."

"That is my hope. And if she does not, there are always other options."

Odelle shivered. She knew without being told what those other options were. *Daashu. If Irana Kalanis ended up in that pit of despair, she would never come out again. No one ever returns from Daashu.*

"Hopefully it won't come to that. A few threats should work. Perhaps we can make her seem like an incompetent instead of a traitor," Odelle said. The chancellor thought over the suggestion for several moments, and the lack of an immediate response made Odelle panic. "Besides," she added, "sending someone of Irana's rank away could cause dissent."

That got the chancellor's attention. Dissent was the only thing she feared. "Very well. I trust you to take care of this, Odelle. I'll be in touch."

Before she could reply, Chancellor Corvis signed off, and the datasheet screen dimmed. Odelle placed a hand to her forehead and slumped over her desk, breathing a sigh of relief. For now, at least, Irana wasn't slated for a slow, painful death. She would have a few days to think up a more permanent solution and to figure out what Sorra's plan was. She latched onto that question, hoping it would distract her from her darker thoughts.

Odelle pushed the datasheet aside and stood up. She had stayed at work for too long already. Even as she yawned and stretched, she could feel the fatigue in her muscles. Another exhausting day and what had she accomplished? *Aside from stalling a friend's death sentence for a few weeks, not much.* Firmly and deliberately, she pushed Irana from her mind. The problem of what to do could wait until after a good night's sleep.

Odelle took a private transit home, waiting numbly for her stop, and ended up at her front door in a fog. It had only been a little under a day since she had last come home, but it felt like it had been a year. The lights were dark but flickered on as soon as they sensed her movement. A soft chirping sound came from beneath her feet, and Odelle looked down to see her tutara, Tazmar, looking up at her. The small, scaled creature crooned up at her, touching a claw to her shoe. *Hungry, no doubt.* For the first time since leaving for work that morning, she smiled.

"*Sorra did a double take.*" Odelle bent down and scooped her pet up into her arms. "I gave you second helpings and extra food for tonight." Still, the creature rested its pointed, scaled face against her chest and stared up at her with unblinking eyes. She gave in and placed him back on the floor. "Just a small treat, then."

Tazmar scampered after her into the kitchen, his four wiry legs skittering across the tiled floor. She tried not to make a face as she fetched the jar of preserved insects and fished one out for Tazmar. As cute as he was, her pet ate the most disgusting things. She had picked him out primarily because of the blue shade of his scales. His easy-going temperament had been a fortunate bonus.

"You wouldn't believe the day I had," she said as Tazmar ate his treat, long tongue wrapping around the insect's body. She started to tell Tazmar about Irana, but another face floated to the front of her mind instead. A face that always filled her thoughts, even when it was inconvenient. "Sorra called. She's up to some new scheme, probably full of unnecessary risks."

Tazmar looked up at her and tilted his head to the side. She liked to think he was agreeing with her.

Odelle turned away from him and walked into the bathroom. Another perk her unsettling career granted her was a spacious home. The halls were paved with stone, and the open rooms featured the most up-to-date décor of low sitting chairs and hanging miniature gardens. The plants required little upkeep with the home's naturally high humidity. The light in her bathroom flickered on as she walked in, and she caught her reflection in the mirror. She looked exhausted. Her pale grey complexion lacked its natural glow, and the wrinkles under her eyes were more pronounced. The usual vibrancy of the pink shading across her eyes had dimmed. Her cheeks were hollow. People would start to talk if she let it get any worse, despite the hard work of the makeup artists hired by the Dominion.

She looked away from her reflection and shed her clothes. Her muscles ached, and it was a greater struggle than it should have been. Even though she knew she should collapse in bed and enjoy the few hours she had to herself before she returned to work in the morning, she glanced at the large, temperature-controlled tub in the corner of the washroom. She had installed it herself when she bought the home. Her nightly soaks were practically the only thing she looked forward to anymore. *Well, those and Sorra's calls.*

It only took a few moments for temptation to get the better of her. "Just a few minutes," she said as she switched on the controls. It did not take the water long to rise, but she avoided glancing at herself in the mirror as she waited. Staring at herself would only make the exhaustion she felt more pronounced.

At last, the tub finished filling. She sank into the water and sighed, closing her eyes and allowing herself to be lost in the pool for a few moments. Soon enough, she heard the clacking of Tazmar's claws on the tile, and she broke to the surface again. Her pet huddled by the rim of the tub, staring up at her with large eyes. He was always concerned by her desire to sit in water. "Just because you don't like it," she teased, splashing a water droplet close to him.

He scooted away.

"And yet you're here anyway, despite the danger." Odelle watched fondly as Tazmar settled down on top of her clothes, curling up. "Though you wouldn't die from a little water..."

Tazmar ignored her.

"You'd think Sorra would explain herself more clearly." She grabbed a cloth from the rim of the tub and soaked it in the water. "Or she could at least call for social reasons once in a while. It's not like any of her aliases are compromised." But, as long as Sorra kept calling, it meant she was still alive. "Back in school, she was always calling me in the middle of the night with some stupid plan. We went swimming in the institute's pond one time...naked."

Odelle stopped talking as the memories came back to her. It had been over twenty years since she and Sorra were students together, but the memories were still fresh and sometimes painfully so. Their parting had been slow, messy, and confusing. Neither of them had wanted to end the relationship, but outside pressures had forced them to leave each other. Before she knew it, she was working for the institution she had always complained about secretly in school. It had required long hours, and Sorra's calls became less and less frequent. Soon, they stopped altogether.

There had been more than a few arguments scattered through those last few months as well. Sorra had despised her career choice. Like many of their classmates, Odelle had harbored more than her fair share of resentment for the Dominion. The work she did for the Dominion had put a strain on their relationship too great to overcome.

The sound of Tazmar's trilling tugged Odelle out of her memories, and she realized she had not even started to wash herself. She hurried to finish in the tub, knowing if she lingered any longer, she wouldn't get enough sleep to function the next day. She didn't even bother drying off completely as she stepped out of the tub. The extra moisture felt good on her skin. Tazmar scuttled over to her and darted back and forth between her legs, nudging against her calves as she pulled a bathrobe on.

"No more food for you," she said, herding him from the bathroom. She walked into the bedroom, pulled on a nightshirt, and settled into bed.

Tazmar curled up on her stomach, making her groan as his weight settled on top of her. His species did not grow to be very large, but he was also slightly plump from too many treats. "No more snacks for you, either," she said, even though she knew it was a lie. After a while, the sound of his steady, wheezing breath made her close her eyes. Even though her body was exhausted, she could not get her mind to quiet down. Irana, the chancellor, and Sorra kept intruding on her thoughts.

"What is she up to?" Odelle murmured, opening her eyes. The shadowed ceiling did not answer her, and Tazmar did not even flinch. "Does she really think this is the right time?" When she and Sorra had reconnected in their new lives after spending so many years apart, they had come to an understanding. One day, Sorra and the rebellion would seize the chance to change things. When that time came, Odelle would be able to use her position to help.

She would only have one chance to do serious harm to the Dominion. She needed to be sure that Sorra's plan was tenable, whatever it turned out to be. If not, then she and Sorra could die, or worse—they could be taken to Daashu.

The thought of Sorra being tortured kept Odelle awake more often than she liked to admit. This night was no different.

***

When Rachel had accused her brother of being an arms dealer, she had thought it was a clever joke. She stared around the hangar in shock, mouth gaping open. It was full of weapons, ships, and alien supplies, almost enough to compare with one of the Coalition's warehouses. She glanced back at Ben and Ellie, who stood behind her, both grinning. "This can't be legal," she said, turning back to the trove of weaponry. They practically had enough to fund a small army.

"It's salvage." Ellie took a step forward and nudged her. "What do you think happens to all the ikthian ships that crash here?"

"Don't they send retrieval units?"

"Not if the crew is dead." Ben walked over to a table scattered with weapon parts and picked up a half-assembled gun. "And even if there are a few survivors, they sometimes just leave them. They're not safe groundside. Their ships might outclass us, but bullets work the same on all species."

"Thanks for the lecture. I'll tell the army when I get back," Rachel said. Ellie punched her in the arm. "Ow!"

"Smartass." Ellie walked further into the hangar and gestured for Rachel to follow. They walked through the rows of gun racks. There were maybe twelve half-repaired ships scattered around, most of them single pilot. "We give a lot of the tech back to the Coalition. This is just a stash to ensure the planet's defense."

"And who defends it? You and Ben?" As impressed as she was, Rachel hardly liked the idea of her siblings fixing up aliens crafts so they could be vigilantes.

"There's a small militia. I'm mostly a scavenger." Ben nodded in their sister's direction. "Ellie is the mechanic."

Rachel found herself genuinely smiling for the first time in a while. She had spent over a year worrying about her family's safety while she was away on duty, but apparently, they could take care of themselves. It did not surprise her at all that her brother and sister had stepped up to defend their home. "And I'll bet she's damn good at it. Both of you are. So...what now?"

"That depends on you." Ellie stepped over to one of the abandoned ships, resting a hand on its curved hull. Rachel had to suppress a shudder. She had seen too many ships like that on her deployments. The shape was too large and too round. For lack of a better word, it looked alien. "You can forget the Coalition and stay here with us, or I can fix one of my babies up for you and stock it with enough weapons and ammunition to take out an entire platoon by yourself."

Even though Ellie tried to hide it, Rachel could tell which option her sister preferred. The sad look on Ben's face was just as easy to interpret. They both wanted her to stay. And it was more tempting than she wanted to admit. It had been a long time since she had seen her family, and she knew things would become difficult for all of the colonists, no matter how many ships and weapons they stockpiled. They wouldn't stand a chance if the ikthian armada decided to pay Signus a visit. But she couldn't stay here.

She needed to find Taylor. Not to help the Coalition or to get back into her superiors' good graces but because it was necessary. Her homeworld was in danger, and her best friend had been brainwashed by an alien, all because she hadn't acted soon enough. She might not be able to save Earth on her own, or even Signus, but she could fix this one mistake.

"I'm sorry, Ellie. Ben. But you know I have to go."

Ben lowered his head, kicking his foot against the concrete floor as he stared at the ground. "Yeah. We know."

Rachel looked over at Ellie. Tears shone in her sister's eyes. Ellie cleared her throat and turned back toward the ship, swiping a hand over her face. "I can get this ship ready for you in another day," she said, her voice shaking. "It only needs a few adjustments. I've already got the main guns working, and the propulsion system is online again. The VI's locked out, but I'm sure you can fly this thing without it."

"Will you show me?" Rachel wanted to get into the cockpit and see how the ship handled. The Coalition had not let her fly since her training, and this one looked like a naledai ship, completely different than anything she was used to. The ikthians had stolen the design from them, just like they had stolen Nakonum.

"Yeah. Shouldn't take long for you to get the controls down. Most people learn to fly them pretty easily." Ellie touched a panel on the ship's side, and the cockpit hissed open. She grabbed a stepladder and swung it open against the ship's hull. "The fishfaces have decent ships, I'll give them that."

Rachel climbed up the ladder and swung over into the cockpit. The small, circular pod was spacious enough. She stretched her legs and leaned back into the seat. It fit her body surprisingly well. She reached out and touched the controls, all within a comfortable distance. "You'd think it was made for humans."

"Yeah. It's better put together than most of our starships." Ben climbed up the side of the craft and looked down at her. "Guess it makes sense. They're pretty close to us in height and shape."

Rachel nodded. Some of Taylor's words came back to her, about how the ikthians weren't so different. She pushed the thoughts aside. "So, how much firepower does this baby have?"

Ben grinned. "I'm glad you asked."

Chapter Six

TAYLOR GROANED AND RESET the flight controls for the third time. She had been dying to pilot one of the sleek naledai starships ever since she had seen them, but getting it to take off proved to be more of a challenge than she had expected. First, the VI system had flashed a "maintenance required" symbol at her. Once she finally got it to shut off, she accidentally activated the autopilot. The ship had almost left the docking bay without her. It was true Taylor had almost no flight experience, but everyone had told her this was supposed to be easy. It wounded her pride to struggle.

Maia had already taken off. To Taylor's embarrassment, she did not seem to be having any trouble with her ship. She careened through an asteroid belt, and if the sounds coming in over the comm channel meant anything, she was having the time of her life. Taylor had never heard Maia shout and cheer like she did when flying. She wanted to be part of the fun.

"Try again. This time, don't ease up on the throttle so fast," said Sorra, her voice crackling over the radio system. She sat on the observation deck, guiding Taylor through the process of getting the fighter in the air. She had assured Taylor any idiot could fly one, but her instructions were difficult to follow.

"I didn't ease up too fast," Taylor snapped. "Something must be wrong with the ship."

She could imagine Sorra smirking at her. "I have a diagnostic readout of the ship right in front of me, and everything looks fine."

"Okay, okay. It's just a little different from what I'm used to." A lie. She had nothing to compare it to, for a start. Flying had to be the biggest weakness in her years of military experience, and it showed. Something always went wrong, and even though she didn't want to admit it, she was starting to think the problem was with her, or with the fact she had failed to explain her utter lack of experience.

Sorra's smug voice drifted into the cockpit again. "Try again. The ship is running, right?"

Taylor bit her lip. Sorra was trying to get on her nerves, and unfortunately, it was working. "Yeah, it's on," she mumbled. She wasn't going to give Sorra the reaction she was looking for. "What next?"

"All right. We'll start back at the beginning." Sorra took on a more serious tone. "This fighter's design is gyroscopic. It doesn't have a 'nose' like the military aircrafts you're used to. You can go in any direction without turning, because the cockpit inside rotates without moving the body of the ship. The engine propels you whichever way you're facing, and the front and rear guns move along with you."

"Well, you made more sense than Maia did earlier," Taylor said. Maia had tried to explain how the ship worked on their way to the hangar, but her explanation had been so technical most of it had gone over her head. Sorra might be irritating, but at least she was concise.

"Glad one of us is finally getting through to you. Look down at the controls. What do you see?"

Taylor stared. The sheer number of buttons, switches, and levers overwhelmed her. "Too much to describe. Can you narrow it down for me?"

"Fine," Sorra said. The eye-roll was audible in her voice, and Taylor pressed her lips more firmly together. "Focus on the steering controls. You do know how to steer, don't you? The ship turns with you, so just pull in the direction you want to go. The pedal beneath your feet is for propulsion—"

Taylor gripped the joysticks. "Got it. I'm ready to test this baby out in the air. Space. Same thing."

"It's not the same thing at all," Sorra continued. "There isn't any air in space, or gravity, so turning will be…" Taylor slammed her foot down on the pedal, and the ship flashed forward so fast her safety harness dug into her chest. She shot straight out of the open hangar bay and into the empty blackness. "…different. When your ship gets ground to dust, don't complain to me."

Taylor eased up on the propulsion and yanked the joysticks to a hard left. "Come on, slow down," she said through gritted teeth. Instead of stopping, the craft banked sharply to the side. The stars spun around her. She tried turning the joysticks the opposite direction, but only succeeded in making the spinning worse. A warning light blinked on. At least, she assumed it was a warning light by the bright red glare. The next time she tried to tug on the joysticks, nothing happened. "Sorra!" she yelled over the intercom. "Sorra, help!"

"I already did!" she snapped. "And stop yelling. The mic is very sensitive. I shut off the propulsion system until your gyroscope stabilizes. Then maybe you can stop your craft from hurtling toward the asteroid belt."

"Won't I just keep spinning forever?" Taylor could already feel the adrenaline spike taking over. Her hands trembled, and she tightened her white-knuckle grip on the joysticks.

"The pod has an automatic orienting system that prevents the center from spinning too much, unless an inexperienced pilot pushes the engines like you just did." Taylor could already feel the pod slowing. The stars did not zoom past her anymore. "There, see? You're already back to neutral, the normal state for the pod to hang. Now why don't you listen to me before your ship gets vaporized? That debris can pick up a lot of momentum."

Taylor tried not to sigh. "What do I do?"

"Gently press down on the propulsion pedal, about a quarter of the way, and turn both the joysticks to the right, about halfway. Stop when the station comes into sight."

Taylor did as she was told. The craft lurched as it stopped its current trajectory. She eased up on the pedal and let go of the controls as the station came into sight. The craft stopped moving, and she could see the space station above her, a faraway pinprick.

"Good. You managed to cancel out the craft's inertia. You'll stay put there until you press down on the pedal again. Each joystick controls an engine on either side of the pod, so you can move in all sorts of directions depending on how hard you push each engine and in what way."

Even though she knew Sorra could not see her, Taylor nodded. "Anything else I should know?" She tried inching forward and up, and the craft began creeping toward the station.

"The triggers on the control handles activate the front guns. The buttons on top of the controls activate the rear guns. They fire energy bullets."

"Right, I knew that." Taylor remembered the lectures on space combat she had received years ago.

Sorra laughed. "It's hard to assess the extent of human ingenuity with only you for a sample."

The insult made Taylor bristle, but before she could respond, a loud whoop of joy came over the radio. "Taylor, have you taken off yet? This is wonderful! Come see!" The sound of Maia genuinely enjoying herself made Taylor smile. They had both been too anxious for their own good.

"Having fun?"

"It's so beautiful out here. Perfect. I...perhaps it is a silly comparison, but piloting has always reminded me of swimming. I can move wherever I want. I feel free."

Despite her annoyance, Taylor laughed. "I'm glad you're enjoying yourself." She pressed her foot down on the pedal, correcting her course as the space station loomed in front of her. Suddenly, a blur of motion streaked in front of her, followed by soft trails of purple light. Maia's ship curved up in a graceful arc, hanging above her for several moments before it curled away in a falling spiral. Taylor gasped. She hadn't expected Maia to handle the ship so well on her first flight.

"Catch me!" Maia's breathless voice came over the radio.

"That probably isn't a good idea," Sorra interrupted. Taylor had almost forgotten that the other ikthian listened in on their conversation. "I think Lieutenant Morgan needs some remedial flight school lessons before she can follow you."

"She can do it," Maia insisted. Taylor eased the pressure on the pedal when she saw Maia's ship settle to a stop in front of her. "I'll help her."

Taylor wanted to protest she didn't need help, but she did want to learn how to handle the ship, and Maia was a far more tolerable teacher than Sorra. "All right. You lead the way, and I'll try to keep up." She tightened her grip on the joysticks, careful not to activate the triggers. She didn't want to embarrass herself by shooting at Maia's fighter.

"Are you ready to follow me?"

Taylor grinned. "I'll follow you anywhere."

"Just stay away from the asteroid belt, please," Sorra said. "These fighters were expensive, and I don't want you wrecking one of them."

"Thanks for the vote of confidence." She didn't have time to say anything else, because Maia swooped up into the blackness above them, urging her to follow. Taylor tapped the pedal and jerked her joysticks up. The world spun around her, and she cried out in surprise as she began hurtling backwards.

Sorra's voice snapped over the radio almost immediately. "What did I tell you about gunning the engine? Push lightly the other way before you throw up on the seats. If you do, you're cleaning them."

Taylor corrected the ship's course faster this time and caught sight of Maia's ship in the distance. When she tried to follow again, she did not slam her foot down on the pedal. The ship moved in a smooth arc toward Maia.

"You're doing great."

"Thanks." Taylor knew Maia's compliments were likely exaggerated, but it felt nice knowing someone appreciated her efforts. Sorra made her feel like an incompetent child. "We'll have to come practice again. I want to be a piloting ace when we bring the fight to the Dominion." She stopped her ship close to Maia's.

"I'd rather avoid a space battle," Sorra said. She sighed over the comm. "They're notoriously good at space battles. We'd want to catch them on the ground, unawares."

"What are you thinking?" Maia asked. Taylor could imagine Maia glaring at Sorra with the same questioning glare. Maia did not completely trust Sorra. She had made that much clear.

"Nothing I'd expect a well-researched scholar like you to understand." Silence crackled over the comm. "It isn't relevant to our current flight lesson. Now, let's see if we can get Taylor to plot and follow an actual trajectory. Then maybe we can try landing in the hangar without destroying it."

Sorra began barking orders over the comm channel, and Taylor tried to follow the directions. Flying frustrated her, especially since simple and trusted concepts like down and up no longer existed. She took in a deep breath and reminded herself that the moment they were on the ground for sparring, she would have the upper hand, unless Sorra was some martial arts genius in addition to being a smartass. With the way her day had turned out so far, that would not surprise her.

***

Sorra glanced at the time again as Taylor and Maia finally landed their ships in the hangar. In one graceful motion, she pushed out of her seat and stalked out of the control room. She didn't have much time to spare. She watched tapping her foot as Taylor and Maia exited their ships. The human's strange, pale skin looked a little greener than usual, but otherwise, she seemed unharmed.

"Good training so far, but I think I'll give the two of you the rest of the day off," Sorra said once they were within earshot. "Just stay out of the hangar and out of the comm rooms. The rest of the station is yours to explore." She reached into her pocket and pulled out two data cards to hand over to them. "I've created alias identity cards for you. They have credit loaded on that is usable at the station if you need anything." Taylor scrunched up her face in an odd way, and Sorra narrowed her eyes. "What?"

"You in a rush to get somewhere?" Taylor asked.

Sorra crossed her arms. "Actually, I have an important meeting coming up. I'll be going if the two of you are comfortable finding your way around the station." She wanted nothing more than to sprint back to her quarters, get dressed, and leave. Her fingers twitched as she resisted the urge.

"Well…" Taylor hesitated on purpose. Sorra could tell that the human sensed her discomfort. "We should be fine, but…"

Maia placed a hand on Taylor's shoulder. "Let her go."

"Thank you, Maia," Sorra said through a forced smile. "At least one of you has good manners. Now, if you'll excuse me." She left without waiting for a response, striding out of the hangar and through the nearest set of doors. As soon as they hissed shut behind her, she walked faster, brushing past several startled-looking maintenance people on her way. Most of them stepped aside as soon as they saw her. Everyone on the station knew better than to get in her way when she had somewhere important to be.

It seemed to take ages to board the lift and ride up to her private quarters in the upper ring, but when Sorra checked her comm, she realized she had far too much time to pass, still. She was jumpy and rushing herself, and even though she didn't want to admit it, she knew the reason why—nerves.

"Not nervous, just eager," Sorra said aloud as she headed for her bedroom, stripping off pieces of clothing along the way. She dropped her shirt on the couch in the living room, and kicked her boots off in a pile halfway down the hall. She left her pants at the door to the bedroom and headed for the closet. On her way, she caught a glimpse of her naked reflection in the mirror. She paused, slightly surprised by the dark flush her cheeks held. "Maybe a little too eager." She took in a deep, calming breath. Her usual confidence returned, and her lips curled into a smirk. Perhaps anticipation was a better word. It had been a long time, months since she had seen Odelle in person and years since they had been anything more than acquaintances.

Pleased with the better outlook, and even more pleased with her appearance, she gave her reflection a wink goodbye and turned back toward the closet. She opened the doors and took stock of her choices, groaning as her eyes settled on a stretch of deep red. "You will do perfectly." It wasn't a commonly worn color among her people, although she had noticed other species often used it. She reached out, running her fingers over the soft fabric of the skirt. "Too much, or just enough?"

Just enough. Everyone else at the party would be showing off. No reason she shouldn't do the same. Sorra lifted the dress out of the closet and draped it over her arm, carrying it over to the bed. She grinned as she imagined the way heads would turn when people saw her, but first, she needed to wash. She headed for the bathroom, but before she could open the door, the sound of a clearing throat made her turn around. Joren stood in the doorway, eyeing her with a look of curiosity. "Hot date tonight?"

Sorra shrugged her shoulders, unembarrassed by her nakedness. "Sure. Date, espionage, what's the difference?"

"For you? Not much." Joren's gaze settled on the dress stretched across the bed, and he shook his head. Whether it was in amusement or approval, she couldn't tell. "Red? Really?"

"What's wrong with red?" she asked, placing a hand on her hip. "I look damn good in that dress."

"I'm sure you do. If I was actually your partner, I'd be the envy of the Empire."

"You already are, and that's just for the privilege of looking." She stepped into the bathroom and started the shower, relaxing her shoulders as steam drifted out past the curtain. "The envy, I mean."

"I got the joke." Joren followed her into the spacious bathroom and leaned against the vanity while she stepped into the shower. She ignored his presence, moaning as the water flowed over her parched skin. "As tempting as you are, I know better than to partner with you."

Sorra pulled the shower curtain aside and flashed a smile at him. He stared back, the corners of his mouth turned down as he glared. "No one else seems to know better." She let it fall back into place and grabbed a bottle of scented soap, pouring a generous amount into her cupped hand. As much as she joked, it was rare for Sorra to bed anyone, especially after the recent months of speaking with Odelle again.

"Not many know you like I do," Joren said. "Although poor Odelle has known you longer, and she still clings to her insane infatuation."

"It's not insane." Sorra lathered her body and allowed the soap to rinse off under the spray.

"It is when it threatens her life."

Sorra shut off the water and stepped out of the shower, extending her hand as Joren passed her a towel to dry off. "I'd never intentionally put her in harm's way." Joren frowned, obviously skeptical. "I'm just meeting her at a party, and I thought it would be nice to show off since everyone else would be."

Joren arched his brow until the green coloring on his forehead wrinkled. "You're going to talk to her at a party where other Dominion officials are present?"

"It's better than having her sneak off. No mess. No trail. No loose ends. I know what I'm doing, and so does Dalia." She walked out of the bathroom, shaking the last drops of water from her hands as she scooped up the dress. She carried it over to the mirror, holding it in front of her and turning to make sure the lines complimented her figure. Once she was satisfied, she draped it on a nearby chair and opened her wardrobe to choose the rest of her outfit. She smirked as she pulled out a particularly scandalous pair of underwear.

"I'm not questioning those reasons."

Sorra paused in pulling on her matching bra and met Joren's worried gaze in the mirror. He stood behind her, hands folded behind his back, and his expression contradicted his words.

"If you're implying that I care too much for Odelle, then—"

"I am implying the two of you are emotionally connected, more than is healthy for this line of work. Why do you think you and I get along so well?"

Sorra finished hooking the back of her bra before pulling on a sheer slip. "I don't know. I think it's the trust between us, like how you trust me not to fuck Odelle on the chancellor's dining room table."

Joren's eyes widened. "That's not what I meant!"

Sorra pushed past him and picked up the dress. "Well it certainly sounds like you think I'll turn into an emotional wreck at the sight of her." She stepped back into the bathroom and slammed the door shut.

"Sorra..."

She sighed and rested backwards against the door. "Just because I'm seeing her in person instead of through a comm link doesn't change things. Both of us know nothing can come of this." *At least, not until the Dominion is taken care of.*

"Are you sure? Are you willing to stake your life on it?"

Sorra's eyes narrowed and she pushed off from the door. "You know the way out." She locked the door behind her. "I'd show you myself, but I'm too preoccupied with my emotional turmoil and poor, reckless decisions." She was being harsh, she knew, but she hated when Joren tried to advise her on matters he knew nothing about. After a few moments, she heard the bedroom door open and click shut. Joren had known her for a long time, and he had learned when to leave her alone.

Sorra sighed as she looked down at the dress in her arms. Maybe Joren had a point. Perhaps she was more emotionally invested in Odelle than she wanted to admit. It had been years since they were romantically involved, but she had never forgotten.

She banished the memories from her mind and pulled the dress over her head, letting out a sigh as the edges of the skirt fell down past her hips. She wasn't traveling back to Korithia to visit with Odelle and reminisce about the past. No, she would not entertain thoughts of when they first met. She had an important job to do, and if she wanted to stay alive, she needed to focus.

"Just work tonight," she told her reflection in the bathroom mirror. "Nothing more." It was a shame she had always been a liar. She turned away from her own gaze, pushing back thoughts of a lush university campus and the fumbling new student Odelle had been.

Sorra smirked at the sight of the new students marching into their dormitories. She lounged on the grass, stretching her hands above her head as she attempted to find a more comfortable spot. She preferred to be out by the lake rather than in the middle of the chaos as the other students settled in. She had deposited her items in her room and then promptly escaped. It was easier out here. She closed her eyes and sighed, allowing the warm humidity of the day to seep over her. Moments later, a shadow covered part of her face, and she opened her eyes. Someone stood over her, hands full of bulky luggage.

"Excuse me?"

She squinted and sat up, cupping her hand over her eyes to get a better look at who disturbed her. It was a young woman with a narrow frame, and her luggage practically dwarfed her as she set the cases down. "Can I help you?" Sorra asked, making note of the way the stranger's delicate features pulled together in a frown.

"I'm sorry to bother you, but I was wondering if you could provide directions to this place?" She gestured to a location on a datasheet.

Sorra sighed. The building wasn't far off, but she did not like the idea of such a small creature tugging her belongings that far. She stood up and brushed the loose grass from her clothes. "I'll show you." She took one of the heavy pieces of luggage and dragged it off toward the proper dormitory.

"Hey, wait!"

Sorra grinned as she heard the clumsy banging of luggage as the newcomer gathered the rest of her things and ran to catch up. "Um, thank you?"

Sorra shrugged. "Don't worry about it. I'm Sorra, by the way."

"Odelle Lastra. It's my first year…"

That much had been obvious, but Sorra didn't say so. She had learned to recognize the fresh ones. They all stared at the large buildings with wide, hopeful eyes, completely oblivious to the way the universe actually worked.

"I'm a graduate student."

Sorra did a double take. Maybe her guesswork wasn't as accurate as she thought. She gave the young student—Odelle—a closer inspection. She stared back, wide- eyed, which probably made her look more immature than she was. The delicate curves of her face also spoke of youth, but Sorra could see the beginnings of wrinkles set into the smoky skin. Although Odelle had the young, fresh-faced look of someone new and was carrying at least twice as many things as she really needed, there was something interesting behind the naiveté. She wanted to find out what it was.

"If you're starting your graduate studies, why are you living on campus? Most people hate living on university grounds. I would have left if I wasn't short on funds."

Fortunately, Odelle didn't seem to mind her prying. "I've spent the last year offworld. I need some time to readjust to Korithia." She took in a deep breath, and a soft smile spread across her face. "It's good to be home. The air just isn't the same on other planets."

Sorra noticed the slight hesitation. She spared a glance around the courtyard, making sure the other new students were too distracted to listen in on their conversation. "Are you sure Korithia is home? It sounds like you enjoyed your time on…where did you say you were?"

"Nakonum, if you would believe it," Odelle said.

Sorra's breath hitched, and she coughed. She struggled to turn it into a throat-clearing, and then hid her surprise by adjusting the large piece of luggage she carried, only a little envious of the drones shuttling everyone else's bags around. "You finished your last year of school there? The planet was only just taken. Bet that made admissions a little leery when they saw your application."

Odelle laughed, a bright, musical sound that made Sorra's stomach flutter. "That would be an understatement. Oh, here we are." She came to a stop, and Sorra paused beside her, looking up at the tall building. Although the outside had been purposely worn, she could catch a glimpse of new metal in a few places, particularly near the biometric scanners. Academia could never decide whether it wanted to appear old and prestigious or modern and sensible.

"I thought I was supposed to be leading the way?" Sorra asked, giving her a suspicious glance. "How did you know we'd arrived?"

Odelle winked. "Maybe I just wanted an excuse to talk to the interesting stranger I saw lying out in the courtyard, or perhaps I simply wanted help with my bags. I'll let you decide which is true." She headed for the door, sweeping by in a surge of confidence.

Sorra stared after her. How in the galaxy she could have mistaken Odelle for an inexperienced, bumbling first-year?

"Well?" Odelle asked, looking over her shoulder. "Are you coming?"

Sorra laughed and shook her head. She had a feeling that bringing Odelle's luggage the rest of the way to the elevator would be worth it.

Chapter Seven

ODELLE SIGHED, LETTING HER mind wander as one complaint blurred into another.

Nalia Drematis had cornered her, and was not about to let her escape before exhausting every single piece of conversation. "And with all the donations the Foundation receives, is it too unreasonable to expect a coat-checker at the door? I mean, really. We have a certain image to uphold here."

She was the vice president of the Foundation's Committee of Resource Distribution, a title nearly as long winded as she was. Listening to her was so boring physical pain would have been preferable.

"I understand," Odelle murmured at the first possible pause, even though she had no idea what Nalia had just said.

"I know," Nalia sniffed. She made a disgusted motion with her free hand. The other wrapped around a full wineglass. Odelle sighed. Hers was tragically empty, and she knew if she tried to excuse herself for a refill, the vice president would just follow her. "And I clearly explained my allergies to the Secretary before she selected the menu. It's impossible to find good help these days."

"You're right, of course." Odelle's gaze wandered around the room. Part of her hoped Nalia would sense her detachment and move on to a fresh victim. She was trapped with little hope of a reprieve. All she could do was endure. At least the scenery was nice. She lingered on a particularly well-shaped ikthian in a red dress. Their back was turned to her, but the view was still worthwhile. Unfortunately, another group of partygoers passed in front of her and blocked her line of sight. With a sigh, she turned back to Nalia.

"So when I made my complaint to Chancellor Corvis, she said she would resolve the issue. At least she knows how to get things done." Odelle gave Nalia her politest smile. She knew the chancellor far better than most, and "resolving the issue" was politician-speak for "go away." She wished she could say the same thing before her brain leaked out of her ears.

Just when she thought she couldn't stand another moment of Nalia's company, she caught sight of the ikthian in the red dress again. She stood casually next to the open bar. Her energy could be felt even from a distance, and Odelle's eyes widened when she finally caught a glimpse of her face. "Oh!"

"Oh indeed!" Nalia said. "That's what I told her. But—"

"I'm sorry, Madam Vice President, but I'm afraid you'll have to excuse me." Odelle glanced down at her wrist, pretending to receive a message on her communicator. "Something important has just come up."

"We'll have to catch up later!" Nalia called after her.

Odelle ignored her and pushed through the crowd. The woman at the bar caught sight of her and grinned, picking up her wine and strolling toward her. They met in the middle of the room, and Odelle hurried to pull her aside.

"What are you doing here?" Odelle hissed. "Do you want to get carted off to Daashu?"

Sorra laughed. "I see my reputation precedes me. Did they at least include all the juicy details on my criminal record?"

"Never mind that. You're here—"

"You're right. Dalia is here. Nobody knows any different except for you." Sorra swallowed the last of her golden wine and deposited the empty glass on a tray held by a passing staff member. "And you're the only one causing a scene. Relax. I bet you're secretly thrilled to see me."

Sorra's smile calmed her, if only for a moment, and Odelle had to admit it was nice to see her in person instead of over a comm signal. At least, it was nice somewhere underneath her terror. "Perhaps a little."

"See, was that so hard?" Sorra linked their arms and led her through the crowd. Several people stepped aside as they passed, and Odelle suspected it had something to do with the flashy, revealing dress Sorra had chosen. "I thought this would be an excellent place to meet and discuss our plans."

"But it's so crowded," Odelle said. There were a few benefits to hiding in plain sight, but something about Sorra's demeanor suggested this meeting was more about showing off than actually working.

"Would you prefer somewhere more private?"

Yes. Odelle swallowed. "No."

"Are you sure?" Sorra led them away from the buffet and out across the ballroom floor, sidestepping couples as they danced. "There are an awful lot of onlookers, after all. I wouldn't want to cause a scene."

Odelle rolled her eyes. "A scene is exactly what you had in mind when you showed up here."

Sorra led her out onto a clear spot on the dance floor. She extended her hand, a clear invitation. "That depends on what you'll let me get away with."

Their gazes met, and Odelle found it difficult to think with those hazel eyes staring at her so intensely. Sorra challenged her, dared her. It had been like this ever since they had reconnected, each of them dancing away from any serious examination of their relationship when they flirted too much.

With a sigh, she reached out and grabbed Sorra's hand, allowing herself to be pulled forward. Sorra's palm settled at her waist, resting just above the curve of her hip and guiding her into a traditional dance pattern. Odelle could remember the many times they had danced together. Though they lacked the intimacy they had shared, they still danced like lovers. They moved in tight circles, bodies pressed close as their hands searched for a hold on one another.

The music peaked as they danced, and Odelle gasped as Sorra's fingertips slid further along her back. "Be careful," she murmured, although she didn't make any effort to redirect Sorra's hands. "You're playing a dangerous game here."

"Which part?" Sorra eased her into a twirl, catching her halfway through and folding an arm around her waist from behind.

Odelle was still aware of the closeness between them. The weight of Sorra's chin tucked over her shoulder, and warm lips moved just beside her cheek.

"Coming here? Dancing with you? Or maybe trying to destroy the Dominion?"

Odelle frowned and pulled herself out of Sorra's arms. She took over leading, placing her hands where Sorra's had been moments before. "You can't say things like that on Korithia," she said in a low whisper as they glided across the room. "The chancellor has ears everywhere. You can't trust anyone."

"I can trust you."

The statement took Odelle by surprise, and she nearly stepped on Sorra's foot. "Why are you so sure about that?"

Sorra's lips melted into a soft smile. "Because I know you, Odelle."

Odelle's heart skipped a beat. Somehow, she knew Sorra was not only talking about their business arrangement. "What do you know about me?"

"I know you'll be able to figure out the best way to use the weapon I'm about to give you."

"A weapon?" Odelle laced her fingers even tighter through Sorra's as they spun past the other dancers. They shifted their direction as one. *Even after all these years, she hasn't forgotten how to read me.* She stared into Sorra's eyes, although she wasn't sure what answer she expected to find there. "What kind of weapon?"

"I've found Irana's daughter."

Of all the things Odelle had expected Sorra to say, that was the last. For the second time since they had started, she almost fell out of step. She recovered in time and leaned in close, speaking as softly as she could. "Maia? I thought she was dead. Are you sure?"

"Very sure. She's back on my station, speaking in five-syllable words and sticking her nose where it doesn't belong. Even worse, she's fallen in bed with a human. I've spent the past few days putting up with them, but it will all be worth it if you can turn her research into something useful."

They maneuvered past another couple and drifted to a quieter corner of the ballroom. "That depends on what it is," Odelle murmured. "May I look at it?"

Sorra snorted. "What, you think I was stupid enough to bring it with me? If you want to see what I have, you'll need to pay me a visit."

Odelle sighed and let Sorra guide her into another spin. Perhaps dancing wasn't the best idea. It brought back too many old memories, and even more unwanted physical contact. *Well, not exactly unwanted.* She shook herself, trying to erase her thoughts. "That isn't a good idea. You can't expect me to just warp off to Tarkoht whenever you need me there."

"I'm not the only one who wants you there. Kalanis has been asking for a chance to present her research formally for days. She picked out a conference room and everything. I'm sure she expects an impressive audience." Sorra leaned forward, so close that their cheeks brushed, and whispered, "And you certainly are impressive."

Odelle gasped and Sorra smirked. *Some all-powerful trader of secrets I am.* She hated and loved how easily Sorra flustered her. "And what does that mean?" she asked, trying to recover.

The music ended and the dancers stopped. Sorra led her off the dance floor, ignoring her question in favor of listening to whichever politician had taken the stage with the musicians. "It means I want you to come to Tarkoht."

"Because of Maia Kalanis, because of the Dominion and what we're trying to accomplish, or because you actually want me there?" Odelle asked before she could stop herself.

Sorra's eyes softened in a way that made Odelle's heart ache. "Yes, I want you there because it's important. Because I think we finally have the chance to finish what we started. I wouldn't ask you to come otherwise. But is it really so hard to believe I want you there because I still enjoy your company? When was the last time you paid me a visit?"

Odelle had to think back. She honestly could not remember anything recent. "It was a long time ago," she murmured, averting her eyes. Years, actually. Her gaze followed the crowd, and fortunately, most of them were preoccupied with the speaker now that the dancing had stopped. She even caught a glimpse of Nalia near the punch bowl, where she had trapped several more unwilling victims.

The soft brush of fingertips against her arm startled her. She turned around to see Sorra standing intimately close to her. "Then come see the station. Say you're going on vacation. Fake an illness. Have a hysterical fit or something." Odelle recognized the same, soft pleading tone Sorra had relied on so often back in school, usually trying to convince her to come out for a night.

She knew it was a bad idea, but she found herself reaching down to take Sorra's hand. Their fingers threaded together. "I hardly think a hysterical fit will be necessary," she whispered. "If this research is as important as you say, I should hear it in person. Then, we can decide on the best way to distribute it."

Sorra nodded. "Right. Find where it will do the most damage." She stepped back, letting their grip loosen and break away. "You still have the coordinates?

"Yes. Tarkoht is still Dominion property. Perhaps I can put a few ideas into the chancellor's head. It's been a long time since anyone's checked up on Joren and Dalia Talamakis." Sorra rolled her eyes at the mention of her partner. Odelle had met Joren before, and she knew Sorra had absolutely no interest in him, but the reminder of her arranged partnership always stung.

"It has been a long time, hasn't it?" Sorra's flirtatious smile returned. "If the chancellor does send you to investigate, I'm sure you'll find a few things on Tarkoht to keep you occupied."

Odelle sighed. She was not ready to think about what she would find if she did visit Tarkoht. The weight of her responsibilities returned, and she shifted her gaze back to the crowd. The orchestra struck up again, and Sorra held out an upturned hand, inviting her back onto the dance floor. "I can't make any promises." She took Sorra's hand, but instead of stepping back into her arms, she gave it a brief squeeze and backed away. "What we're doing is dangerous. If anyone discovers…"

"No one is going to discover anything." Sorra took another step toward her. "We'll be careful."

"This isn't just about us," Odelle hissed under her breath. "You're treating it like some kind of game. This is about the Dominion, the entire galaxy. We can't let this become about what we used to have."

Sorra's eyes widened then narrowed. The last traces of her smile vanished. She let her hand fall back to her side and stepped away from the dance floor. "I take my job very seriously, Executive Lastra. You just concentrate on doing yours, and that includes coming to Tarkoht. If we're lucky, Kalanis and her research will help both of us get what we want." Odelle opened her mouth to speak, but Sorra cut her off again. "And believe it or not, what I want does not rest solely between your legs."

"I never said that." Odelle crossed her arms. "I just meant…You know what? It doesn't matter." Sorra was infamous for letting arguments spiral out of control, and she refused to give her any more openings for a witty comeback. "Thank you for coming all this way just to speak with me. I'm sure it must have been difficult for you."

"It wasn't too hard even though I'm glad you appreciate the effort."

Odelle took a step closer, though she kept her arms crossed. "You'll have to tell me how you managed to get Dalia an invite. I'm sure it's an interesting story."

"I'd be happy to regale you with the full details somewhere more private." The seductive look returned to Sorra's eyes, and as much as Odelle wanted to say yes to the offer, she knew it would be a mistake.

"I…thank you, but I'm afraid I can't." Odelle walked toward the open balcony at the end of the ballroom, not wanting to meet Sorra's gaze and see the disappointment there. The clack of Sorra's shoes against the stone floors followed her.

"Well, that doesn't have to mean the night's over." Together, they stepped out into the warm, humid air. Only one other couple occupied the balcony, and they lingered in the far corner, talking to one another in whispers. Odelle ignored them, resting her arms against the balcony railing. "What are you walking away for? Do you want to be alone?"

"I don't know what I want." Odelle stared out past the railing and over the grounds. The institute rested in between a lake and an expansive city, and the balcony overlooked the lake's shore. Its surface reflected the nighttime sky, black and smooth as obsidian. She almost wanted to dive in, just to see if she could shatter the surface.

There was a soft noise beside her, and she felt rather than saw Sorra join her at the railing. "You think it's any different there?"

Odelle tore her eyes away from the glassy water and glanced over at her. "Where?"

"Wherever that world is." Sorra nodded at the lake. "I remember growing up and being told the water reflected another world parallel to ours. My parents always told me it looked exactly the same, but was different in ways we could not imagine. That was why the reflection mirrored us. They didn't want us ever trying to cross over."

Odelle smiled, remembering the folklore from her childhood. "There's a perfectly viable explanation for water's reflective surface, you know." Sorra did not respond, and she sighed, moving closer so that their arms brushed together. "But if there is another world, perhaps they don't have war. Maybe they watch us, with our egos and self-inflicted problems, and laugh...or weep." It was probably a good thing Sorra did not know how much weeping she had done.

Sorra laughed softly and moved so their arms were not touching anymore. "Why am I not surprised? Even when you aren't working, you still worry about what other people think."

Odelle frowned. She was too high up to make out her own reflection in the lake, but the light from the party behind them cast shining ripples across the water, breaking through the polished blackness. "It's habit. The chancellor pays me to worry about what other people think...or, more accurately, she pays me to make sure they think what we want them to think. And if anyone disagrees..." She closed her eyes, trying to ignore the sudden heaviness in her chest. She didn't want to imagine a world in which Sorra was taken prisoner by the Dominion. Warm fingers slid across her shoulder, and the touch sent a jolt through her. She took in a shaking breath. "Don't. You need to leave before anyone sees us like this."

"I've already been seen. I picked this dress for a reason."

Odelle knew Sorra had worn it for her benefit. "It was a good choice," she said weakly. "I'm not making any promises, but I'll see if I can convince the chancellor to let me visit Tarkoht. If you want to help, ask your naledai friends to act a little more disgruntled than usual. The orbital station is an important hub near Nakonum, and she won't want to loosen her hold on it."

Sorra let go of her arm. "I'll see what I can do. Just be there. I'd appreciate it if you were."

Odelle did not respond as Sorra walked away. She did not want to cause a scene. That would only make Sorra's departure harder, and she had probably stayed too long already. Instead of watching her leave, Odelle looked up at the sky, the stars washed out from the bright city lights, no shining bulbs of distant planets. No reminders of the trillions of lives she gambled with. She could not tell if she preferred it that way or not. She closed her eyes and leaned on the railing.

At least for a few hours that night, she had been able to forget about those responsibilities. That was part of Sorra's charm. She helped Odelle put aside her burdens, and the starless sky looked more like an empty canvas than a barren wasteland.

***

Odelle's stomach twisted into knots as she waited out in the dark. Her eyes darted toward every small noise she heard, and she tightened her fingers around the grip of the stunner tucked in her jacket. She desperately wished Sorra would hurry up. The only thing worse than sneaking off to a dangerous, forbidden student meeting in the middle of the night was sneaking there alone.

"Hey!"

A hand gripped her arm, and she cried out, jerking away. She whipped around to face her shadowy form of attacker, brandishing the stunner with a shaking hand. The person raised their arms in surrender and laughed. Odelle sighed as she recognized Sorra's chiseled features, her grin twisting as she tried to stifle more laughs.

"You awful person!" she hissed, lost for a proper insult. She stuffed the stunner back into her jacket. "I was about to hurt you. What were you thinking?"

"I was thinking I would have a little fun by scaring you. Relax."
When Odelle remained silent, Sorra sighed and nodded down the alley.

"Come on. If you're going to stay mad at me forever, at least come with me so we're not late."

After glancing over her shoulder to make sure no one else had heard her scream, Odelle followed Sorra down the alley. Despite the childish prank, she didn't want to return to her room. The meetings subjects were too tempting to resist, and if she was being honest with herself, so was the idea of spending more time in Sorra's company. She often found herself surprised by Sorra's insights, and she wanted to discover more of the depth of her character, if possible.

"So, what makes a good girl like you want to sneak out to an 'illegal gathering of dangerous, antisocial dissenters'?" Sorra asked as they crept around a corner.

Odelle recognized the quote. It had been on the news a few months ago, when the Safety and Justice Department had broken up a similar meeting. According to the rumor mill, several students hadn't returned to classes the following week. "You just don't seem like the type."

Odelle peered over at her companion. "If I don't seem like the type, why did you ask me to come? I could've turned you in."

Her eyes adjusted to the dark, and she saw Sorra flash her a confident grin. "I knew you wouldn't." Sorra drew closer to her as they walked, their shoulders almost touching.

The possibility of contact made Odelle's face heat up. "You still haven't answered my question. Why did you invite me? We've only known each other a few months."

Instead of teasing her, Sorra fell into silence for a few moments before giving her answer. "Maybe it's the way you talk about the naledai you met on Nakonum. You use their names. You get this little furrow in the middle of your brow when you talk about some of the things you saw." She shrugged, and her careless smile returned. "I figured this would be right up your alley."

"Being sympathetic to aliens is a large jump from openly opposing the chancellor and her council," Odelle pointed out.

"Not so large. Anyone with a brain and a conscience knows what the Dominion's doing is wrong. You don't have to go all the way to Nakonum to see it. Plenty of ikthians end up dead or worse right here on Korithia. Problem is most people are too scared to do anything about it. But you aren't scared, are you?"

Odelle narrowed her eyes. "You're right, I'm not scared. I barreled right past it and ended up at terrified when you grabbed me in the dark."

"Hey," Sorra protested, her lower lip sticking out in a pout. "I said I was sorry."

"Actually, you didn't."

"Well then, I'm sorry. No, really," Sorra added when Odelle snorted and turned her head. Warmth covered her hand, and her breath hitched as Sorra's fingers laced through hers, urging her to look. "I shouldn't have snuck up on you like that. Guess I like getting under your skin a little."

That confession took Odelle by surprise. She came to a stop just behind one of the buildings, and Sorra stopped with her. "That's an odd way of putting it, getting under my skin. What about me is so interesting to you, Sorra?"

"Well, what about me is so interesting to you? Don't tell me you only came for the rebellion and not for a little extra quality time with me."

Odelle sighed. Sorra's annoying habit of redirecting questions would drive her insane one of these days. She was already well on her way there. "You'll have to speak plainly with me eventually." They continued on, reaching the student home where the meeting was to be hosted. Lights were on in the upper floor windows, but shadows still flooded the lower levels. As they approached the entrance, Odelle frowned. Two Safety and Justice officials stood outside, turning people away from the door. Another university staff member had dragged some students aside and spoke quietly with them. "Sorra, we should leave," she said, tugging on Sorra's arm.

She pulled away from Odelle and shook her head. "Just a minute. I want a word with them."

"Sorra, don't!" Odelle tried to grab her arm again, but missed. She watched in horror as Sorra marched right up to the officials.

"What are you doing here?"

Odelle groaned and buried her face in her hands. It was too painful to watch, but she heard one of the officials speak in an apathetic, low tone. "Return to your dormitory. This place is off-limits."

"Why?" Sorra asked.

"Because we say it is. Return to your dormitory, now."

Before Sorra could reply, Odelle moved forward. Thinking quickly, she flung her arms around Sorra's neck, drawing her into an affectionate embrace. "Oh, my dear, let's just go. You promised to share a bath with me once we get back to our dormitory."

Sorra turned to stare at her, but her shock was short-lived. She adapted to the situation quickly. "And you'll get one, my love," she ground the words out in a growl. She pulled Odelle's arms off her. "But first, I want to know why I'm not allowed inside public property. I thought this building was open to all students?"

"We are currently conducting an investigation," said one of the officials. Both of them glared at Sorra. "Details will be released after all criminals have been detained and questioned."

"Criminals?" Sorra repeated. "What? Were the students getting too uppity in their freethinking? Couldn't have that, huh?"

"Sorra, let's go," Odelle said again, pulling at her elbow. This was it. This was how Sorra would get them killed.

"Listen to your friend," said one of the officials, nodding in Odelle's direction. "You don't want to get involved with this. Leave, or we'll have to detain you, too."

"She's not my friend." Sorra shoved her away and took another step closer to the officials. "Now tell me—"

The soldier didn't bother arguing. Before Odelle could react, one of them drew his arm back. His fist broke across Sorra's face with a sickening crack. She staggered backward, bringing one hand up to her face, but the blow had disoriented her.

Odelle rushed to Sorra's side, catching her before she lost her balance or tried to throw a punch of her own. "Are you all right?"

"Get her out of here," said the official. His knuckles were smeared dark with blood, and Odelle could see even more spurting out from between Sorra's fingers.

"I will," she said, pulling Sorra away. Sorra sagged in her arms, every step weak and faltering. "Let's get you home, now. Come on."

"Odelle?" Sorra asked in a weak voice. She looked up, and Odelle could see that her nose was crooked. "My face hurts."

"We'll take you to the health clinic. Come on." She helped Sorra loop an arm over her shoulder, pulling her weight up so they could walk. She took a deep breath, trying to calm herself, ignoring the wetness on her face, the stinging in her eyes. She had to get Sorra help first. The rest could wait.

Rae D. Magdon & Michelle Magly

Chapter Eight

MAIA SMILED AS TAYLOR gestured out over the surface of the lake.

"Wow, I had no idea Nakonum's moons had water, let alone something as large as this!" Taylor said.

Her lover's excitement was infectious. "I am glad you approve. I hoped this spot would appeal to you. I never got to see much of Earth, but I have been told this landscape is similar." She reached back to adjust the straps of her biopack where they rubbed against her shoulders. Her legs were a little sore from hiking up over the last ridge, but the expression on Taylor's face was worth it. She looked happier than Maia had seen her in a long time.

"I more than approve. This is incredible!" Taylor lifted her hand, shielding her eyes with her palm. Nakonum's sun hung high overhead, casting a rippling glare on the water. "A place this beautiful should be a tourist destination or something."

"Perhaps it was before the war." It certainly seemed plausible. The rocks around the edge of the water were smooth, as if other people had worn them down. Giant trees stretched toward the sky, and although they did not look like the Korithian foliage she was used to, she could tell the area near the lake had been cleared for easier passage.

She turned back to Taylor, watching the wind ripple the short, dark strands of her hair. "And now it is again, at least for the next few hours."

Taylor sighed. "I'd spend more than a few hours here if I could, but it'll have to do. Hey, pass me the water?" She gestured at the pack on Maia's back.

"Why?" Maia adopted her most innocent expression. "Did you lose yours?" She knew Taylor hadn't actually lost her water at all. It was underneath all the other things they had packed before their flight, and Maia suspected she simply didn't feel like digging for it.

"Fine," Taylor huffed. "Make me pull out all the useless stuff you asked me to bring." Despite the annoyance in her voice, she still seemed cheerful as she swung her own biopack off her back and tossed it onto the ground. "Think this is a decent spot for a picnic blanket?" she asked, unsealing the top compartment. "The view's great, but the wind might get a little cold."

Maia knelt beside her. "Then it's a good thing we brought more than one blanket."

"Your idea." Taylor unfolded one of the sturdy outdoor blankets, flicking it open and draping it over the flattest patch of ground. "I'm glad you insisted on it."

"Personal experience. I spent many of my days in a laboratory back on Korithia, but I did my fair share of fieldwork as well. Someone has to collect the samples for study, and you can't always trust graduate students."

"Why not?" Taylor asked. "Sorry, I don't exactly know much about higher education."

"They might collect the wrong sample or label the data incorrectly. Of course, the professionals aren't much better. It's a risk that comes with having anyone else do your own work. There was also the risk they might take it to the authorities, especially with my controversial work."

"So you did it all yourself?" Taylor asked. She knelt down and dragged food out of the bag. Maia joined her.

"That is often how it is with any contentious work. There are no other options," she said with a shrug. "I couldn't trust anyone."

Taylor watched her for a moment. The corners of her mouth twitched down, and her forehead wrinkled. "It must have been lonely."

"It was." Maia rarely talked about her past with Taylor, mostly because it had been uninteresting and controlled by others. Even now, she did not feel like talking about the days she had spent with no contact from another living being. Well, aside from her samples.

Silence settled between them, and Maia watched Taylor pick at her food. She currently held a steamed fish wrapped in seaweed and stuffed with local grains. Taylor took a bite and Maia watched her expression, trying to discern if Taylor looked disgusted or intrigued. Maia had not quite figured out how eyebrow-related expressions worked.

"It's like sushi," Taylor said at last. She took another bite, which had to be a good sign.

"I don't know what that is," Maia said.

Taylor held up the wrap. "Same ingredients, kind of. Meat, rice, maybe some vegetables, and a seaweed wrap on the outside. Your seaweed, or whatever this flaky stuff is, looks kind of weird though." She scrunched her nose and picked at a piece dangling from the bitten portion of her food. She stuffed the rest into her mouth and swallowed.

"Looks weird, but tastes pretty good. Anyway, my mom made this stuff all the time. She said it helped her connect to her heritage."

Maia paused to take a bite from her own food. "Was your mother really so different than your father simply because she was born in a different place?"

Taylor shrugged. "It's hard to explain. You ikthians don't seem to make a big deal out of regional differences."

"When you exist as a galactic entity, the borderline between identities is usually drawn at the species. We used to separate ourselves by region, but that was ages ago." Maia paused and considered her words. "But that does not mean we are all the same. The different cultures and ways of life are still there, just not as pronounced as in human culture. At least, it seems that way to me, but I don't know much about your species."

Taylor nodded, though Maia wondered if she was humoring her. She held up the wrap. "So what would you call this if it isn't sushi?"

"In my native language? *Angatha*. It's a very popular dish on Korithia, and several other species have adapted it for themselves, like the naledai."

"*Angatha*," Taylor repeated, testing the word in her mouth. "Why didn't my translator change that word when you said it?"

"Perhaps it doesn't have an English equivalent." Instinctively, Maia reached up to touch the small scar above the edge of her jaw. It was so close to the small ridges along her neck it was hardly noticeable, and she could not see it when she looked at her reflection, but she was aware of its presence. She had been so scared then, drugged and strapped to that horrible table while the strange human scientists implanted her translator. Now, she was surprisingly grateful for it. If she hadn't been able to communicate with Taylor, she never would have escaped, and she might have died of loneliness long before the Coalition or the Dominion ever got around to killing her.

"Does it hurt?" Taylor asked in a low voice.

Maia's eyes flicked back up to her face. "No. It doesn't hurt and hasn't for a long time. Without it, we wouldn't be able to speak at all."

"Well, maybe we should fix that." Taylor shifted on the blanket. "Teach me some of your language. I want to learn Ikthian. You know, in case one of us loses our translator." She raised her eyebrows. "Or if one of us wants to curse in another language."

Maia laughed. "There is no language called Ikthian, Taylor, just as there is no language called Human. I speak *Cetacean*, and we mostly use it in the south. It's the most common dialect on our planet." She leaned closer to Taylor as a gust of wind whipped across the lake. "But if you wish to learn, I would be happy to teach. Are you able to turn off your translator?"

Taylor grinned. "Yep. But then how am I going to understand the dirty parts?"

"I'm not sure obscenity should be your first lesson," Maia said. "Let's start with something simpler. Are you ready?"

"Ready." Maia watched her reach behind an ear and tapped the translator off.

Maia thought for a moment then gestured out at the lake. "Anapos."

Taylor reached back again and turned her translator back on. "What did you just say? Lake?"

"Water," Maia said. "It's the most basic word I could think of...and probably the most useful. The words for 'mother' and 'home' use the same root."

"Anapos," Taylor repeated. The word flowed easily. Maia had no problem dissecting the vowel sounds. She smiled. "Water. Okay. How's my accent. Good?" When she didn't respond right away, Taylor sighed. "That bad, huh?"

"Actually, I didn't have any problem understanding you. You are an excellent imitator."

Taylor smiled once more and leaned back on her palms. "All right! Give me another one. I want to be able to say something in a full sentence to Sorra. Preferably something insulting. That'd wipe the smug grin off her face."

Maia shook her head. "She won't let you get away with that so easily. Sorra is known for her wit first. All other traits come second." When Taylor frowned again Maia added, "But I'll teach you some good replies to use on her."

"Really? You think I can be that good?" Taylor asked. She looked less confident than she usually did. Her shoulders were relaxed and her head bowed, not the usual display of power Taylor managed to exert.

"I don't see why you can't be."

"Oh, well...you know." Taylor shifted. She looked anywhere but at Maia. "I'm not the smartest human. I didn't do well in school. When I had the choice to go to college, I joined the military and became a jarhead. I figured it was something I could actually be good at."

"Taylor." Maia knew little about Taylor's life before the military, but it sounded difficult. "You're a very intelligent person. I don't know if I would have been attracted to you otherwise."

"Yeah, but..." Taylor gestured vaguely to her. "You're a scientist with a PhD or some ikthian equivalent. You're a genius, a vital asset to your people, even if they did use you for evil. I doubt the Coalition even felt a loss when I jumped ship." Taylor grew silent and stared at the ground for several long seconds. Maia waited for her to say more. At last, Taylor met her gaze again. "So, let's see if you can teach me anything."

Maia smiled and reached out for Taylor's hand, squeezing it gently. "Certainly."

***

The foul smell of smoke and sweat made Rachel wrinkle her nose as she stepped into the dimly lit bar. Apparently, some things transcended language and culture, because even though this dive was on one of Nakonum's less-secure moons, it was uncomfortably similar to the run-down Earth bars she had seen. She ran a finger over the nearest table, picking up a layer of grime. Dirtier even.

She drew a few curious stares when she entered, but fortunately, the patrons of the bar, mostly naledai, with a few other stragglers mixed in, followed the same rule humans usually did in this kind of place—mind your own business. Once they decided she wasn't an immediate threat, they turned their backs. She ignored them, straightened her shoulders, and approached the bar, her hand hovering near the grip of her pistol.

There were several open seats, but none of them faced the door. Reluctantly, she chose one at the far end, close to the window. If one of the fish squads patrolling the streets under the guise of "peacekeeping" decided to peek in, she might get some advance warning. Once she was perched in the corner, she braced her elbow on the edge of the bar and observed her surroundings more closely. Most of the naledai present did not seem to be armed at first glance, but she suspected that several of them were carrying despite the planet-wide ban on weapons.

"What'll you have?"

She turned to face the bartender, who had finally decided to make his way over. He wasn't naledai, and his slitted nostrils reminded her of a serpent's nose. His waxy skin made him look like a corpse, pale and tight-lipped. He was Rakash and probably hired because of the extra arms. Most human bartenders would have been envious of the way his six hands deftly wielded different glasses and bottles. The tall, slender alien kept his four eyes focused on her, but managed to continue serving and passing drinks to other patrons without missing a beat.

Rachel glanced at the flickering letters on the board behind the bar. None of them made sense to her, since her translator implant was only auditory. She shrugged. "Something smooth, not too strong. I'm working." The bartender gave her a skeptical look, or at least she thought it was skeptical when his grey, murky second eyelids blinked beneath the first set. He walked off, and Rachel resumed her vigil.

The longer she studied the other people in the bar, the more she began to doubt her information. The brief reports the Coalition had provided her before banishing her from Earth had listed Aureus as a hotbed of rebel activity, but she suspected the reports were outdated at best and inaccurate at worst. A few drunks stared into their glasses and a small group of gamblers shouted at one of the better-lit tables in the back, but mostly, the people here were fighters. Street thugs with the bulk and scars to prove it. Even if they did know where the rebels were, she doubted any of them would be friendly enough to volunteer the information or smuggle her past the ikthian blockade around Nakonum's atmosphere.

"Not every day you see a human in this place, let alone a female."

Rachel knew by the gruffness of the voice that it was a naledai. She forced a smile, but the naledai only stared at her with glittering dark eyes. "And it's not every day you find a naledai smart enough to figure that out. Good job."

He snarled, revealing pointed teeth. "You're calling me stupid? I'm not the one who walked into a bar on a hostile planet. Leave now. If the ikthians catch you here, what they do to us won't compare to what they'll do to you."

Rachel leaned back against the counter, trying to look relaxed, but her hand drifted closer to her pistol. She tried to keep her breathing even in spite of her racing heart. "I didn't know having a drink was such a risky occupation." The bartender returned with her glass and slid it over to her. She picked it up and took a slow sip of the biting liquid, refusing to break eye contact with the naledai.

"I haven't seen a human here in over a year," the naledai grunted. "What makes you so special?"

"I wanted a vacation." Rachel set her glass back down on the bar. Some of other patrons shifted around, glancing over at her. Others got up to leave. None of them looked friendly. Her fingers twitched beside her hip. "And even if I'm here for something else, why should it bother you? We're allies, aren't we?"

The naledai leaned in closer. "Not on Nakonum. Not while the fish are listening to every word we say. Get out before we all pay the price."

"Leave the human alone," the bartender said. Rachel glanced at him and her eyes widened when she noticed that he had drawn a weapon in one of his hands.

The naledai noticed, too. His fur bristled. He lunged past her shoulder and over the counter, swiping his claws at the bartender's weapon. He wasn't fast enough. A shot blasted near Rachel's ears, and she jumped back just in time, drawing her own weapon. She stood, willing her hands not to shake as the naledai slumped over on top of the bar. His arms twitched a few times, and then he went still, leaving nothing but the acrid smell of burnt flesh and a slow-gathering pool of blood.

"Well, shit," Rachel said. She didn't think the bartender was a threat, but she kept the nose of her weapon trained on him just in case. "That escalated quickly."

The bartender ignored her. He tucked his weapon away behind his lowest set of arms and leaned closer to the naledai. "You're worth more dead," he hissed to the corpse. She glanced around at the other patrons, but all of them looked away. They must have seen the shot, but either they were too afraid or too smart to get involved.

"So..." Rachel's eyes flicked back toward the naledai's corpse, and she swallowed when the blood spilled off the counter. "I guess this is the part where I pay you for the drink and back away slowly."

The bartender glanced at her pistol, and then at the half-empty glass sitting on top of the bar. Miraculously, it was still undisturbed. "The drink is free, human. It's nothing compared to the fortune I just made by killing him."

"So it wasn't his lack of manners that earned him a bullet?" Cautiously, Rachel lowered her pistol and tucked it back into its holder.

"He was caught selling secrets. The rebels here are thin on the ground, and General Oranthis can't afford to waste lives."

Rachel narrowed her eyes at the rakash. "You're with them?"

"I'm with whoever pays the most. General Oranthis asked Sorra to take care of this problem. Sorra paid me to do it. Everyone's happy."

"Yeah," Rachel muttered, glancing at the dead naledai. "Everyone but him."

The bartender shrugged. "What do you care?"

"I don't." She picked up her glass and finished off her drink. "So, you probably know who I need to talk to about getting in touch with the rebels."

"You don't need to. They will be here momentarily."

"What?" Before Rachel could even reach for her weapon, the bar doors opened, and two naledai walked in. Unlike the other people in the bar, they were heavily armed, and they did not bother hiding it. They found her gaze immediately, and she took a step back, wishing she had not been so quick to put away her pistol.

"You're coming with us."

Rachel backed up, bumping against the edge of the bar. "Wait a second." She pulled out her gun and pointed it at the approaching naledai, but they continued walking toward her. Rachel swallowed. If by some miracle she did manage to get a shot off first, the other naledai would be sure to take her down. "I'm just trying to find someone. Another human."

"Then look for them on Earth," the larger naledai growled. "You're going to get everyone killed if you stay here. And put that thing away." It nodded at her pistol. "Do you want the fish to shoot you on sight?"

"I've managed to avoid them this long, and if they do come in...well, let's just say I think they'll be more concerned about the two rebels waving their weapons around."

The other naledai barked and grabbed her by the arm. It was smaller, and Rachel was almost certain it was female, but its grip was painfully strong. "You come with us now, or the ikthian patrol outside finds you and guns down everyone in this bar." She leaned in closer, and Rachel shuddered as claws pierced the sleeve of her shirt. She felt naked without the protection of her body armor. "This isn't one of their homeworlds. They don't care about bystanders."

Rachel cast one last look at the bartender and made a decision. Before coming to the bar, she had tucked her ship away in a relatively safe hiding place, and she put her most important supplies in her biopack. It was probably better to go along with what the naledai wanted, especially since finding the rebels was the first step to finding Taylor. They would probably be able to take her planetside, if nothing else. "Fine. I'll come with you." The smaller naledai reached for her weapon, but she narrowed her eyes and tightened her finger on the trigger. "I don't think so. I'll keep mine, and you keep yours."

The smaller naledai looked as though she was about to protest, but the larger one shook his great, shaggy head. Reluctantly, the two of them stepped back and gave her enough space to reach for her pack. She swung it onto her shoulders, trying not to look at the corpse lying a few feet away. The bartender gave her a sarcastic little wave, and Rachel wasn't sure whether to be grateful to him or angry at his deception. "Goodbye, human. You just gave me the best tip I've ever gotten in this place."

"Yeah, well..." she muttered as she followed the two naledai out of the bar. "You should work on your customer service."

***

"Madam Chancellor." Odelle pushed out of her chair, standing up behind her desk. "It's good to see you." Over the years, that simple lie had become easier and easier to tell. Her job dealt in lies every day, and she was good at crafting them.

"You were the one who wanted to see me," the chancellor reminded her. Although there was a comfortable seat in front of the desk, she made no move to take it. Her gaze drifted around the room instead, as if she were there for an inspection instead of a meeting.

Odelle forced herself to smile, her cheeks straining with the effort. "And I'm very grateful you made time out of your busy schedule to come and see me. I'm afraid it's urgent, and the topic is sensitive. Discussing it via messages would have been inappropriate."

The chancellor nodded and finally took her seat. "Well, I'm here now. Let's resolve this quickly. I have an appearance to make at the Performing Arts Center later this evening."

The simple statement sent a pulse of fear down Odelle's spine. No matter how much time she spent with Chancellor Corvis, she could never quite get a handle on what was going through her head. One moment, she was a smiling, bright-faced leader, the face of the council and devoted to making the lives of her people as smooth and worry-free as possible. At least until any of them dared to complain about the alien slave labor that made their easy lives possible or questioned the lies of superiority the Dominion told. Then, she was a violent, merciless enforcer, unashamed to get blood on her hands in service to the "greater good."

Odelle took her cue from the chancellor and sat down as well. "That sounds like a pleasant way to spend your evening." She folded her hands over the desk and waited for a response, but the chancellor looked at her. "Anyway, I asked you here to propose I visit the Tarkoht orbital station. I had a conversation with one of the station managers recently, and there appears to be unusual activity in the area."

The chancellor's expression remained outwardly calm, but Odelle could tell that she wasn't pleased. "Unusual how?"

She slid the datasheet across the desk and flipped it for the chancellor to read. The records were faked, but it hardly mattered. Any mention of rebel activity was usually enough to make the chancellor wary. "We've noticed irregular traffic patterns. Questionable shipping orders. The station is either home for too much illegal activity or is becoming a hotbed for dissenters. It is conveniently close to Nakonum."

"Rebels," the chancellor murmured. She took the datasheet and scrolled through it. "And why should I send you? This is a problem for the Seekers to solve."

Odelle nodded. Outwardly, she maintained a neutral expression, but her insides twisted. "Normally, that would be correct, but the head of the station and his partner recently invited me to come visit. I have a perfectly acceptable excuse to go. Surely you can appreciate the advantages of a subtler approach. Tarkoht is one of our most profitable trading ports, and if anything goes wrong while the Seekers are there…" She paused deliberately. "We don't want any bad publicity over the next few months. I'm better suited for the job."

The chancellor gave her a calculated look, and Odelle tried not to shift under the steady gaze. "The station managers are old friends of yours, aren't they?"

"Joren's partner Dalia was my schoolmate," Odelle said. The more truth her story held, the less likely she was to arouse the chancellor's suspicions. "We reunited at the Foundation's party. Talking to her got me thinking, and when I began planning my visit, these irregularities came up."

The chancellor sat without saying anything for a long time. She switched between studying the datasheet and staring off at nothing. Finally, she sighed and leaned back in her chair. "I suppose looking into this wouldn't hurt. I don't like the idea of you being gone during reelection."

"It will be a short stay." A smile tugged at Odelle's lips at the thought of visiting Sorra. "I'll be back in plenty of time to keep an eye on your campaign." Truthfully, it was a "campaign" in name only. The chancellor's victory was already assured, the rest just for show. "I promise, you won't even notice my absence."

"Very well. But be careful, Odelle. I'm going to start thinking this is just a clever ploy for some vacation time." Odelle's smile receded, and the chancellor stood up. She took one more glance at the datasheet before smoothing the front of her dress. "I expect comprehensive reports delivered daily while you're gone, especially concerning Irana Talamakis' activities. You are free to leave any time you wish, but give my assistant a full itinerary of your travel details before you do."

"Thank you, Madam Chancellor." Odelle stood up in a show of respect as the chancellor paused at the door.

"No, Odelle. Thank you for your work. People like you keep our society held together." She flashed one more smile at Odelle—a warning, possibly. "Remember that while you're away."

Chapter Nine

SORRA GLANCED FROM HER station in the viewing deck down into the hangar, looking everywhere but at the sealed doors of the docking bay. Only a small escort of two guards waited with her, just in case. Aside from them, she had ordered everyone else to leave. Odelle would arrive any second, and she did not want an audience. Preparing for the visit had earned her enough laughter from Joren already.

"What time is it?" she asked, not bothering to look at the guards beside her.

One of them glanced at his communicator. "Two standard hours past Odelle Lastra's departure and twenty seconds past when you last asked me. She should arrive any second."

Sorra glanced at the control tower, but the technician sat at her post, waiting with the rest of them. No communication with an incoming vessel, at least not yet.

Just as she looked back at the hangar shields, a blip appeared in the distance, a splash of color against a black. "What is that?" she asked, pointing at the approaching vessel.

"Incoming ship requesting permission to dock," the technician said over the intercom. "Bio identification shows an ikthian female. Positive match with Odelle Lastra."

"Welcome her aboard, then." Sorra took a deep breath to calm her nerves. She wanted everything to be perfect. Since their falling out and reacquaintance, she and Odelle had barely shared a few hours together at a time, not enough to get used to one another again. She hoped a couple weeks on the orbital station would allow them to recover some of their lost friendship.

The hangar bay's translucent docking doors slid open, and the body of a ship lowered onto the landing strip. Sorra leaned forward, her breath fogging up the viewing glass. She searched for the ship's exit before fixing on the row of lights along the far wall. They flashed from red to yellow, and the doors sealed again. Waiting for the pumps to finish adjusting the air pressure only took a few seconds, but the moments crawled by.

She headed for the door as soon as the lights flashed green, leaving the guards behind. Part of her wanted to take the stairs to the hangar entrance and save herself a few seconds, but she forced herself to resist. It would not do to look desperate, even if that was pretty close to how she felt. She was, however, eager enough to hop the railing instead of opening the gate that led to the elevator pad.

She touched down on the lower level just as a metal walkway descended from the belly of the ship, and her heartbeat leapt into her throat when she saw a slender figure walk down the ramp. Even from a distance, she recognized Odelle. Sorra swallowed, forcing her lips into a careless smile. "You're late," she said, making her way over to the ship at a more measured pace.

Odelle shook her head, but Sorra was relieved to see her smiling. "Fashionably on time. I don't have enough hours in the day to be early for everything."

"Not even for me?" Sorra had meant the question to sound teasing, but when it escaped, the squeak in her throat horrified her.

"For you, I managed 'on time' instead of late, Dalia."

The sound of the wrong name caused a catch in her breath, although she could not articulate why. It never bothered her when the other people on the station used it, especially since most of Tarkoht knew her by that identity. Still, hearing it from Odelle felt wrong. "Let's get out of here," she said, holding out her elbow. After a moment of hesitation, Odelle took it. "I've got a few plans for you before our meeting."

Odelle's gaze darted around the docking bay. "Are we safe to speak freely?"

Sorra smirked. "I guess the Dominion doesn't realize what a hotbed of rebel activity this place is. Most permanent staff members are on my payroll or against your little regime. I'm very good at keeping my identities separate."

Odelle relaxed. "That's comforting to hear." They stepped onto the lift and rejoined the guards. Sorra nodded, and they allowed her to pass, before trailing behind them out of the hangar. "So, what do you have planned for me first? I travelled across the galaxy. I thought you'd at least let me rest."

"Someone will collect your things and bring them to your room. I can take you there if you're too exhausted from travel." Sorra tried to keep her expression neutral, but she dreaded Odelle might not want to spend the evening with her. She had bribed too many people to recoup the losses.

"No, I'm looking forward to spending some time with you. I just thought I might change into something more appropriate for an evening out."

Sorra glanced back at Odelle. She wore what could already considered to be a rather tasteful set of flowing blue robes, though someone in politics might consider it work clothes. "You look stunning, though my opinion is biased." She grinned when Odelle's pale cheeks flushed. "I thought I'd take you out somewhere quiet for a meal, and then let you have some time to recover from your flight."

"How thoughtful. I might be touched if I didn't think this was an elaborate ploy to get me alone."

Sorra led her down a turn that would connect with the restaurant she had chosen. "We both know all I need to do is ask."

The grip on her arm loosened a little. "You think I'm that easy?" Odelle pulled away and walked ahead. "You're the one that practically begged me for a visit."

One of the guards behind them tried to stifle a laugh, but he was not subtle enough. Sorra shot him a glare. "Leave us, both of you," she growled. The guards obeyed, although she noticed with some displeasure they still grinned.

Odelle stopped, waiting for her to catch up. "You know, I think I would appreciate a shower before dinner. Your station is more arid than I expected."

Sorra had to fight to keep her expression neutral. She had already made reservations for dinner, and the timing on everything would be ruined if they delayed. "Blame the naledai. They shed if I keep it too humid."

"I'm sure they do, but I'd still like to refresh myself, if you could show the way."

"Of course." She gave a short nod in the direction of Odelle's rooms. "This way."

Unfortunately, Odelle saw through her. "Relax. We have all night, and our meeting with Maia isn't until tomorrow morning."

But she could not relax, even when Odelle's arm wove through hers. "Yeah, all right." Assuming Odelle took a ten-minute shower, she would have to call the restaurant and push their reservation back by thirty minutes, and then send some extra money over to make sure the quartet was still playing when they arrived. If they lingered at dinner, she would have to push back the rest of their itinerary or skip it entirely.

She was still lost in her head when they finally reached Odelle's rooms, and it took her a moment to realize they were both standing outside the door. "I've set up a profile for you," she said, hoping to cover the awkward pause. Odelle pressed her palm onto the scanner and the doors swished open.

Odelle smiled, looking around the spacious front room. "This is beautiful. I have to say, I'm impressed. I didn't think Tarkoht had these kinds of accommodations. I was under the impression it was just a trading port."

"Part of my cover. You know how the Dominion operates. It always demands the best, even if that means stealing resources from alien worlds to do it. Korithian officials expect a certain amount of luxury, even ones who aren't as beautiful as you." She paused and followed Odelle into the room, shutting the doors behind them.

"I still get the feeling Tarkoht is different than most ports," Odelle said.

Sorra shrugged. "Well, naledai and other aliens are actually allowed to live on my station instead of being worked to death shelling out Nakonum's moons. I feed them more than once a week." Her smile faded. "The Dominion officials still treat them like animals when they come for inspections, but at least they aren't quite slaves. Not here."

Warmth surrounded her hand, and Sorra looked down in surprise. Odelle's hand clasped hers. "One step at a time, Sorra. You and I both know this is wrong, and we have a plan to change it, which we can discuss tomorrow."

With a nod, Sorra allowed the change of subject. She almost never got to see Odelle in person, and she didn't want to spoil their time together. The galaxy had been in turmoil for years thanks to the Dominion's selfishness. It wouldn't collapse any further overnight.

"These rooms have even been refurbished since the last time someone used them," she said, gently withdrawing her hand. She left out the fact that Odelle's visit was the entire reason the rooms had been refurbished in the first place. "Anyway, they're yours for the next few days. The only other bio-signature coded to the reader is mine."

Odelle glanced back toward the door. Perhaps it was wishful thinking, but Sorra thought she saw a hint of hunger in her eyes. "Somehow, that doesn't surprise me. Now, if you don't mind, I'd love to start that shower."

Sorra opened her mouth, nearly offering to join her, but she stopped herself. She needed to reschedule their reservations if she wanted to salvage the night. "Go ahead. It's down the hall to your left. I'll be in here once you're finished, and I'll make sure someone brings up your bags."

"Thank you," Odelle murmured. "I promise I won't be long." She headed for the hallway, leaving Sorra to wonder if the note of disappointment in her voice had been real or imagined.

As soon as Odelle left, she pulled up her communicator. Several minutes and even more frantic messages later, she had their entire itinerary pushed back. Luckily, 'Dalia' had enough pull on Tarkoht to make miracles happen. She just managed to end her final message before Odelle stepped back into the room, wrapped in one of the plush white towels from the bathroom. Her body was still slick with stray water droplets, but she looked much happier.

"That was quick." Sorra allowed her eyes to linger on Odelle's legs for a moment, admiring the smooth silver skin on display beneath the towel's hem. "And while I more than appreciate the view, I'm sure you want something fresh to change into. Check the closet in the bedroom. There should be something appropriate in your size."

Odelle nodded. "You're behaving quite well today. I'm shocked."

"Or perhaps I've just grown up since we've last spent time together." She watched Odelle turn and walk away, her gaze following the sway of her hips.

"Or you're scared," Odelle said as she entered the bedroom. "I rather like that possibility. The last time you were this timid was before our first date."

Sorra bit back her response and waited for Odelle to change. Part of being older meant she could give Odelle the grand romance she had always wanted to when she was young and poor. Instead, she had settled for spontaneity and lust. "I'll admit to being nervous," she said at last. There was nothing wrong with flattering Odelle with a little truth. She heard the closet click open and tried to think of something other than Odelle undressing.

"Whatever could you be nervous about?" The teasing tone in Odelle's voice was obvious even from the next room, and it was almost too much for her to bear. The party had been Odelle's realm, and Sorra had taken great pleasure in disrupting it. She could act suave and powerful there, and the risk of getting caught only made her feel more in control. Here, however, on her own space station, she could not quite shake her nervousness. Part of her could hardly believe Odelle had actually agreed to come and visit her. She belonged light-years away, not within touching distance. It was enough to upset the delicate balance Sorra struggled to maintain.

"I'm nervous about a lot of things." Sorra heard footsteps approaching and Odelle stepped out of the bedroom. She wore a thin, flowing dress that looked like darkness rippling over her body. It contrasted well with her skin, and Sorra smiled. She had been confident in her choice, but the way the dress clung to Odelle's breasts and hips had her wanting to tear off her own clothes.

"Am I acceptable?" Odelle asked, twirling the skirt.

Sorra walked forward and took Odelle's hand, raising it to her mouth and brushing a gentle kiss across her knuckles. "More than."

***

"I didn't realize Tarkoht had such luxurious restaurants." Odelle turned her head, partially to take in the wide dining room and partially to break eye contact with Sorra. The heat of her gaze burned. "According to the reports I read, it's mostly a resource refinement facility."

"Oh, Tarkoht is much more than that." Sorra waved at the host, and they were ushered into the restaurant despite the line of people waiting outside. "In fact, I'm surprised you didn't find an excuse to visit me earlier. The upper ring is becoming quite a fashionable vacation spot among Korithia's elite, and you certainly fit in that category."

Odelle cleared her throat. "Please, let's not talk about that."

They stopped beside a table near the back, far enough away from the other diners to offer them some privacy, but with a clear view of the sparkling water fountain in the center of the room. Odelle smiled. Their seating had obviously been arranged in advance. The fountain bore a remarkable resemblance to the one beside the library at their old university.

"Why not?" Sorra asked, stepping past the host to pull out her chair.

Odelle sighed but took the seat that Sorra had offered her. "Because even after all these years, I still feel like I'm pretending sometimes." Another thought pushed to the front of her mind, but she knew better than to speak it aloud. She had spent most of her life pretending. Pretending to be a socialite, pretending to be loyal to the

Dominion. Sorra was one of the only people in the galaxy who truly knew her.

Sorra circled the table and took the other seat before addressing their host. "My usual for the wine, please, and if you wouldn't mind, the humidifier could use some tweaking. Thank you." The ikthian gave a polite nod, assuring them he would return soon.

Odelle smiled as soon as he left. "You know, that's one reason I always liked you. You might have been rude to our teachers, our classmates, and anyone in a position of authority, but you were always polite to waiters."

"And you," Sorra murmured, leaning over the table. The new closeness made Odelle's pulse flutter. "I was always polite to you."

"'Polite' isn't the word I would use," she said.

"Oh? What word would you pick, then?"

In all fairness, Sorra was one of the more socially graceful people she knew. "I suppose I'd use suave. Yes, that fits you well, I think. You treat everything like some grand show, like you're playing your role perfectly and expect the other parts to be played in turn."

Sorra's smirked. "Are you saying my life is a production?"

"I'm saying you enjoy your schemes too much. That is, until you lose your temper and everything falls apart at your feet." Odelle glanced around the restaurant. Sorra had not changed in their years apart. She still preferred grand gestures, and she still had little patience.

The waiter returned with Sorra's requested drink, and she took a small sip from her wine. "I like to think of myself as careful these days, if anything."

Odelle nodded. "It's certainly a good quality to have. Especially in your position, where nothing can be left to chance. I would say that thinking things out is a new development for you."

Sorra shrugged. "I've grown up. It's nice having the odds stacked in my favor."

"Then why take the risk of inviting me here?"

"I happen to think you're worth a few risks."

The compliment called some heat to Odelle's cheeks. She looked down at her lap and tried to think of all the reasons she and Sorra should not be sitting together and sharing a romantic meal. For the sake of her life, she could not recall one. She just wanted to enjoy herself without the burden of her career catching up with her.

The waiter returned and they placed their orders. "I'll have a glass of wine as well. Whatever you served her." She nodded at Sorra.

The waiter left to put in their order and Sorra arched her brow. "Loosening up, are we?"

"One glass won't hurt. I'm supposed to be enjoying myself, aren't I?"

Sorra raised her glass. "Your pleasure is my intention."

Odelle groaned. "You can stop with the one-liners now. Your intentions are fairly clear."

Before Sorra could come back with a response, a small music quartet began playing beside the fountain. Odelle glanced over at the musicians, and her hands shook in her lap. They played a classic ikthian melody, one of her favorites from when she was younger. She had thought Sorra had slept through all the concerts Odelle had dragged her to. Apparently not.

"You've really outdone yourself," she whispered, keeping her eyes focused on the musicians so she would not have to look at Sorra. "The room, the dress, the fountain, the music...It must have taken a lot of planning." She could usually control herself on the rare occasions that they met in person, but this was entirely different.

Thankfully, the waiter returned with their meals before she could say something she regretted. When the steaming plate of fish was set in front of her, she turned away from the musicians and made a conscious decision to relax. Tomorrow, the spell would be broken, and she would be forced to deal with the present again. But for tonight, at least, what harm would it do to pretend this was her life?

Odelle ate quickly, although she could not resist offering commentary once in a while. "Did you arrange for the flowers, too?" she asked after she had drained the last of her wine. There was no centerpiece at their table, probably to encourage more intimate conversation, but the others were all decorated with brilliant white blooms. "I suppose I shouldn't be surprised you remembered my favorite."

"Flattered." Sorra pointed her fork at Odelle. "You're supposed to be flattered. Perhaps even impressed."

"I am," Odelle replied. "It's a nice gesture. You should be proud."

Sorra beamed. "Just nice?"

"Nice enough I think we should ask the waiter for our bill."

"Already taken care of. If you're ready to leave, I would be more than happy to escort you wherever you want to go next."

Odelle pushed back her chair and stood up. Sorra stood and circled the edge of the table before reaching out her hand and threading their fingers together. "I think I'd like to go back to my room, if you don't mind."

"I don't mind at all."

"Then let's get out of here." They walked out of the restaurant hand, and the old but familiar contact made Odelle feel giddy. She almost feared they would get caught and scolded, but no one cared. People walked past them without sparing a second glance. All the while, her heart pounded heavily against her ribcage. She was no longer young and reckless, but Sorra still had a way of making her feel youthful.

At last, they came to a stop outside Odelle's apartment door. All she had to do was let go of Sorra and press her palm against the ID pad, but she couldn't find the strength to part their joined hands and lift her arm.

Finally, Sorra cleared her throat. "Would you like to go inside?"

Odelle nodded. She could not decide whether to run or to pin Sorra against the wall as soon as she stepped through the door. They had done this so many times before, even if it was years ago. Why was tonight so different? "Here," Odelle said, finally pressing her palm against the reader. A second later, the door opened, and they stepped inside.

Sorra wandered away from her, heading toward the kitchen. "Would you like another drink?"

Odelle swallowed. She wasn't sure whether to be relieved or disappointed at the physical distance between them. If she spent another second pressed against Sorra's side, she feared her legs would have given out. "I think that might help, yes," she murmured, trying not to admire Sorra's retreating form for too long.

"Hold on. I'll just be a minute."

Once Sorra was out of sight, she took in a deep, shuddering breath and moved on to the living room. The low couch occupying most of the space gave her some relief, and she sank down onto it with a grateful sigh. She barely had time to fold her legs and assume a casual pose before Sorra returned with two glasses. Her fingers trembled as she took one of them from Sorra's outstretched hand. "What did you bring?" she asked, hesitant to try the glass of dark liquid.

Sorra smiled, her lips barely teasing the rim of the glass. "Something we distill right here on Tarkoht. It's a mild mead. Don't worry, I know what you like."

Odelle glanced down at the drink again. She honestly did not know what she was doing anymore. Here she was with Sorra, free of any obligations that would whisk her away, and she had insisted on having another drink. Sorra stretched out along the couch and draped an arm behind Odelle, and the back of her neck tingled.

She took a sip and found the alcohol to be sweeter than she expected. A perfect blend of her favorite flavors. Sorra did know what she liked. "This is delicious," she said, lowering the glass. Their evening together had shown Odelle that Sorra remembered everything about her, everything from when they had been together. Sorra cared about her. She must have always cared.

The realization shook something in Odelle. She set down the glass.

"Is everything all right?" Sorra set down her own glass and placed her hand on Odelle's back. The touch sent sparks along her spine. "Odelle? We don't have to do anything. I just wanted to..."

Before Odelle could stop and question herself, she leaned in and caught Sorra's mouth with hers, cutting off her words. At first, she feared Sorra might pull away. It had been years, after all, and some of those years had been spent in bitter silence. But Sorra only remained frozen for a split second before parting her lips. Odelle groaned at the warmth, bringing her hand to the back of Sorra's neck and pulling her closer.

They kissed slowly at first. Odelle explored cautiously, but soon remembered her old habits. Sorra's hands wandered to her waist in a familiar hold, and Odelle shivered. It had been years since they had touched each other like this, but with her mouth covering Sorra's, she could not understand why they had waited so long.

She was not surprised when Sorra distracted her, breaking off their deep kiss to brush her mouth with several smaller ones. The edges of Sorra's teeth caught her lower lip and tugged, and Odelle moved her hands to Sorra's shoulders. "Please," Odelle murmured as they broke away. "I..."

"I know."

The low, soft glide of Sorra's voice made her pulse spike, and Odelle kissed her again. She lost her balance and tipped over, pushing Sorra back against the arm of the couch. Fortunately, her old lover didn't seem to mind. The hands around her waist moved up to roam along her back, dragging her forward until she found herself straddling Sorra's waist. She gasped for air, trying to ignore the rapidly building pressure as Sorra's knee shifted beneath the skirt of her dress.

"I have missed you," Odelle murmured between kisses, too desperate to part their lips even long enough to speak in sentences. "Didn't realize how much."

Sorra did not answer. Odelle's breath caught as she felt her hips being guided in a rocking motion instead. A low, shuddering throb started between her legs, and each push only made it grow. Things were quickly spiraling out of control. She no longer cared. Sorra's body felt so good beneath hers, and her mouth tasted just the way she remembered. She could not bear to pull away.

Odelle brought her hands between their bodies and bunched up the fabric of Sorra's shirt, pulling up and away. Her palms glided over Sorra's stomach, causing her to let out a low sigh as they kissed. For a moment, she managed to forget all that troubled her and focus solely on them.

"*Incoming message.*" The automated voice was accompanied with a loud, incessant ringing. Odelle jerked away from Sorra and nearly fell off the couch as she looked around for the communicator. She had instructed the device to sound an alarm for only two callers, and one was in the room with her.

"Damn it!" Odelle tried to stand up as Sorra took hold of her hand.

"Where are you going?" Her brow had furrowed and her thumb traced small circles into Odelle's skin.

"That's the chancellor." Odelle pulled away and searched the room for her communicator. She managed to dig it out of a travel bag and turned on the information screen, frowning at the *missed call* symbol. "And she's already called twice today."

"So let her call again. She'll get over it." Sorra sat up and leaned over, elbows braced on her knees. Even though she sounded irritated, she looked concerned.

"Or she'll send a team of Seekers to tear this place apart."

"You don't know that." Sorra looked up at her with pleading eyes. The communicator persisted.

"I don't want to risk..." She let the unspoken words hang between them. *I don't want to risk this opportunity? The rebellion? Us?* She had no idea, but the thought of Seekers swarming over the station chilled her. They would find reason to vaporize everyone on board in seconds.

Sorra stood up from the couch.

"Are you leaving?"

"You need to answer that, and I don't want to put you in danger by being here." Sorra gave a sad smile. "I enjoyed my time with you tonight. I'll see you in the morning."

She left before Odelle had a chance to change her mind or call her back in. With a sigh, she accepted the incoming transmission. *This had better be worth a ruined evening.*

Chapter Ten

MAIA GLANCED AROUND THE shopping plaza, trying to decide on a destination. Several crowded shops and stands lined the busy walkway, most decorated with flickering advertisement screens. The stalls were crammed nearly on top of each other, and the storefronts were dirtier than the establishments she was used to frequenting on Korithia, but most of the vendors seemed to be doing a brisk business. She hummed in thought, not necessarily knowing what would make Taylor happiest.

"Why don't you decide where to start? You were the one who suggested coming here for lunch."

Taylor shrugged. Although she had seemed eager to go on another "date" at first, some of her enthusiasm had waned at the sight of the bustling street. "I don't know. I didn't really think this through. When Sorra mentioned there was a shopping center here, I thought it would be a nice place to spend some time together. I wasn't expecting it to be this busy, or this sketchy-looking."

Maia looked from the moving signs to the crowd. Most of the people were naledai, since the ikthians kept to themselves in the upper ring of the station, but there were a few other species mixed in. Some passers-by gave Taylor odd glances, and Maia felt her heart sink. She knew Taylor was having trouble adjusting to such an alien environment. Surely the stares made things harder.

"Was there anything you wanted to see in particular? Anything you needed?" The fact Taylor had left most of her possessions behind during their escape from Earth still ate at her from time to time. If she could help replace some of the nonessentials, she would jump at the opportunity.

"You know, I wouldn't mind some new clothes," Taylor said after a moment's thought. "I'm getting tired of wearing the same two outfits over and over again."

Maia smiled. "Then new clothes it is. Come on." She took Taylor's hand in hers, heading for one of the nearest shops. It was the nicest of their lackluster selection, although the naledai mannequins in the window were missing a few body parts. "I don't want to offend Sorra by wasting her line of credit, but I'm sure she won't mind if we spend a little money here." Maia took a moment to admire Taylor's broad shoulders in the simple military shirt she wore. "You look wonderful no matter what, but it would make me happy to choose something new for you."

A soft blush colored Taylor's cheeks, but her lost smile returned. "Yeah. Okay. Look around and tell me if you see something you want me to model."

Maia took her time browsing, wandering past the disorganized shelves and broken racks. Most of the clothes in the shop were designed for naledai, and the few items that would fit an ikthian were fancier than she would have liked. She dismissed the more impractical garments immediately. *She needs something simple. Something she'll get a lot of use from.* Moments later, she saw exactly what she was looking for. A brown jacket hung above one of the dusty shelves. It looked like it would fit, but she held it up anyway as she removed it from the hangar. "Here. Try this on."

Taylor's mood brightened even more as she felt the smooth material. "Nice. Is this some kind of leather?"

"Basically. Try it on please?"

Taylor grinned as she slid her arms through the sleeves. "It's a perfect fit," she said, twisting to make sure it wasn't too tight. "Who knew you were so good at picking out clothes? It probably would have taken me ages to find this. I suck at shopping."

"I have a keen eye." Maia admired the way the jacket's cut highlighted Taylor's body. It almost made her wish she hadn't suggested waiting. They needed to talk about where their relationship stood, but the time wasn't quite right. "My profession probably helped."

Taylor laughed. "Being a scientist makes you good at picking out clothes?"

"Not exactly. But you do learn how to ignore large amounts of extraneous data while trying to find what you're looking for."

"Well, you picked a winner this time." Taylor slid the jacket off and draped it over her arm instead of putting in back on the hangar. "Come on, let's go pay for this. Maybe then we can find somewhere a little less crowded to spend the afternoon."

They paid and left the shopping level for the menagerie. Fewer pedestrians meandered on the walkways, and Taylor sighed once they left the worst of the crowd behind. "Thank God," she muttered, running a hand through her hair. Her fingers left it messier than it had been before, and Maia had to resist the temptation to reach up and straighten it. "I was getting claustrophobic back there." She suddenly seemed to realize what she had said and hastened to clarify. "I was still having a good time. I always have a good time when I'm with you."

Maia took Taylor's hand. "I know," she said as they turned a corner. There were two entrances, one for the menagerie and one for the botanical gardens. "Let's walk through the gardens," she said when she noticed Taylor looking suspiciously at the menagerie sign. "It's right between the upper and lower ring. I've heard that Sorra collects all kinds of plant life native to Korithia and Nakonum."

"Probably a good idea," Taylor agreed. "I don't want anyone to mistake me for one of the exhibits."

Maia gave Taylor's hand a slight squeeze. "You know Sorra doesn't actually think of you that way, don't you? She respects you for bringing me here, even if she has a funny way of showing it."

"I don't care what Sorra thinks," Taylor said, a little too brusquely. "But let's not talk about her right now. I want to focus on spending time with you." She pulled her hand away, tugging on the sleeve of her new jacket.

"Are you sure you like it?"

Taylor stopped fidgeting and took her hand again. "It fits great, yeah." Her eyes darted downward to their feet as they walked beneath an arch of flowering tree branches. They walked along the garden path before branching off into a grassy clearing. Taylor sat down and leaned against one of the trees, bracing her elbows on her knees. "It's nice. I'm just afraid of ruining it. I tend to do that a lot."

Maia sat down next to Taylor and crossed her legs. "What do you mean?"

Taylor looked over at her, a lost expression on her face. "I haven't done the best job with us, have I?"

"Oh, Taylor." Maia scooted closer, resting her hand on top of Taylor's forearm. At first, she was afraid her touch would make the situation worse, but Taylor seemed to relax at the contact. "You haven't ruined anything. And you need to stop this self-pitying attitude. It isn't like you." Taylor did not respond. She trapped her lower lip between her teeth, exhaling through her nose and staring out across the clearing. Maia knew she still wasn't convinced. "I asked for us to slow down because I think we have a chance. Back on Earth, I thought I only had a few weeks left to live."

"So, what were we then? An impulsive decision?"

"No," Maia insisted. Taylor's words hurt, but she put her own sadness aside, knowing she had to explain. "I wanted to be with you, but I didn't think anything serious could come of it. Now, I'm not so certain. You saved my life. You left Earth and came all the way here for me. You're risking your safety to save your people from the Dominion, and my people from themselves."

Taylor's face softened, and Maia reached up to cup her cheek. Her heart started pounding faster. She had forgotten how smooth Taylor's skin felt beneath her palms. "I admire you, Taylor. I care about you very deeply. The next time we have sex, I want it to reflect that. I want it to mean something. You are an incredible person."

With a soft smile, Taylor tilted her head and kissed Maia's palm. "I think I can manage that."

"I don't want you to think this slower pace is so easy for me, though," Maia said, withdrawing her hand. "That connection is still there. It's just a matter of controlling my impulses at this point. And I control them only because I would rather spend what little time we have learning all I can about you, not just the physical side. We are going to be buried in work within the next few days. I want to treasure these small moments while we can." When Taylor frowned, she readjusted so they sat next to one another. She leaned into Taylor's side, resting a head on her shoulder. "Do you mind if we stay here a while?"

An arm snaked its way over her shoulder as Taylor held her close. "I think that sounds wonderful, actually."

***

"Maia?" Taylor pressed her ear to the closed bathroom door, listening. She thought she could hear the sound of Maia's voice beneath the hiss of the water, but she couldn't be sure. "You all right in there?"

There was no response. She sighed and rested her forehead against the warm metal of the door. She had bitten her tongue and concealed her disappointment when Maia asked to shower alone this morning, but she had been in there for nearly an hour. Too long for a regular shower, even when she said she needed to hydrate her skin.

Taylor waited a few more beats, trying to convince herself she didn't need to intrude on Maia's privacy. *She's been in there so long though. What if something happened? What if she got sucked down the drain?* The silliness of the thought struck her, though she could not resist glancing at the time again. They still had twenty standard minutes before their meeting with Sorra. Enough time to get ready and make their way to the conference room they had been assigned, but only just.

She sighed and sat down on the edge of the bed, resting her elbows on her knees. Her thoughts drifted to more rational reasons Maia would take so long. *What if she was sick? What if...*She took in a slow, deep breath. *Maia can take care of herself. A long shower doesn't mean I have to go in after her like it's some kind of rescue mission.* Before she could finish convincing herself, the door to the washroom hissed open. Maia walked out. Taylor grinned at her.

"Taylor?" Maia returned her smile, waving away steam with her hand. "Sorry, I had the settings on high. I needed it."

Taylor swallowed. Maia only wore a towel, probably to enjoy the last of the water droplets clinging to her skin. Taylor rested her hands on the mattress so that she wouldn't be tempted to touch. "I don't really mind," she muttered.

"Are you all right?"

Taylor nodded, though she didn't move. She didn't trust herself to refrain from anything that would make Maia uncomfortable. "It's just that you're..."

Maia glanced down at herself, then back at Taylor. The soft pity in her expression was unmistakable. "I know space has been taxing on you." She smiled sadly. "Just a little longer, though. Things are getting better." Taylor's heart jumped as Maia stepped forward and caressed the side of her cheek. "Next time, I'll let you come in with me. I promise. I just...I am nervous today. This meeting is important."

Taylor reached up to keep Maia's palm pressed against her face. "You don't have anything to worry about. If someone like me can understand your research, I'm sure Sorra and her 'special guest' won't have any trouble."

Maia's eyes narrowed. "What are you implying when you say 'someone like you'?"

"Someone without a formal education."

Maia sighed and drew her hand away but not before leaning down to press a kiss against her forehead. Taylor's face flushed, and she tried not to stare at Maia's chest wrapped tightly in the towel. "You are more brilliant than you give yourself credit for." She pulled her hands away, and Taylor had to resist the impulse to bring them back. "What time is it?"

"We've got..." Taylor glanced over at the clock again. "Oh shit, about seven minutes."

Maia pulled back with a start and rushed over to the closet. "Seven minutes? That's not enough time. What will I wear? I hardly have anything appropriate for this." She tossed clothes over her shoulder, and Taylor dodged a pair of pants that went flying past her head. Maia managed to pull on her undergarments without much fuss before running back to her and holding up two robes. "Which robe should I pick?" She held the sheer fabric up. "This one or this one?"

Taylor shrugged. The formal wear for ikthians was different. It was not strictly gendered. The males and females both wore flowing robes any time they wanted. The aquamarine robes Maia had selected looked nearly identical. "What's best for the situation?"

Maia frowned and tossed the first robe aside. "I suppose this one will work." She slipped it over her head and grabbed her datasheet. "I'm ready if you are."

They arrived on time—or they did by Taylor's standards. Maia continued to insist she would have been better off with an extra five minutes until they walked through the door. The conference room itself was small, with enough seating for about ten. Only a handful of people had been invited to attend the presentation: seven total. This included Akton, who gave her a friendly nod as she entered the room, as well as Sorra and her visitor. They sat together at left side of the table.

"Kalanis. Good to see you," Sorra said. Her voice was smooth, although not exactly friendly. Taylor frowned when she was not included in the greeting but remained silent. "Allow me to introduce everyone else. This is Joren Talamakis." She gestured at a male ikthian seated close by. "He's the owner of this station, as well as a trusted confidant."

Joren stood to greet Maia, holding his head high with respect. Taylor noted the shimmering green tint that bathed the hollows of his cheeks and washed down his neck. She often wondered what ranges of color were common for ikthian skin. While Joren and Maia murmured pleasantries to each other, pressing their palms together in greeting, Taylor made her way to the other side of the room, toward the only empty chair left at the table, right next to Sorra. Sorra narrowed her eyes but continued the introductions. "You already know Akton. The other naledai is General Kross. He's one of the highest-ranking officials left from Nakonum's former military."

"It's an honor to meet you, General Kross," Taylor said, and even though she wasn't certain the gesture would translate, she gave Kross a respectful salute. They hadn't shared any words, but she was already certain she would prefer his demeanor over Sorra's.

"You're military," General Kross said in a gravelly voice, eyeing her up and down. "Good. Sorra's little games of espionage have gotten us useful information so far, but eventually, we're going to need action."

"That's why you and Akton are here, Kross," Sorra drawled. "But before we get to that, please allow me to introduce Odelle Lastra." Her frown softened as she said the name. "She currently holds the title of Executive Media Coordinator back on Korithia. Her attendance here is strictly confidential and absolutely vital to the success of this project. I don't want anyone mentioning her name outside this room."

"I understand," Maia said. "Thank you for coming. I know you are taking a great personal risk to be here, and I am grateful for any advice you might have about the best way to distribute my research."

Taylor instinctively turned to look at the other ikthian. She had somewhat familiar pink markings highlighting her eyelids and cheeks. *Where have I seen her before? How could I have seen her before?*

Odelle smiled. "It's a risk worth taking. I look forward to your presentation, and afterward, if it's not too much trouble, I would like to speak with you further."

While Maia nodded, Taylor felt a sharp nudge against her side. "Stop staring and sit down," Sorra hissed. "You look like an idiot standing there."

"Right. Did you save this seat especially for me?" she asked, pretending to ignore the Sorra's irritated look.

"But of course."

"Oh, hush." Both Sorra and Taylor glanced at Odelle. "You must be the human Sorra's been talking about, Taylor Morgan. I've been wanting to meet you, though we should probably save that conversation for after the presentation."

Taylor's grin widened at the annoyed look on Sorra's face. "That sounds great," she said, trying not to laugh as Sorra's frown deepened. "I'm glad you both were kind enough to allow me to sit with you."

"Of course. You are a stranger here. It would be terrible of us to ignore you. Wouldn't it, Sorra?" Odelle gave Sorra a look, one she seemed to ignore.

Taylor found herself liking Odelle more and more. Her charisma was certainly refreshing after having to put up with Sorra's arrogance.

From what she had observed, however, Sorra respected few people to begin with. At first, she had thought to attribute it to her age. Sorra was not a young ikthian that much she could tell. If she had to guess, Taylor would have put her at around middle age. The more time she spent around Sorra, however, the more she realized that the ikthian's sarcastic treatment extended to everyone, regardless of age, species, or station. It seemed simply part of her nature to argue and get under people's skin.

Maia stood at the head of the table, datasheet in hand. Her skin looked closer to a pasty chalk. However, she cleared her throat and entered a code on the sheet. A screen lit up on the wall behind her, displaying figures and statistics in a foreign language to Taylor. "Thank you all for coming today." Maia took a hesitant step forward and glanced down at the datasheet again. "As you all know, I am here to present my latest findings during an excavation of site 41623, a historic ruin found on the planet Amaren."

She pressed a sequence of keys on the datasheet again, and the screen behind her flickered, revealing a series of photos. Taylor recognized the planet surface where her squad had been ambushed and killed by ikthian Seekers. She had also found Maia there.

"I discovered several fossilized samples of DNA from a variety of species still present in the galaxy today. I took samples from human, ikthian, and naledai remains, along with several other sentient species." The screen flashed again and pictures of carefully excavated remains appeared. "Putting aside the astounding fact that these samples were gathered at the same site, they are hundreds of thousands of years old and reveal an interesting correlation between all sentient species."

Another flash. Charts appeared. Taylor thought she recognized the double-helix strand of human DNA, but it was difficult to understand in the foreign format. "This image displays the fundamental genetic codes present in most sentient species today. They are almost identical. The strands have a few marked differences in them, which I've highlighted below, but that's something you would expect from the DNA of different species."

Taylor squinted and leaned forward in her chair. She was not sure if speaking up was appropriate, given how little she knew on the subject, but the chart seemed off. "I don't see much of a difference."

"Exactly," Maia said. "There's hardly any difference at all."

"Just how much similarity are we talking here?" Sorra said. "Ikthians share a little under half of our genetic code with some of the plants on Korithia, and even more with the animals. How much more do we share with naledai and humans?"

"A lot more," Maia replied. "The variations I mentioned account for just under two percent of our genetic code. Now, watch what happens when I compare the older samples." The screen flashed again, and a chart appeared with no recognizable features. The lines were compressed together in a tight blur of images. "This graph displays the DNA from those same species, only from the tissue samples from site 41623. The sequences have almost converged together on this graph, suggesting that sentient species held even more in common all those years ago. That two percent just got cut in half."

"So you're saying we're all the same?" Joren asked.

Maia looked at him. "Not quite, but the evidence clearly shows our species were present together on another planet all those years ago, even though none of us had achieved space travel at the time. Furthermore, it shows we started out more alike than we are now, practically cousins in scientific terms. Our species all came from a common ancestor and adapted to the different environments of our home planets." Maia gestured with her hands. She paced back and forth, looking to different attendees in the room.

"But how did we get separated?" Sorra asked. "If we all come from a common ancestor, we should have developed on the same homeworld instead of diverging."

Maia smiled. Taylor had never seen her so animated before. "I have a theory about that, although it isn't the main focus of the presentation. I believe the ikthians weren't the first sentient species to master space travel. Another race came before us, and they were partially responsible for our genetic development. It also explains the genetic similarities between the plant and animal life on our homeworlds. This ancient species terraformed our planets and guided our evolution along with it."

A silence fell across the room. "I hate to say it, Maia, but that's going to be hard for a lot of people to accept," Akton said. "Admitting we're descended from a common species is strange enough. But a whole other species guiding our evolution? It's bound to grate against a lot of religious beliefs on all our worlds. You're basically saying we're an experiment."

"Perhaps," Maia admitted. Her brow creased, but her confidence did not waver. "But it also completely undermines the ikthian doctrine of species superiority." Maia's explanation made Taylor uneasy. It was controversial, at least to the people in the room. She began to wonder how humans might react to a similar problem. Darwin's whole theory of evolution had a rocky start, after all, and he was asking people to accept an even milder claim.

When she paused, the naledai general, Kross, spoke up. "So, your research proves we're related and the ikthian propaganda is faulty. What makes this revelation so powerful? If anything, we should be fighting to overthrow ikthian oppression because it's simply the right thing to do. As sentient creatures, we recognize enslavement and rigid social hierarchies are dangerous."

"You make a valid point, General Kross," Odelle said, turning to face him. "But I would urge you to view this research from a different perspective. Ikthians on Korithia and the other nearby planets exist in what feels like a perfect world. It's false, of course, and it takes the exploitation of other species to keep it that way, but most of the population is ignorant rather than malicious. Everyone is vaguely aware the situation is different away from our homeworld, so the Dominion has presented them with lies to make them feel better about the state of the galaxy. 'Ikthians are genetically superior.' 'The other sentient species are better off under our control.' 'The leaders of the Dominion are always correct' are lies common to our people." She paused to glance around the rest of the table. "If we force the citizens of Korithia to question the first statement, what's to stop them from questioning the others as well? It's a crack in the foundation, a vulnerable opening we can exploit. If they have lied about this..." She glanced around the room. "What else have they lied about?"

"This is only a tool to undermine the hierarchy," Maia said, picking up where Odelle had left off. "I know it will not win the war alone, but it was dangerous enough to try and have me eliminated. They fear this research. Why not use it?"

"How?" asked Joren. "It's not like we can distribute pamphlets."

"Actually, the idea I had was not far off." Odelle glanced back at Maia. "Thank you for sharing your research." Maia nodded and turned off the presentation screen. "The ikthian government elections are approaching, and I happen to be responsible for running the campaign of our most highly regarded official."

"Chancellor Corvis," Kross murmured.

Taylor turned away from Maia and stared at Odelle in shock. She finally remembered where she had seen her face before. "You were on the holo," she blurted out. "When the Dominion was trying to negotiate for Maia's return...you were standing next to her mother." She narrowed her eyes, studying Odelle's face.

Odelle remained silent for a long moment. At last, she nodded. "Yes, I was in attendance for most of those transmissions. I'm grateful you took Maia away from Earth when you did. My own efforts to hamper the negotiations were falling apart. I'm not sure I could have gotten her away from the Coalition alive, even with all of my connections."

"We're getting off track," Sorra said quickly. "What does the chancellor's campaign have to do with Maia's research?"

"Haven't you guessed, Sorra? We're going to interrupt the candidates' speeches," Odelle said.

"Why?" Kross asked. "The elections are rigged anyway. The chancellor picks her opponent herself, and they usually end up with a council position as payment after they lose. I doubt most ikthians will even bother watching."

"That's where you're wrong." Odelle smiled. "Viewing is mandatory on Korithia and the other ikthian homeworlds. We'll have a captive audience. And guess who is in charge of organizing the entire production?"

Taylor grinned. "You're going to share Maia's research with all of them at once? That's great. How?"

"That's where I come in," Joren said. He stood up from his chair and turned to Maia. "I'm going to help you condense all those graphs into something the average ikthian can understand. I don't have much of a scientific background, but I think that's an asset. We need to translate your presentation into simpler language."

"If you really want to go with simple, you should use Taylor," Sorra said. "Then we'll know the simple minded can understand it."

Taylor was about to object, but before she could say anything; Odelle shot Sorra a chastising look. The ikthian averted her eyes and fell silent without another word. Taylor found herself liking Odelle even more.

"I wouldn't have put it so rudely, but that's an excellent idea nonetheless," Odelle said. "Between Taylor and Joren, we have two people of two different species and backgrounds to help Maia translate her research. Once you do, I'll make sure everyone on the homeworld sees it."

Kross folded his arms across his chest. "Then what happens? Once we do this, you can't take it back. The chancellor's grip on the empire might be destabilized for a while, but you'll be outed as a traitor, and Nakonum will still be under Dominion control."

"They will try to spin the story so I'm a villain. They will reveal all the horrible things I've done over the years, and they will claim ignorance to the propaganda I've helped spread." Odelle grinned. "But I don't care. This opportunity is too important to waste. I have a few plans in place, but they will only stall ikthian attempts to blame me." She glanced at Sorra. "I'll need to go into hiding."

General Kross sighed and leaned back in his chair. "If you're aware of the risks, I think it's time we make our move."

Sitting in that room with so many great minds, Taylor felt a rising panic. These people were what a resistance should be. Her people on Earth had been a petty, disorganized squalor in comparison.

Chapter Eleven

"SO, HOW DO YOU think it went?" Taylor asked. "Good, right?"

Maia gave her a small shrug. "I am not sure if I would be the best person to answer that." She paused as they slipped out into the hallway, leaving Joren and General Kross behind in the conference room. Sorra and Odelle had already exited, and from the looks they had been giving each other, she could hazard a guess as to why. They stood a little too close together, touched hands a little too often. The soft smile that tugged at Sorra's lips would have been enough to give it away.

Taylor's arm flung around her shoulder, giving her a reassuring squeeze. "Well, I think you did great. The slides were a bit hard to process, but you were really clear."

Maia gave Taylor a grateful look, leaning in to graze the side of her cheek with a kiss. A pink blush spread across Taylor's face, and the color made her smile. She had learned to recognize it as a sign of pleasure. "That is sweet of you to say, Taylor, but I am not sure." She caught sight of a figure standing at the other end of the hall. Odelle was waiting for them, and to Maia's surprise, she appeared to be alone.

Odelle smiled and nodded her greeting at both of them. "Actually, I agree with Taylor's assessment. You did a wonderful job, Maia."

The compliment made her fumble, and she ducked out from under Taylor's arm. "Thank you, Executive Lastra—"

"Don't bother with titles, dear. We haven't the time. In fact, I need to have a quick word with you. The sooner the better."

Maia furrowed her brow. "About what?"

Odelle's eyes drifted over to Taylor. "I'm sorry, Lieutenant Morgan. I have a great deal of respect for you, but I think this news would be best delivered in private."

Taylor opened her mouth, but Maia cut her off with a shake of her head. "Go back to our room. I'll find you later."

"You sure?" Taylor's face tightened with concern. "I don't want to intrude, but..."

"I am sure. I promise I will be quick."

"All right. I'll be waiting in our rooms, okay?" Reluctantly, Taylor made her way down the hall, although she cast one last glance over her shoulder before she turned the corner.

"Why don't you walk with me?" Odelle nodded toward an empty hall, opposite the direction Taylor had chosen. They set off together, and Maia tried to ignore the sick feeling in her stomach.

"I know we're only familiar with each other in passing, but I'm afraid I have some unfortunate news," Odelle said, "and I think it's best that you hear it from me."

"Unfortunate news?" Maia's smile vanished. "Please, tell me. I doubt it's any worse than being one of the most wanted ikthians in the Dominion."

Odelle hesitated. "Your mother has been targeted by the chancellor."

It took a few moments for the words to sink in, but when they did, her heart dropped. "Why? My mother and the chancellor have always been allies. One of the reasons I ran away was to protect her." She stopped walking, and Odelle waited for her. "I...suppose that was naive of me, wasn't it? To think they wouldn't use her to get to me?"

Odelle sighed. After a moment, she reached out and put a hand on her shoulder. Maia didn't shake it off, but the contact was numbing instead of reassuring. "She took your capture and loss badly and voiced her opinions on getting you back a little too loudly when it became clear that the Coalition had you. I don't even know if she realized the chancellor wanted to execute you once you were brought back to Korithia."

Maia swallowed, searching for her voice. "So, what are they planning?"

"Right now? Only to undermine her reputation. The chancellor wants Irana to leave the council at the very least. But if that doesn't work..." Maia suddenly realized that Odelle was upset, too. "If she refuses to step down and fall in line, she will be sent to Daashu."

The word sent a pulse of fear down Maia's spine. She shuddered, pulling away from Odelle's hand. "Daashu? Because of me?" Images flashed in her mind. Dark walls. Her mother screaming in pain. She had never been to Daashu—no one went there and came out alive—but it had to be even more horrible than her own imprisonment on Earth. "But that's worse than a death sentence!"

"She hasn't been taken yet," Odelle said. "They respect her enough to issue a warning first, one I hope she takes to heart. But if she continues to speak out on your behalf, I'm sure you know all too well what the Dominion does to traitors."

Tears blurred her eyes, and Maia pressed her lips together, blinking back the sting. "Why are you telling me this? What do you expect me to do about it?"

"I'm telling you because Irana is my friend. And there isn't anything you can do, but there might be something I can do. I'm the one in charge of unseating her from power. Hopefully, she will step out of the public view before anything worse happens."

"And what will happen once my research leaks? The chancellor and her followers will consider me a greater threat than ever. Before, I was just a disobedient scientist. Now, I'm actively helping the rebellion."

"If your mother is as smart as you are, she'll read between the lines and leave Korithia before that happens." Odelle gave her a pitying look. "Go find Taylor. She's probably worried about you."

Maia let out a soft laugh and crossed her arms. She blinked back more tears, but felt one crawl down her cheek. "Sometimes, it seems like worrying about me is all she does."

"That might not be such a bad thing. We're about to turn this rebellion into a revolution. When things start falling to pieces, it's good to have someone worrying about you." Her expression turned wistful for a moment. "Thank you for listening. If I receive any more news about your mother, I'll be sure to tell you. I'm staying on Tarkoht for the next several days. If you need to speak with me, just ask Sorra."

"I will." Maia glanced over her shoulder, looking in the direction Taylor had gone. "I suppose I should go if there is nothing else you need."

"That sounds like a good idea. Sorra is probably looking for me by now as well. It would be best not to keep them waiting for too long." Odelle nodded goodbye and turned back down the hall.

As soon as she was alone, Maia started off in the other direction. She headed for her room as fast as possible, hoping Taylor waited for her there. Thoughts ran through her head, each one contradicting the last. Her stomach had knotted tightly with worry. *Of course the Dominion would use my mother against me.* Not once had she stopped to consider how those close to her would be affected in the aftermath of this. Truthfully, she had no one close to her. Even her mother had felt almost like an acquaintance over the past few years.

Normally, Maia isolated herself when she was sad or afraid, but things had changed in the last few months. She had learned how to look outward for comfort and reassurance. And after hearing the news about Irana, she needed it more than ever. She swallowed back her tears, struggling to maintain composure for just a little longer.

Thankfully, Taylor was waiting for her in the bedroom. She sat perched on the edge of the mattress, drumming her fingers across her knees and trying to look like she hadn't been waiting. Maia saw her smile when she looked up, but it faded quickly.

"What happened?" Taylor stood and hurried toward her. "Are you okay?"

Maia did not answer. She could not answer. Her mother's life was in danger, and it was all her fault. Instead of explaining, she threw herself into Taylor's arms, burying her face in the warm, familiar hollow of her neck. Her stifled sobs finally spilled free, and she cried.

Taylor held her close, rocking her gently. She pressed a kiss to the top of Maia's head and rubbed a soothing hand up and down her back. "Hey, it's all right. Whatever it is, we'll fix it. I promise."

"There is no way to fix it," Maia gasped, her chest still heaving. "This is all my fault."

"No, it's not," Taylor insisted.

For a moment, her sobs turned to laughter. "I haven't even told you what I'm crying about," she said, shaking her head. She sniffed, wiping away her tears with the edge of her sleeve, but they kept coming.

"It doesn't matter. Anything that's left you this upset, you wouldn't do on purpose."

Maia could come up with a thousand arguments to that statement, but she did not. In the end, it didn't matter whether her mother's fate was her fault or not. There was nothing she could do to change it. But at least she had Taylor. The longer she spent with the human, the more certain she became of her feelings. They were real, not just a product of her imprisonment.

"How have you grown to know me so well in such a short time?" Maia stared into Taylor's face. It was already so familiar to her. She knew every line, every freckle, every subtle shift that showed how Taylor was feeling. At the moment, her forehead was puckered with worry and her eyes shone with concern.

"Because the more I learned, the more I wanted to know." Taylor began moving, and Maia followed, allowing herself to be led back toward the bed. "Come on. Let's lay down for a while. You can tell me about it, or I can just hold you. Whatever you want."

Maia's eyes stung with a fresh round of tears, but this time, they weren't entirely unpleasant.

***

Odelle returned to her quarters and found Sorra lounging on the couch, head propped against the armrest. She continued staring at the ceiling, but Odelle noticed the slight tensing of her body as the door hissed shut.

"What kept you?" Sorra asked without bothering to look at her.

Odelle frowned. Sorra knew exactly what had kept her. Either she was waiting for an apology, or she could not decide what to say. "I needed to have a word with Maia. Sorry about that."

"Don't apologize," Sorra murmured, still avoiding her eyes.

Odelle walked over to the couch and sat down. "If you don't want me to tell you I'm sorry, what do you want?"

"A few answers. Where do you have to be to execute your part of the plan?"

"Korithia, though not for very long," she admitted reluctantly. "I have to monitor the campaign speeches personally. If I assigned someone else to the job, they might discover Maia's research and the rebellion's statement embedded in the files. I need to be the one coordinating things up until the campaign's release."

Sorra finally met her gaze. Most people would not have been able to interpret the tightness of her jaw or the way her lips pressed together, but Odelle had known her for years. Sorra was afraid. Afraid for her. Fear was at the root of her anger. "So you'll be there when Chancellor Corvis realizes you're a traitor?"

"It is a gamble," she admitted.

"One you're willing to make?" Sorra's eyes finally met hers, and they shone unnaturally bright. Odelle's heart clenched. She could not remember the last time she had seen Sorra close to tears.

"If it will help put an end to the Dominion, yes."

Sorra looked away. Odelle tried to place a hand on her shoulder, but she moved out of reach. "It's stupid, you know? That you think you have to die to save the galaxy."

"I never said I was going to throw my life away. I have every intention of staying alive. But I refuse to pretend I'm immortal. I am well aware of the fact I might die in this war. Any one of us could."

Sorra pushed herself up from the couch and stepped back. "Well, you don't have to speed up the process with terrible choices."

"This conversation sounds awfully familiar, doesn't it?" Odelle stood as well, face clouding with anger. "After all the times you risked your life back in school, you have no right to criticize me. You kept pushing again and again, even when I begged you to stay safe." Sorra tried to avoid her gaze, but Odelle moved back into her line of sight. "Now, it's my turn. This is our best chance, and you know it. What I need from you now is support, not a pathetic attempt to show you care by belittling my carefully thought-out plans."

That caught Sorra's attention. She stared at Odelle, wide-eyed and clearly upset. "You, how dare you—"

"No. How dare you?" Odelle jabbed her finger into Sorra's chest, pushing her back. "You think I'm not terrified of what happens if this fails? You think I'm not scared of the ramifications? Of losing you? I know exactly how much it hurts, and after the number of times I've watched you run off into danger without a thought for my feelings, I have no sympathy."

Sorra took hold of her hand and moved the threatening finger away. "Odelle, I didn't think—"

"You never think, you idiot!" Before she could stop herself, she was kissing Sorra, and her heart was launching into space without her.

Sorra responded almost instantly. The lips beneath hers moved, and a low groan vibrated against her mouth. Odelle clutched the back of Sorra's neck with her hand, holding her in place. Part of her was afraid that if she let go, the moment would shatter. She closed her eyes so she would not have to see the pain written on Sorra's face, pouring all of her anger, all of her fear, and all of her confusion into the kiss instead.

They broke apart and Odelle dragged her lips down to the soft spot behind Sorra's jaw. She did not want room to speak, think, or breathe. The last thing she wanted to do was talk herself out of this. Sorra's hands clutched at her hips, pulling her close, and she shuddered as their bodies melted together. It was still a perfect fit, familiar and brand new all at once.

"Odelle—"

She stopped Sorra's mouth with hers, cutting off her words. Her nails raked down the back of Sorra's neck, clutching the collar of her shirt. She surrendered to her instincts, pressing her tongue against Sorra's lips until they parted for her. The grip on her waist tightened and pulled her back toward the couch. She stumbled along as best she could without stopping. She was determined to kiss Sorra until she simply couldn't anymore.

The world tilted, and she was finally forced to release Sorra's lips when she felt herself being whirled around. Instead of pulling her onto the couch, Sorra threw her onto it. Sorra's eyes flashed with a familiar hunger, and Odelle smiled. Some things had not changed. She reached for the hem of Sorra's pants and dragged her forward, undoing the front and tugging down. Sorra kicked the pants away and pulled her shirt up and over her head in one smooth motion.

A shiver raced down the middle of her back as she stared at the display before her; familiar, yet different in subtle ways. There was a new scar along Sorra's side, and her hips had filled out a little since their university days, but the shimmering silver of her skin and the tight muscles of her stomach were still the same. Her fingers moved up to trace the familiar outline, and she grabbed Sorra's hips and dragged her forward onto the couch and on top of her.

Sorra caught herself at the last moment, but Odelle did not wait for her to find her balance. She stroked up along Sorra's tense arms, enjoying the smooth curve of her shoulders until her fingers came together at the center of her chest. She could feel the hammer of Sorra's heartbeat under her palms, thudding fast and hard inside of her chest. It was firm and reassuring, exactly what she needed.

Before she could explore further, Sorra wedged a knee in between her thighs. The pressure made her buck, and her hands flew up, clinging to Sorra's shoulders instead. Warm lips ghosted over her neck, planting small kisses against the skin there. Sorra began stripping her clothes away, hiking up fabric where she could and tugging ties free. She lifted her hips and allowed Sorra to tug her clothes off, but her skin burned even hotter once it was bare.

They paused as Sorra tossed the fabric aside. Their eyes met, and Odelle saw Sorra's pained expression: the faint glimmer in her eyes and the creases on her forehead spoke of deeper conflict. On any other night, she would stop to ask if she was all right, but all she could bear to do was stare silently.

Sorra raised a hand to her cheek and cupped it gently. "You're beautiful," she whispered.

This time, Sorra's lips found hers. They shed the rest of their clothes as quickly as they could, and Odelle groaned as Sorra's bare skin met hers at last. She had forgotten how good it felt to be wrapped in Sorra's arms. Other lovers never held her the way Sorra did, cradled close with barely enough room for movement. She wanted to stay here forever and forget the rest of the world.

Sorra's knee rode higher between her legs, and the grind made her gasp. She drew her in for another kiss as Sorra's hands wandered down the side of her body. They dragged along her stomach, her hips, burning as they went until they finally stopped at her thighs. She arched into Sorra's touch. She desperately wanted to relearn Sorra's body, every inch of it, but that took time. Time neither of them had.

The pressure between her legs drew back, and she swallowed down a whimper. It broke in her throat, becoming a sigh of relief when Sorra's fingers trailed over her. The knot in her stomach unraveled, and she dug her nails into Sorra's shoulders, struggling not to close her eyes. She wanted to keep looking at the beautiful face hovering above hers. "Please," she said, unable to keep silent any longer. "Don't make me wait."

Sorra's fingers slid up, teasing with just a hint of pressure. It was enough to draw out a pulse of wetness from Odelle. Her muscles went stiff, and Sorra trapped her lower lip, tugging her into a kiss. Things had changed in the years they had been apart but not this.

Sorra moved her hand with slow, deliberate strokes, drawing Odelle up to a pinnacle of pleasure every time, only to stop just short. Odelle hooked a knee around Sorra's hip and rocked forward, shuddering as the angle of her fingers changed. She arched and cried out, seeking that same pleasure again, but Sorra's hand withdrew.

"You're still a tease," she groaned against Sorra's throat. Her hips sought Sorra's hand again.

Sorra smirked at her. "I'm only a tease if I don't give you what you want."

Odelle could not find the strength to argue with her. She shuddered when Sorra pressed two fingers against her swollen clit. The pressure made stars swim in front of her eyes, but it was not enough. She needed more. She pried her hand away from Sorra's shoulder, pulling back just enough to make room for it between their bodies. "Inside," she gasped, catching Sorra's wrist and trying to drag her down. "Don't stop, just…"

Sorra pressed inside her once more. There was no more teasing, only a blissful, satisfying stretch as Sorra took her. Another spike of heat rushed between her legs, and the deeper Sorra pushed inside of her, the harder her core throbbed.

One more pulse and she released. The tension in her body uncoiled with wave after wave of pleasure. The rest of the world was swept away, replaced with nothing but the sensation of Sorra pressing against her. She clung to her lover tightly. The world soon pieced itself back together. First the couch, then the cool apartment air, and finally the rest of the cosmos. Sorra stared down at her, brow furrowed. "How are you feeling?"

Odelle smiled and leaned up to kiss her. "Much better."

The look of concern melted away to a cocky grin. "Looks like you just needed a good lay."

Odelle smacked Sorra's arm. "Stop it. Don't ruin this moment with your false bravado."

"No promises." Sorra bent down for another kiss and Odelle backed up, giggling. Finally, Sorra caught her lips in a sweet kiss. Briefly, she wondered how life for both of them might have been if she had only chosen another career path, something not so entrenched in politics.

Well, we would never be here. That thought was almost enough to wash away the regret she felt for the empty years. She sighed and closed her eyes, thinking back to the night on the balcony. Sorra had told her the reflected world in the pool hid its perfections by reflecting imperfection. The other world could keep its perfections, as far as Odelle was concerned. She had Sorra in her arms again, and that was enough for her.

***

Odelle checked her communicator for what felt like the hundredth time, but the screen remained stubbornly blank. Sorra still hadn't called or messaged. There had been no word from her since Odelle had woken in bed alone, with the other side of the mattress cold. She lowered her arm, breathing deep to loosen the knot in her chest. According to the news, the university was crawling with peace officers. Their presence on campus had been constant for the past year, but there were even more squads patrolling the grounds than usual. If Sorra wasn't with her, it meant she was out there, risking her life—again.

With one more disappointed glance at her comm, she gathered her things and left her room. Despite the frequent spurts of violence between the peace keepers and the student rebels, it was usually safe to walk in daylight if you kept your head down and avoided eye contact. The Dominion was still invested in pretending everything was normal.

Once she exited the building, she searched the usual places Sorra retreated to when she wasn't attending class. She did not find her in the library, by the fountain, or in either of the dining halls. She finally checked Sorra's room, her very last hope, but there was no answer to her knock. She glanced at her comm again as she headed back out into the sunlight, squinting at the glare. Still no missed messages.

"You there!"

Odelle turned to see a peace officer approaching her. He was wearing full armor, and his visor prevented her from seeing his eyes. All she could see was her own terrified reflection. "Yes?"

"Return to your quarters immediately. This area isn't secure."

"Of course," she murmured. Odelle never gave the peace officers trouble. Sorra would have asked why, or maybe even challenged the officer's orders, but she was far more cautious. She hated their presence, but her main focus was survival. She sympathized with the rebels, and even looked for ways to aid them when she could, but she was practical about it. She would be of no use to them dead—and neither would Sorra.

Reluctantly, Odelle headed back to her dorm. She had no other options. Until Sorra contacted her, all she could do was return home to wait and try not to drive herself crazy. Thanks to her tendency to worry and Sorra's increasingly risky behavior, she had a lot of practice fighting that particular battle. She rarely won.

She arrived back at her room and was surprised to find the door ajar. She froze, listening for some sound. "Sorra?" she called, waiting for a reply. No one spoke. She went inside and shut the door behind her. She could hear running water in the bathroom, and it eased some of her fears. Surely the peace officers wouldn't barge in just to use her sink. "Hello?" she called again as she walked down the hall. "Is that you, love?"

A low groan floated from the bathroom in response. The sound was clearly one of pain, and she sprinted the rest of the way down the hall, throwing the door open. "Sorra!"

Her lover was hunched over the bowl of the sink, splashing water on her face. Bruises covered the left side of her cheek, and blood wept from her split lip. One of her eyes was swollen completely shut, and her normally crooked nose looked even worse than usual, as if it had been broken again.

Odelle forgot her shock and rushed to Sorra's side. "Ancestors, what happened to you?" She tilted Sorra's chin up with gentle fingers. Her injuries looked even worse under the harsh ceiling lights. They were recent, a few minutes old at most.

"I'm okay," Sorra muttered, though her speech was slurred through swollen lips. "You don't have to..."

Odelle's concern rapidly shifted to anger. She whirled away from Sorra, snatching a washcloth from the bar beside the mirror and running it under the faucet. "Be quiet and hold still," she ordered, wiping the blood from Sorra's face. She needed to see what she was doing before she could apply anything else. "What were you thinking? You promised me you wouldn't go to any more meetings."

"Please," Sorra said, wincing as the cloth touched her lip. "Don't be angry."

"I'm past angry," Odelle snapped. She threw the bloody washcloth back in her sink and opened the medicine cabinet, withdrawing a half-empty tube and some gauze. "I woke up in bed alone. You didn't call. You didn't message. When I went outside to look for you, there were twice as many peace officers skulking around than usual. Then, you show up out of nowhere with your face broken, telling me how I should feel about it. Don't you dare."

A flash of guilt appeared in Sorra's good eye, but it was quickly replaced with indignation. "This isn't a game. You know exactly what the Dominion is capable of. How many worlds are burning because of them? How many of our friends have been carted off to Daashu just for speaking up about it? Do you really expect me to stay in bed with you and pretend everything is normal?"

"I expect you to stop trying to get yourself killed," Odelle snapped Sorra's nose back into place, relishing her yelp of pain a little too much. "I hate the Dominion as much as you do, but running around and taunting the peace officers is foolish. At best, it will get you shot. At worst...how many of those friends you mentioned have ever come back?"

Sorra jerked away from her, lips peeling back in a snarl. She snatched up the tube and applied the gel on her own. "What do you want from me? I can't pretend all of this is normal. Our campus is a warzone, our fleets are committing genocide, and our leaders are murdering anyone who complains. And the rest of the population is too brainwashed to care."

Odelle clutched the side of the counter, eyes stinging with hurt. "You...you think I'm condoning this? Simply because I don't have a death wish?"

Sorra threw the crumpled tube aside, reaching up to wipe the last of the gel and blood beneath her nose. "Well, sometimes it sure fucking seems like it."

They remained silent for a long moment, staring at each other with torn expressions. Odelle couldn't stand it any longer and turned away from Sorra, exiting the bathroom, walking back down the hall.

"Odelle? Odelle, wait…"

Odelle whirled around, fingers clenching into fists. "Don't. I thought I could handle your lies. Your stupid risks. The injuries and the near misses. But I can't be with you if that's truly how you think of me."

Sorra opened her mouth, but no words came out. It might as well have been a confirmation of all her worst fears. She left without another backward glance, storming toward the front door.

"Odelle, I wasn't…I didn't mean…Please, come back."

Odelle slammed the door behind her, cutting off the rest of Sorra's words. Tears rolled down her cheeks as she headed for the elevator, but she didn't bother wiping them away. She had thought that love would be enough. Had told herself over and over again that love was a source of strength. But as she left the building alone, with no idea where she was going, it felt like her greatest weakness. And through it all, she couldn't banish the sickening thought that maybe Sorra was right.

Chapter Twelve

TAYLOR TURNED IN THE copilot's seat to look at Maia as they soared away from Tarkoht station. She would have preferred to get some more practice piloting, but she had suggested the trip to make Maia feel better. While Maia seemed to enjoy flying, Taylor noticed the shadow of worry clinging to every smile. "I really appreciate the jacket," she said, tugging on the leather.

"You clearly wanted it." Maia's response was short and clipped.

Taylor sighed, leaning back into her seat. The goal of the compliment had been to draw Maia out of her sour mood, but it seemed she would have to try something else. "So, where are you taking us this time?"

Maia stared out through the forward shield, though her shoulders finally lowered from their hunched up position. "I thought we could go to Storik. It's a small naledai planet I once visited as a student. There are magnificent mountains." Her fingers loosened slightly around the controls. "That was before the Dominion took an interest in my work. Research projects were a lot simpler then."

"Simpler how?"

"I could learn for the love of learning, without worrying about how the knowledge would be received." A soft smile pulled at her lips. "Surely you have similar memories, before the war at least."

Taylor shrugged. "That depends on what you mean. I have fond memories of growing up. Not so many fond ones of learning. I told you I was never good in school." She gave Maia a hopeful look. "While we're down there, maybe you can give me another language lesson? Maybe you're just good at what you do, but I don't feel clueless when you're the one teaching me."

Maia let out a small laugh. "I would not call you clueless. You underestimate yourself. Perhaps you should give me a lesson this time? I could learn a few words of that other human language. What did you call it? Japanese."

Taylor's smile faltered for a moment. "I don't like speaking it. It has...too many memories attached to it. My mom taught me, mostly. It's hard to think about her, sometimes." Already, thoughts of her mother's funeral came flooding back to her, along with her father's heartbroken expression. When she noticed Maia's frown, she added, "Maybe some other day?"

"All right." They lulled into a silence that made the cockpit feel cramped. Taylor regretted her words. Maia had not said much about her private conversation with Odelle, but the glassy look in her eyes filled in the gaps. And she had said the taboo word from the last few days—mom. "Is your mother okay?" she asked when she could not stand the emptiness anymore.

Maia pulled up on the controls, turning the ship in a smooth arc. The brilliant orange surface of a planet grew larger and larger in the viewport, but Taylor studied Maia's face instead, waiting for an answer and wishing she knew what else to say. "I am not sure," Maia said at last. "Executive Lastra was understanding, but the news she had to deliver was awful. My mother has been criticizing the chancellor since the failed attempts to bring me to back to Korithia. If she does not stop..." She left the sentence unfinished.

"I'm sorry," Taylor murmured. "It's always hard being separated from your family during a war. I know it isn't the same, but every time I heard about another bombing raid, I couldn't breathe until I heard the coordinates and confirmed that it wasn't my Dad's town. You feel so powerless."

Maia released a held breath and pulled their ship into a descent. A low rumble filled the cockpit as they began breaking through the atmosphere. The black around them shifted into streaks of white, then blue, and Taylor gasped as her safety belt pulled at her chest. For several seconds, the noise was too loud for either of them to talk.

Once the rumble quieted down, Maia turned to look at her. "I'm not only powerless, I'm responsible. I'm the reason my mother is in danger. If I had gone back to Korithia, or if I had not offended the Dominion in the first place, she would not be in danger."

"That still doesn't make it your responsibility," said Taylor. The g-forces of the plane pulled her back even as she tried to lean forward. "The Dominion is threatening your mother's life, and it's their brutal tactics that put her in danger in the first place. They want you to feel responsible, to throw you off balance. If that makes any sense."

Maia looked away from her and toward the planet's surface as she activated the landing protocol. "On the contrary. You make more sense than most people I have encountered in my life."

The ship leveled out as it crept toward their chosen landing spot, a cleared-out plateau in the middle of a string of mountains. It touched down with a jolt, and Taylor undid her safety harness. "Is it safe to hop out?"

Maia nodded. "Yes. This planet's atmosphere is remarkably similar to Earth's. It is a frequent stop for survivalist expeditions or geological studies."

The cockpit opened, and Taylor inhaled the rush of air as the gritty heat of the planet washed over her. "It's a desert," she said, climbing out of the ship. The gentle sting of sand against her skin had never felt more comforting.

"Yes." Maia climbed out and jumped down onto the surface next to her. "Is that a problem?"

"No, it just reminded me of home." Taylor glanced around at the mountain ranges, dark edges standing out sharply against the washed-out blue of the sky. She could imagine her father climbing over one of those ridges, his pack shouldered and the brim of his hat pulled low to spare his eyes.

"You grew up in the desert?"

Taylor shrugged. "The Mojave. San Diego base is pretty close by. My dad would take me hiking in the mountains every weekend." She took a step forward and glanced back at Maia. "Want to take a hike with me?"

Maia glanced between Taylor and the ship. "I...one moment." She clamored back into the cockpit and dug out a provisions pack. She chucked it down to Taylor before climbing back out. "There."

Taylor pointed to a gentle mountain slope. "Let's get moving." They walked down the slope and toward a dried-out river valley. As they hiked, Maia went over various ikthian phrases and terminology with her. She had gotten to the point where she could speak a handful of sentences competently.

About halfway down the mountain, Maia stopped. Taylor glanced back at her. "Something wrong?" Maia touched a hand to her forehead, and Taylor noticed the papery look of her skin. "Is it too dry?"

Maia nodded. "Sorry. I never intended to walk away from the ship."

"Let's head back." They turned around and started back toward the ship. They had made it a mile or so before turning around, an acceptable hike. She dug around in the pack for water, passing the liquid pouch to Maia.

"Thank you," she whispered, her throat raspy.

As they walked, Taylor tried not to panic about dragging Maia into the middle of a desert. Instead, she focused on their surroundings. The mountains really were stunning, exactly as Maia had said. The tall, jagged peaks stretched to the sky, making the horizon line mimic a razor sharp maw. The panic receded. Just when it had vanished completely, her foot caught in a dip in the ground. She stumbled forward before catching her balance.

"Ouch," she muttered, stopping by the track pressed deep into the sand.

"What is it?" Maia asked.

"Tire tracks."

Maia took one look at them before setting off toward the ship. "Skedova."

"I'm sorry, that didn't translate," Taylor said.

"Scavengers, though a much more impolite term for them."

Taylor grinned, following after her. "You know, it's kind of hot when you swear in another language."

"Now is not the time for jokes." Maia glanced back at her. "Do you have a weapon?"

Taylor pulled her jacket aside to reveal a holstered pistol. "Don't worry. Maybe they aren't even scavengers. They could be tourists like us." Maia did not respond. They continued walking quietly toward the summit. The crest of the mountain blocked their view, so while they had the advantage of stealth, they also had no idea what waited for them over the ridge.

The tire tracks grew thicker the closer they got. There was definitely more than one vehicle in the area. "What do you think the chances are that they aren't waiting at the ship?" Taylor whispered as they neared the edge of the plateau.

"About as likely as they are to be friendly," Maia murmured. "That is, slim to nonexistent." She drew her pistol, but her hand shook.

"Let me go first." Taylor drew her own pistol.

Maia shook her head. "If these Skedova are ikthian, they will be less likely to shoot me on sight."

Taylor narrowed her eyes. "Until they realize exactly who you are, you mean."

The sound of a revving engine drowned out their whispered conversation, and Taylor dragged Maia to the ground behind the nearest rock formation. Dust rose around them in a cloud, and she lifted her free hand to shield her face. "Shit," she muttered, peering out from behind the rock. A dark vehicle sped toward them over the mountainside. "That's a Seeker rover."

The rover jerked to a stop, and several armored ikthians stepped out. They carried their weapons with bare hands. A firm grip around the throat was the easiest way to down an opponent with toxins. Quietly, Taylor ducked behind the rock formation.

"They are between us and the ship," Maia breathed. Taylor could hear the crunch of their footsteps against the dirt. Her heart rate sped up. It had been a while since she had seen combat, and their current position reminded her too much of being cornered on Amaren. "How are we going to escape?"

Taylor peeked out around the edge of the rock again. The ikthians were not quite in their way. Although they were far too close for comfort, they were not directly in their line of escape. She did not answer Maia's question, but she did hold up one of her hands, silently urging her to wait.

The Seekers walked further away from their rover, talking as they pointed out across the desert. There were five in all, one short of what typically made a full squad. One of them knelt and traced a hand over a footprint. Taylor swallowed. It was only a matter of time before their hiding place was discovered. If they were going to make a move, they needed to make it now.

Taylor raised her pistol and aimed at the kneeling ikthian. The blast went right through its skull, and its body slumped to the ground. The others whirled around at the sound of gunfire, and she adjusted her aim, shooting a second Seeker before the rest managed to dive for cover. One of them ducked around the rover, and the other two took shelter behind their ship. She pulled back behind the rock formation just as the Seekers returned fire. "See?" She turned to Maia with a smile. "Two down and four to go."

"Four? I thought there were only—" A grenade tumbled by Maia's foot, and she jumped back, abandoning their cover. Taylor hurried to kick it away, and it rolled down the mountainside. A plume of dust shot up from the ground as it detonated out of range, but the noise sent a spike of pain through her eardrums. Maia's lips moved soundlessly, but it took several moments for her hearing to return. "—you crazy? You could have killed us!"

"There's a very good chance of that happening no matter what I do." Taylor waited for another round to taper off before she aimed at the rover, but there was no room for a clear shot. Sparks exploded beside her head as one of the other Seekers returned fire, and she slammed her back flat against the rock as she waited for another opening. "Damn it. They keep covering each other when one of them can't fire."

"Distract them for as long as possible. I have a plan." Maia brought up her communicator and began typing into it.

"Distraction, got it." Another grenade flew overhead and landed in the dust beside her leg. This time, Taylor caught it and threw it back toward the rover. It detonated before it reached the ikthians, and her head pounded at the piercing sound. She longed for the noise suppressors built into the Coalition's helmets. At this rate, they would deafen her before they killed her.

Taylor tried to peek around the corner again, but a shower of sparks from a round hitting the rocks stopped her. She ducked back behind the rocks and fired blindly at where the ikthians might be. "Whatever this plan is, make it fast," she shouted, barely able to hear her own voice over the ringing in her ears. "I killed two, and there are three left over. There's probably one extra skulking around here somewhere." Maia nodded, and despite the constant pelt of gunfire, Taylor saw a small smile tugging at her lips. "Something funny?"

"It's a somewhat familiar situation, don't you think?"

Taylor grinned at her. "Almost romantic, isn't it?" Before Maia could reply, the sixth Seeker jumped down from an overhanging rock. Taylor raised her gun and shot before it could lay its hands on her. Maia screamed and jerked back as the dead ikthian slumped down between them. "I said almost, didn't I?"

Maia fiddled with her communicator. At first, Taylor could not tell what she was doing, but a few moments later, she heard the familiar sound of an engine. The Seeker's fire paused, and she risked glancing over the top of the rock. Maia's ship hovered several yards off the ground. The ikthians stared up at it in shock.

Taylor lifted her pistol to take advantage of their surprise, but she was not fast enough. The lights along the ship's side flared white, and all of its weapons began firing at once. The front guns blasted off into the distance, but the rear guns aimed straight at the two Seekers who had been hiding behind the ship. They did not have time to start running before they were caught in its beam. The lasers blew holes through each of them, disintegrating flesh.

The final ikthian crouched behind the rover threw open the door and clambered inside, speeding away without even bothering to close it. Gravel and dust spat up behind the tires, and Taylor fired a few useless shots after the trail even though she knew she was out of range. "Can you reach it?" she shouted, but Maia shook her head.

"No. I can only aim from inside the ship. I simply activated its automatic defense systems."

Taylor's eyes widened as she tucked her pistol away. "I had no idea you could do that," she said breathlessly. Maia smiled at her, and her heart continued pounding hard against her ribs even though they were out of danger.

"I didn't either until I read the manual."

"Well, it's a good thing one of us knows how to use that damn ship." Before she could finish complaining, Maia grabbed the back of her neck and pulled her forward, yanking her into a short, hard kiss that made the rhythm of her heart stutter. Taylor froze in surprise, but managed to open her mouth as Maia's tongue pressed against the seam of her lips. Her hands finally drifted down to settle on Maia's hips, but before she could get a grip, she found herself gasping as the kiss broke off.

"You were right," Maia said as her hand fell away. "This was almost romantic."

Maia stood up and Taylor followed. "That was nice," she said, though Maia had switched her focus back to the communicator. The cockpit to the ship swung open and they clambered in. "Hey, did you hear me?"

"I did." Maia pulled the cockpit closed and activated the radar.

"What are you doing?"

"Trying to run a trace on the ikthian who escaped. They were likely off to a ship or base. It would be easier to shoot them down if they were still close by. Now, we run the risk of exposing ourselves to danger again."

"So we let one get away. It's not the end of the world."

Maia continued fiddling with the controls, pulling the ship up and into the air. "Whoever that was is going to have intelligence on us. I do not want the Dominion to find out what corner of the galaxy we are lingering in." Maia groaned and shook her head. "There is no trace."

Taylor slumped down in her chair. "Well, this is a whole mess of problems." Maia nodded and the ship swung up to point to the sky. As they sped into orbit, Taylor began to worry. Maia was right. That ikthian was going to report seeing a human where no human ought to be. It would give them away in an instance. She looked over Maia's shoulder to glance at the ship's readouts, but saw no anomalies.

They left the planet without any further incidents, but Taylor couldn't shake the feeling of being watched. "Can you run a scan on the electronics? I want to make sure the ship isn't bugged."

"Good idea." Maia pulled away from the controls to activate one of the ship's terminals. "If they slipped a tracker on us, they might be able to predict some of our trajectory from the start of our flight path, but this should minimize the damage."

Taylor nodded, but the nervous feeling that gripped her stomach stayed. Her instructors on Earth had never believed in coincidence. She had a hard time believing coincidence had brought the Seekers to their ship. Either way, she and Maia had been lucky to escape with their lives. They might not be so fortunate a second time.

Chapter Thirteen

RACHEL WOKE UP AND groaned. Her back was stiff again, probably because she had yet to fix the naledai bed she had been supplied with. The back support was in all the wrong places, resulting in sore muscles every morning. Still, she rose and stretched in the tiny room. The rebellion had given her standard quarters for any officer in their ranks, though not necessarily out of respect for her. It was easier to know where she was if they only had to account for one body in a room. The bunk functioned more like a prisoner's cell than a private suite. After getting dressed, Rachel entered her access code for the door, another precaution to track her movements. The door slid open, and she stepped out into the busy hall of the naledai base.

"Move it, human," one of the naledai growled, shoving past her.

Rachel bit back a reply and set off in the opposite direction, toward the cafeteria. The startling faces of alien species had somehow blended into the canvas of a normal crowd in the past week since her arrival. Conversely, she became aware of her own presence as an oddity with each passing day. She was called human, not Rachel.

The cafeteria was another previously strange experience. Instead of having lines, the throng of aliens shuffled through an array of food stands, selecting what they wanted from each one before dispersing. She passed next to a fruit stand and selected a bright red globe of a melon. At least, she thought it was a melon. It was edible, from what the naledai generals had told her, and that was all that mattered. Before she could get the rest of her meal, however, a naledai officer approached her. The grizzly soldier would have looked terrifying before she had arrived on Nakonum. His mane of fur grew wild except for a patch of bald scar tissue that ran down his snout and over his neck.

"Human," he said, pointing at her. "Come with me. We've decided what to do with you."

Rachel did not respond immediately to the sharp, growling voice. Instead, she set the melon down and placed her hands on her hips. She had learned through experience that while the naledai expected her to follow orders, they did not respect cowards. She could not allow any of her fear or discomfort to show. "Does that involve giving me back my weapon?" The naledai narrowed his eyes at her, and the scar on his face wrinkled. "No, huh? Guess that's too much to hope for. It did take four of you to steal it in the first place."

"We didn't steal it," the naledai grunted. "We confiscated it. Get moving. The general wants to see you."

"General Oranthis?" she asked, but the soldier was already walking away, heading for the exit at a brisk pace. She followed, too curious to disobey orders. Although she had not met the general yet, she had overheard enough to form a profile. He was the leader of this base, along with several others scattered throughout the region, and a key figure of the naledai resistance on Nakonum. She wasn't sure why he wanted to see her, but she hoped it was because she would finally be leaving this rock. She still had no idea where to find Taylor, and being held on base as an alien prisoner wore on her nerves.

Rachel followed the naledai out of the dining area and down a narrow hallway. She kept her eyes peeled as they turned a corner, trying to memorize her surroundings. Her movements had been tightly restricted by the armed guards stationed around the base, so she had not been given much opportunity to explore. What little she had seen was similar to the Coalition bases she had been stationed at back on Earth. Apparently, being a soldier transcended species and planet.

At last, they stopped in front of a solid metal door. The naledai punched a code into the glowing green panel along the wall. There was a high-pitched whir of approval, and the doors slid open. Rachel stepped forward before her escort had a chance to push her in, as she had learned naledai were fond of doing when they felt someone was taking too long. The room was small and sparsely furnished, although several large monitors covered the walls. A group of six figures waited for her, and Rachel was shocked to see that one of them was not naledai. A female ikthian stood among them, dressed in armor with the naledai colors and carrying a large gun.

Rachel's heart dropped. "Shit," she muttered, reaching for her hip. Her fingers clamped down on air. "God damn it!" She tried to back out through the door, but her escort stood in the way, preventing her from leaving. She pressed her back against the wall, raising her hands into fists.

One of the naledai held up his hand. "Calm down, soldier. No one here is going to shoot you unless you force us to."

Rachel nearly dropped her hands in surprise. 'Soldier' was not how she had expected to be addressed, but she had to admit, it was somewhat better than 'human.'

"What's that doing here?" she asked, jerking her head in the direction of the ikthian.

The ikthian turned her head toward the naledai who had spoken. When he nodded, she approached Rachel. "My name is Elurin. I'm here because the general asked me to be."

Rachel eased away from the wall and glanced toward the door. The only exit. If the ikthian came any closer, her best option was to shove the naledai guard aside and escape past him. "Why do you have an ikthian here?"

The general gave her a searching look. "Not all ikthians are our enemies. Some fight against the Dominion just as fiercely as we do."

Rachel fixed her eyes back on the tall, pale ikthian. She stared back at Rachel with a blank face, her dark eyes betraying nothing. A deep blue tint rose from her neck and stretched over her eyes, giving her skin the impression of war paint. It was like Taylor all over again, except this ikthian was clearly a fighter. What if it was exercising some control over them? "Forgive me if I don't believe you. Usually when I meet ikthians, they start shooting at me a few seconds later."

"I don't expect her to trust me right away," Elurin took a cautious step forward, and Rachel edged closer toward the door. "Just know I won't kill you. Can you believe that?"

General Oranthis moved between them. "We were going to wait longer before forcing you to cooperate with an ikthian, but an incident has occurred I think you will find interesting." He nodded toward a monitor displaying a planet's surface. "This is Storik. We've recorded several instances of Dominion and human activity on the planet recently, and we need to send a reconnaissance team to investigate."

"Human activity." Rachel eased off the wall and stepped closer to the monitor. "So does that mean..."

"It could be a troop of Coalition soldiers, meaning your expertise would be invaluable in this operation. We currently have no other humans on Nakonum and running into a Coalition squad with Elurin on the team could be troubling, to say the least."

"So you just want me along to call off any soldiers?"

Oranthis narrowed his eyes. "We want you along to keep the peace, yes, but also to give you an opportunity. We both hate the Dominion. You could be of use to us, and we can help you fight a common enemy. This is a chance for you to prove your worth to the Resistance."

"I don't have anything to prove to you." Rachel turned toward the exit but stopped when Oranthis spoke again.

"You have something to prove to your other humans, don't you? They didn't fling you to the far reaches of the galaxy for no reason."

The words sent a chill through her. They knew why she was out on her own, and they were going to exploit her for it. Even to aliens, her banishment was obvious. Rachel turned back to Oranthis. She had no other choice. She wasn't getting off this planet, or even out of this base, any time soon unless the naledai let her, and she still had her own mission to think of.

"When do we leave for this recon?"

"Immediately," Elurin said. Rachel frowned at the sound of her voice. Although her translator could handle the ikthian's words, something about her speech seemed off. "General Oranthis ordered me to outfit you with extra supplies. I also have this." She gestured to Rachel's pistol hanging at her side. "If you think you can resist blowing my head off."

Rachel's eyes widened. The sight infuriated her, but she swallowed back her anger. The naledai would never let her off this planet unless she complied with their orders. To her surprise, Elurin withdrew the pistol and extended her hand, offering it to her. Rachel hesitated but eventually reached out to take her weapon back. She had to admit, it was good to be armed again. If Elurin tried to shoot or poison her, at least she would have a fighting chance. "Thanks," she grunted, even though she hardly meant it.

Elurin dipped her head. "You are welcome. Come with me, and I'll outfit you for the mission."

***

Rachel lifted her gloved hand above her eyes, shielding them from the dust. Although Elurin and the naledai had provided her with some lightweight armor for the mission, none of the helmets had been the right fit for her head. She had been forced to go without. *At least the atmosphere is breathable.* She scanned the horizon. Mountains stretched in every direction, and the sun was low enough in the sky to cause an uncomfortable glare. There was no sign of any other life yet.

"You're sure of these reports?" she asked one of the naledai standing beside her.

He nodded. "This is where our scouts picked up traces of human activity." His voice was warped through the filter in his helmet. "The ikthian tire treads aren't far off either."

Reluctantly, Rachel glanced at Elurin. It had become apparent during the hop over to Storik she was actually in charge of the party despite being an ikthian, and that only made Rachel's fears worse. Elurin currently supervised two of the other soldiers as they tucked the strange naledai ship behind a ridge for protection. She wanted to stay as far away from Elurin as possible, but there was no sign of any activity near the landing site. Following the ikthian trail might be their best bet for finding whatever humans had dared to come here.

Elurin finished speaking to her soldiers and headed back in their direction, studying the horizon just as Rachel had. "The coordinates we were given are about a ten minute walk south of here," she said once she reached them. She gave Rachel a grin through her visor. "If Harris can keep up, that is."

Rachel frowned at the sound of her name, even though she had no idea what else she would have preferred for Elurin to call her. "I can keep up," she insisted.

Elurin nodded. "I see the general's words sank in after all. You do have something to prove."

"Yeah, but not to you."

The naledai soldiers gathered around them before Elurin could give a retort, and she turned her attention to them. "All right, we're headed south. Look out for Seekers and Coalition squads. Hold your fire for the humans unless they attack us, but if you see other ikthians, shoot first and ask questions later. Aim to incapacitate. We need at least one Dominion lackey to interrogate."

The other soldiers laughed. Rachel followed them as they traced the tire tracks. Thankfully, there was only one set. If the tracks never joined up with anything else, they would only have a scouting party to deal with.

As they marched along, Elurin turned and said something to the group. The words came out like a garbled mess of vowels. "I didn't get that," she said.

Elurin glanced back at her. "What kind of translator are you using?"

"Standard issue for the Coalition."

"Then I'm guessing it hasn't been updated with any ikthian dialects or languages other than what the Dominion officials use."

Rachel shrugged. She did not want to show her ignorance by confessing that she had hardly considered the ikthians might use other dialects and languages, just as humans did.

"Don't worry," said Elurin. "The human Coalition is very limiting with the information it provides soldiers, from what I understand."

"You should see the ads they make about ikthians to fund the war effort," added one of the naledai soldiers. "It's almost as bad as the ikthian propaganda."

Rachel resisted yelling a slur. They were clearly trying to goad her, and she would not reward them by behaving like an animal. "Well, you know us humans. Not very far from monkeys. Though I guess I'd rather be an ape than a dog or some fish."

Everyone in the group glanced back at her. A hush fell over the company as they walked. Finally, one of the naledai barked a laugh, and the tension dissipated as everyone else joined in. "The human's got a sense of humor. We might just have to keep her around."

"If she's inclined to keep our company." Elurin turned and winked at Rachel, who scowled. From that point, the soldiers traveled in a quiet ease. Rachel did not feel the same agitation as she had when first landing, though she kept her hand near her pistol holster just in case. If Elurin turned on them, or even exhibited some show of control over the naledai soldiers, she would not hesitate to burn a hole through her head.

"Lifeforms ahead," the lead naledai said over their comm channel.

"How many?" Elurin asked.

The naledai glanced down at a small instrument. "It looks like just one, though there's a large metallic object lying alongside it."

"Probably whatever made these tracks," said Rachel. "Didn't you say this is a scouting party?"

"Was a scouting party." Elurin scuffed her boot over the scorched rock. "There were several small-scale explosions here. I would say grenades. Weapon fire as well."

Rachel's lips twitched into a prideful smile. Although she did not voice her suspicions aloud, she was certain the Coalition soldiers spotted near here had taken care of the Seekers before their arrival. She looked back over her shoulder at Elurin. "What next?"

"There was a battle here. We don't know how many survived or which side won." Elurin gestured off to the right, speaking to the naledai with the tracking equipment. "Nordis, head that way with half the squad. We'll make a pincer. Use the comm channel if you see any other life forms on your way. We'll head left around those rocks."

The naledai nodded his head. The squad split in half, lining up behind Nordis and Elurin. Only Rachel paused, unsure which group to follow. Elurin noticed her hesitation and gave her a small nod. "You're with me, Harris. We approach from behind."

Rachel fell into step behind the ikthian and raised her pistol. She was ready. They crept around the rocks, circling the vehicle and its lone survivor. The tire tracks veered left then ended abruptly, and Rachel could just make out a large black shape silhouetted against the sun's glare. She recognized it immediately: an ikthian rover, tipped onto its side. She glanced suspiciously at Elurin, who motioned the rest of the squad forward. There were no enemies in sight. Everything about the situation suggested a trap.

Before she could worry further, the other half of the naledai squad stepped out from behind the rover's large metal side. "Nothing over here," one said over the comm, motioning them forward with a sweep of his large arm.

Elurin's eyes narrowed behind her visor. "Check inside."

Rachel stood closest to the rover's main entrance, and she braced her feet on the ground to haul the hatch open. It came loose with a groan, and she leapt back as a body spilled out over her feet. It squirmed, trying to scramble away, and she pointed her weapon at its head. "Stop!"

The figure stopped. It was an ikthian, dressed in full armor and without a weapon. She shuddered. It didn't have gloves either. *A Seeker, then. But why was it all alone? Seekers always travelled in squads of six.*

"Where are the others?" Elurin snapped, aiming her own weapon at the strange ikthian. "There should be five more."

"Dead," the ikthian rasped. His skin was papery white, his voice, hoarse. "They're all dead, and I will be soon, from the looks of it." He rolled onto his back and slowly lifted himself to rest against the upturned rover.

"How? Who took out your squad?" Elurin stepped closer and motioned for the others to back away.

The ikthian glared up at her. "Another traitor, like you." Elurin lowered the gun toward his temple. "Some ikthian out for a stroll with a pet human." He nodded toward Rachel. "I didn't realize they made such useful slaves."

"Shut your mouth before I blow a hole through it," Elurin snapped. "The next time you speak, it better be to tell me something useful."

"Wait, wait. What'd you say about a human?" Rachel asked. "A human with another ikthian? What did they look like?"

"Didn't get a good look through the gunfire." The ikthian coughed again and wiped his brow. "How about you give me some water? Hurts to talk."

"Here." Rachel shrugged off her canteen and tossed it to the ikthian, wary of touching his hands. The ikthian caught it and drank greedily from the flask. The way he desperately gulped it down made Rachel realize just how taxing being without water could be for an ikthian.

"Thanks," he said between gulps. "Ran out this morning."

"How long have you been out here?" Elurin cut in.

"Days." He tossed aside the canteen. "Lost count."

"And they sent no one to collect you?"

"No one knows we landed here. Just reconnaissance."

"And the human and ikthian? When did you see them?"

"The day I crashed this thing." The ikthian thumped the hull of the rover. "They were in a short-range ship, though."

Elurin narrowed her eyes at the prisoner. "It was smart of you to talk. It means you get to live another day." She summoned several naledai soldiers forward with a brief nod of her head. "Keep your weapons on him and head back for the ship. We're returning to base. The rest of you are going to help me strip this vehicle. I want supplies, data, anything you can find." The soldiers hurried to follow her orders.

Rachel did not join. Instead, she whirled on Elurin. "What else is near this planet besides Nakonum? Any cities? Large ports? Stations?"

Elurin seemed to think on it for a moment. "Well, there's Tarkoht station, but it's technically ikthian controlled. It would not be a friendly environment for humans. Sorra runs the place."

"Sorra," Rachel repeated. *Where have I heard that name before?* Suddenly, it came back to her. Sorra was the name of the person who had paid the rakash bartender to kill whoever had threatened her in the bar. From what little she remembered, Sorra was involved with the rebellion somehow. "Tell me more about Tarkoht station. Any rebel activity there?"

"Officially? None. Unofficially? Half the station is involved with the rebels in one way or another." Elurin holstered her pistol and headed toward the rover, picking up the canteen that Rachel had shared with the ikthian. She shoved it back into her hands, and Rachel almost let go in surprise. She wasn't sure she wanted to touch something an ikthian Seeker had been handling moments before, even if she was wearing gloves. "It's only a matter of time before that place goes up in smoke," Elurin continued, "but believe me when I say that Sorra will squeeze every last drop of usefulness out of it first. That's how she operates."

"Are they our allies?"

Elurin smirked. "Our allies? I thought you didn't trust ikthians, even ones that are supposedly fighting against the Dominion?"

"I don't," Rachel grunted, but she regretted the words as soon as she said them. She needed all the information Elurin could provide if she was going to track Taylor and Maia Kalanis down. "Look, I need to get to Tarkoht station. That human the Seeker was talking about? I think she's a friend of mine, and I know she's in trouble. I have to find her."

"I'm not sure what you expect me to do about it," Elurin said. "The rebellion's strapped thin for soldiers and resources. I can talk to Oranthis about sending you with the next detachment of soldiers going to Tarkoht station if that's what you want, but I'm not going to organize a field trip just for you. You're lucky we let you tag along on this mission in the first place."

Instead of arguing, Rachel nodded and proceeded to help the team break down the rover. She did not need permission to go to Tarkoht, just a little time to prepare. The coordinates would be simple enough to find. It was retrieving her ship that would be the challenge, but she had time to plan for that. For now, she would do as Elurin and Oranthis said, and eventually they would slip up. Then, she could finally find Taylor and Maia and bring them back. Rachel found herself grinning as she worked. She couldn't wait to see the look on General Hunt's face when she actually accomplished this suicide mission.

Chapter Fourteen

SORRA FROWNED AT THE flashing screen of her communicator. The annoying buzz interrupted the serenity of her lush surroundings. She let out a heavy sigh as she read the familiar number. *Joren again, probably with news of another ikthian patrol. Ever since Taylor and Maia had returned from Storik, patrols are cropping up everywhere. Well, there's nothing I can do about it right now.* She touched the screen and dropped the call. *Besides, I've got other things to worry about.*

"Sorra?" The sound of her name made Sorra look up from her wrist. Odelle waited for her a few steps ahead on the garden pathway, smiling over her shoulder. She grinned back. "Is everything all right? This is the third call you've gotten today. Are you sure there is nothing you need to take care of?"

"Nothing urgent. I promised I would take you to visit the botanical gardens, and I meant it. Joren and everyone else will just have to wait a little longer."

Odelle's forehead creased. "It was Joren who called you?"

"It doesn't matter," Sorra insisted. "If it is important, he can send someone to find me."

"All right," Odelle murmured, but she did not seem convinced. "I don't want you to neglect your job, especially with so much at stake. It seems like the two of us have been in a dream ever since..."

Sorra felt heat spread across her cheeks as she thought back over the past four days. Odelle was right. They had remained wrapped up in each other ever since they had finally given in to temptation. Being with Odelle was better now than it had been back at university, even though their relationship was still undefined.

Sorra reached out and took Odelle's hands in hers. "A good dream, I hope." Odelle stared at her with concern. "Let's just keep this going a little longer," she pleaded, running her thumbs over the backs of Odelle's hands. "I need more time. One more day before we're too busy preparing to see each other."

Odelle's face softened. "I suppose one more day can't hurt." She drew her hands back and looked up at the flowering trees that lined the path. "The gardens really are lovely. I've never seen such beautiful plants in space before. The other stations I've visited have all been very..."

"Utilitarian," Sorra finished for her. "I know. But Dalia is rich and eccentric, and the Dominion seems to like how I've turned this place into a tourist destination. No one suspects it's a rebel base." She looped her arm through Odelle's elbow and continued walking down the path. Her eyes settled on one of the yellow flowers blooming along the pathway. "Did you know that humans pluck these to give as gifts to one another?"

Odelle raised her brow. "Really? How odd. You'd think a better gift would be to let it grow."

"That's what I thought. I saw Taylor do it for Maia a while ago. It was a very confusing experience for the both of them, from what I could tell."

"Perhaps they were just happy to be alive," Odelle said. "Those Seekers could have—"

"I don't want to hear about the Seekers." Sorra pulled Odelle gently toward the exit. "Not today, anyway. Today is about you and me, and the only words I want to hear from you are 'Sorra, how lovely you are', and maybe, 'Please, more.'"

Odelle's cheeks flushed, and she ducked her head. "Here?" She glanced around to make sure no one else had overheard. Sorra did not bother checking. She had made sure to close the gardens to the public for the entire afternoon in order to ensure their privacy. "Are you sure that's a good idea?"

"No, not here," Sorra drawled. "We wouldn't want the groundskeeper to see 'Dalia' carrying on with you instead of Joren. But don't act so shocked at the suggestion. I remember you used to enjoy meeting with me behind the fountain at night back in school."

Odelle chuckled softly as they walked toward the exit. "That was quite some time ago. We were both young and foolish."

"It certainly was more fun, not having to worry about responsibilities." They left the gardens and started down the hall toward Odelle's quarters. "I always swore I wouldn't let myself get sucked into anything political. Look at me now."

Odelle smirked, and Sorra elbowed her. "I think you've done a fine job." She gave Sorra a peck on the cheek. "Besides, the universe needs people who would rather not play the political game. Otherwise we would find ourselves overpowered by people like the chancellor."

Sorra frowned. "Don't mention her either. We were having such a wonderful day." They stopped in front of the door leading to Odelle's rooms. Sorra entered the proper commands, and they both waited for the door to open.

"I can think of a way to make up for it, if you want," Odelle said, her voice low.

Sorra smiled and stepped aside to allow Odelle into the apartment first. "After you, then." As soon as she stepped inside, Odelle pulled her into a heated kiss. She staggered backward, balancing against a wall as Odelle's mouth crushed against hers. Finally, she remembered to move her hands and gripped Odelle's hips hard, pulling them flush against her own body. She groaned into the sweetness of Odelle's mouth. "Been waiting to do this?"

"Only all day."

Sorra pushed off the door and began guiding them toward the bedroom. They got as far as the living room before Odelle whirled her around and pinned her against the wall. Her hands roamed over Sorra's body, making it increasingly difficult to concentrate on anything other than the pounding between her legs. "You know, we're never going to have sex on a proper bed at this rate."

Odelle pulled away, and her gaze burned with a need Sorra hardly recognized. "We don't need a bed." After one last breath-stealing kiss, she dropped to her knees. Sorra braced herself harder against the wall to keep from falling to the floor along with her. She swallowed as Odelle began removing her pants, praying she wouldn't embarrass herself. Normally, she preferred making Odelle work a little harder, but something about the insistence of her fingers as they undid the ties and the searing heat of her gaze made the ache in her body throb even harder.

"You always were impatient," Sorra rasped as Odelle finally managed to shove her pants down past her thighs. She tried to step out of them, but Odelle's hands gripped her hips and shoved her tight against the wall, pinning her in place. Her eyes widened, but she did not object.

"Impatient?" Odelle smirked at her as she hurried to strip down Sorra's underwear. "No. I just know how to get what I want."

She dipped her head. Sorra stiffened at the first brush of Odelle's lip over the bare skin of her stomach, biting her lip to stifle a groan.

Odelle had always been something of a tease, and she had grown even more unbearable in their years apart. Sorra clawed at the wall behind her as Odelle trailed a blazing line of kisses between her hipbones, searing the sensitive strip of skin with the heat of her mouth.

"Stop messing around," Sorra gasped, hoping she sounded forceful instead of desperate. Unfortunately, she could not conceal the need in her voice. "I want impatient Odelle back." Odelle laughed, and Sorra felt the vibrations play across her skin. Each heartbeat sent another painful throb between her legs, and she shuddered as the warmth of Odelle's mouth dipped lower. It stopped just short of the place she needed it most, and she groaned, closing her eyes as she tilted her head back against the wall. "Please?"

Moments later, she felt the silken warmth of Odelle's tongue sweep between her outer lips. Her hands shot down to clutch at Odelle's shoulders. She wanted to open her eyes, but she knew that if she did, the sweet pressure building inside of her would become unbearable. Instead, she shifted her weight and spread her legs as wide as the pants around her knees would allow, hoping she would be able to outlast Odelle's patience.

Odelle seemed determined to destroy every bit of resolve Sorra had left before showing her any mercy. She pressed her tongue against Sorra's entrance first. Her hips tried to buck, unsure whether to pull away or push forward, but Odelle's hands kept her in place, limiting her range of motion. With her willpower rapidly slipping away, Sorra moved her hands to the back of Odelle's head.

"Odelle, I'm going to lose it if you hold off any longer," she said, her voice uncharacteristically high and breathy.

She could feel Odelle grin against her thigh. "Imagine that. You always were the impatient one, and I can't remember the last time I had you begging so wonderfully. I think I might enjoy this a bit longer." Sorra felt her tongue drag a slow trail across her inner thigh.

"Or you could give me what I want, and I can promise not to be quite as cruel to you in return." Odelle paused, and Sorra almost screamed. After several tense seconds, the heat of Odelle's mouth finally surrounded her. Sorra groaned. She rocked her hips forward, crying out as Odelle's tongue circled the tip of her clit. "Just like that." Odelle's hands pinned her hips tight to the wall, and though she desperately wanted to rock against her, Sorra couldn't find the strength. Instead, she tightened her grip on the back of Odelle's head, torn between looking down and squeezing her eyes shut in ecstasy.

Odelle was horribly good at giving her exactly what she wanted without providing what she needed. The seal of her lips was just a bit too gentle, and the quick strokes of her tongue a touch too slow and off center. Sorra knew she was doing it deliberately, and she had to bite her lip to keep from cursing, pleading, or both. Need coiled in her lower belly, tightening as her inner walls pulsed around nothing. She wanted Odelle's fingers inside of her but was afraid to ask, simply because she knew her request wouldn't be granted in quite the way she wanted.

Sorra groaned as she felt Odelle's fingertips press against her, sliding down to tease at penetration. The warmth receded, and her stomach tightened as Odelle skimmed over her wet flesh. "You haven't needed me this much in a long time."

Sorra struggled not to look at her. She pushed down and sank onto Odelle's fingers, letting out a deep groan at the stretch. Finally, she gave in and tilted her chin down to stare into her lover's face, the craving she saw there surprised her. Odelle wanted her pleasure as much as she did. Perhaps she even needed it. She let her hand slide down over the curve of Odelle's neck and gripped her shoulder instead, desperate for some kind of connection beyond the physical. *If the need in Odelle's eyes is real, then perhaps... perhaps...*

Odelle's fingers slid inside her the rest of the way, pulling her toward an inevitable release. Her peak rose more swiftly than she expected, and although Odelle made a few small efforts to delay the inevitable, she did not pull away when it came. Instead, she pulled hard with her lips and thrust her fingers forward in a motion that had Sorra crying out for more. Rippling waves started deep within her, pushing out until she couldn't tell when each shudder started. She dug her nails into Odelle's shoulder, scratching the skin there as she thrashed through her orgasm.

Too soon, the soft, rhythmic tug of Odelle's lips stopped, and the thrusts inside of her stilled. Sorra stared down with blurry eyes, breathing heavily and reeling from the power of what had just happened. Her muscles twitched with aftershocks as she watched Odelle remove her fingers and slide them between her lips, cleaning them. The satisfied look on her face was just too much. Sorra kicked her pants the rest of the way off and pounced on Odelle.

They fell to the floor, tangled together as she tugged at Odelle's clothes. After pulling the offending fabric away, she slung one of Odelle's knees over her shoulder. She slid her hand between Odelle's legs and found wetness "You always enjoyed doing that, didn't you?" she panted beside Odelle's ear.

"Yes."

The shaking word eased the knot of tension in Sorra's chest. She dipped her fingers forward, running the tips up and down in a soft line. "I know. I can feel it." She paused at Odelle's entrance, waiting for her breath to hitch before she slid inside, unable to stifle a groan at the warm, clinging heat waiting for her. "Odelle, I...you're..." She could not find the words. Instead, she focused on the tight, needy expression of Odelle's face and leaned down to kiss her creased forehead. She wrapped an arm around her, pulling their bodies closer as her fingers rocked into Odelle once more.

"Oh, Sorra," Odelle breathed. She slid her leg down off Sorra's shoulder and then their lips met again in a desperate kiss. What had started as a war of teasing and suppressed craving had turned into an urgent need to get closer, to draw one another into themselves. Sorra did not think she could get Odelle close enough, and she had been a fool to stay away for so long. They had wasted their years, and it was all thanks to the chancellor and their stupid war. "Sorra." The sound of her name broke her from her thoughts. Odelle pressed a hand to her face. "Come back to me."

She kissed Odelle again, more gently that time as she eased her fingers in and out of her lover. "I'm here," she whispered against Odelle's lips. "I'm here."

Odelle clung to her tightly. "I'm so close."

Sorra thrust into her more quickly, curling her fingers upward and dragging them against the same spot that always drove her insane. She could feel Odelle's walls pulsing around her hand. She was almost there. Just a little more.

With a short, breathy cry of pleasure, Odelle came, pulsing around her fingers. For a moment they lay there, breathing heavily and placing gentle kisses against one another. Then, slowly, they picked themselves off the floor and tried to make it to the bedroom. However, Sorra kept catching Odelle by the hand and pulling her close, kissing her sweetly and tugging urgently at her remaining clothes. They stumbled into the kitchen and stayed there. *Beds are entirely overrated*, Sorra decided.

"What in the name of the cosmos are you two doing?"

The noise made Sorra groan in frustration, and Odelle flinched against her in surprise. That chafing male voice could belong to no one other than Joren. Reluctantly, she pulled away from Odelle and tried to gather what was left of her composure, taking a deep breath and hoping she appeared calmer than she felt. She passed Odelle a recently discarded shirt to cover up and then glared at Joren, placing her hands on her hips. "I'm certain you can figure that one out. Care to explain your incredible rudeness?"

Joren kept his eyes fixed politely on the floor. "I...you know I would never interrupt you unless it was important." The purple flush on his face grew darker, spreading across his cheeks.

"Has something happened?" Odelle asked from behind her, still gathering her clothes.

Joren cleared his throat. "I just thought you both would want to know that Chancellor Corvis is sending a detachment of Seekers here immediately."

"What?" Odelle nearly toppled over, clumsily pushing a leg through her pants.

"Apparently a squadron went missing in this region, and they wish to investigate the nearest station for signs of dissenters." Joren finally looked over at Odelle. "The chancellor expressed concern over you. She seems to think you're in danger."

Sorra's stomach dropped. "That or she's figured you out. We have to get you away from here before she arrives. You need to stay somewhere safe."

"Absolutely not." Odelle folded her arms over her chest, somehow managing to appear confident even while half-dressed and flushed. Sorra began to protest, but Odelle held up her hand. "The chancellor is expecting to find me here. If I leave the station before the Seekers arrive, it will only make her suspicious. I have to do everything I can to convince her nothing is out of the ordinary."

"But it isn't ordinary." Sorra paced the length of the kitchen, hands clasped tightly behind her back. "We're in the middle of developing our plan. If the Seekers find even a hint of rebel activity here, we're all dead."

She stopped short when a firm hand clasped her shoulder. Sorra turned and met Odelle's eyes. The determination in them was unmistakable. "The Seekers aren't going to find anything. You've played this game hundreds of times before, Sorra. Now is no different."

Sorra looked away. This was entirely different. She was used to being "Dalia" in public, used to flying under the Dominion's radar and outsmarting the Seekers when they made their inspections, but this time, there was so much more at stake. Odelle was a traitor as well as a rebel, and the chancellor was known for devising particularly gruesome punishments. If they were discovered, she was worse than dead.

"You aren't going to leave, are you?" Sorra whispered.

Odelle's warm palm slid down along her arm to fold around her fingers instead. "No. I'm not going to leave."

She took in a deep breath and lifted her head. "All right. Joren, put the usual procedures in motion. It's time to give the chancellor what she wants."

Joren nodded. "Of course. But what about Maia and Taylor? I checked the flight logs, and they're on the station today."

"Have Kalanis sent up to me before the Seekers arrive. We need to figure out where to stash her research and her pet human, I suppose."

"Very well." He bent down to check his communicator. "We have a few hours before the Seekers arrive. That should be plenty of time to put things in order."

"Let's hope it is," Odelle murmured. "Is there anything I can do to help before they dock?"

"You can start by making it look like we didn't fuck in every room in the suite," Sorra said. "I doubt we've got time for a cleaning crew, and I'm sure they'll pay a visit here to make sure no one's put a bullet through your head yet." Her voice came out harsher than she had intended, and Odelle gave her a disapproving frown.

"And you can start with a shower. You look like you need it."

Sorra turned away, not bothering with a goodbye as she stalked toward the back of the suite. She hoped Odelle wouldn't follow her. She had known the peaceful illusion wouldn't last, but she hadn't expected it to end so abruptly. Once she took refuge in the bathroom, her shoulders slumped, and she stared sadly at her reflection as she began stripping out of her ruined clothes. She only had a few hours before the Seekers arrived and just a few minutes to make herself forget the past several days and regain her focus.

She paused as she looked down at her hands. Her fingers still glistened with the efforts of their lovemaking. It had been so perfect, the moment when Odelle had fallen over the edge and into her arms. But moments like that were too dangerous—distracting. If she really cared about Odelle, she needed to distance herself until the plan was finished. She only had one chance to make this work, and if it fell apart now, Odelle would pay the price.

Chapter Fifteen

"IN THE ZOO? YOU'RE kidding, right?" Taylor frowned and crossed her arms. "There isn't any other way? Won't the ikthians recognize me?"

Sorra smirked. "You'd be surprised at most ikthians' inability to distinguish one human from another. If I say you're a pet for my exotic collection, then they'll view you as the simple subspecies I claim you are."

"That's awful!"

"No, it's genius." Sorra took a step closer, jabbing a finger at her. "You get to sit around in that zoo, fully clothed and out of harm's way, worrying about nothing while the rest of us run around and try to lie about the whole station."

Taylor clenched her hands into tense fists. What she really hated about the plan was that Maia would have to stay hidden during the chancellor's visit, nowhere near her. "Isn't there anything I can do?"

"No. In fact, the less you do, the better. We need you to appear as uninteresting as possible. So, pretty much act like you normally do." Taylor shot Sorra a glare, but if she noticed it, she didn't let on. "The last thing we need is the Seekers wanting a closer look at you. Now, come on. Odelle is going to take care of Kalanis, but we need to get you into that zoo. You'll need to stay out of the carnivorous enclosures."

Taylor groaned and followed Sorra. She had shared a hasty goodbye with Maia before she was dragged off to help hide her data, but their abrupt separation had left her feeling sick. "This is going to end in disaster," she muttered. All around them, everyone else rushed to get the station in order. Even those not part of the rebellion often conducted legally questionable practices, and they feared inspections as much as anyone else.

"It very well might," Sorra said. She paused and turned to Taylor. Her smug expression had vanished, leaving her features grim. "If something happens and the Seekers attack, get Maia and run."

"Right. Where can I find her?" Taylor could feel her adrenaline kicking in. Her combat training told her now was not the time to sit still. She had to fight against every instinct to remain calm.

"She'll be back in your rooms after we lock down her research. She's going to sleep through the whole ordeal."

"That's still not very comforting," Taylor mumbled, but her complaints were cut off when they reached the entrance to the menagerie.

"Put her somewhere safe," Sorra said, passing her off to the obviously unenthusiastic groundskeeper. He was a tall alien, his sallow skin and large dark eyes reminding Taylor of an Earth horror film more than another species. "Somewhere the animals won't eat her."

Taylor barely had time to give Sorra one last dirty look before the ikthian stalked away, leaving her to her fate. With a reluctant sigh, she turned to the groundskeeper.

"So, where are you stashing me?" Taylor forced herself to give him a friendly smile. It was probably best to stay on good terms with him, especially since he had the power to put her in the wrong hiding place.

Unfortunately, he did not return her smile. She wasn't sure his twisted black lips were even capable of making one. "Come on," he grunted, tugging the side of her arm and practically dragging her down the path.

Taylor realized with some relief the enclosures on both sides looked somewhat clean and the animals inside, while certainly strange, didn't seem very large. A faint shield of purple light separated each one from the path.

"Maybe this won't be so bad." She caught a glimpse of a tiny leaf-like creature. It scuttled across the ground, whirring its ragged wings. "These animals look pretty harmless."

"This is just the insect exhibit," the groundskeeper said. "I have to take you to the right section."

"The right section?" Taylor repeated, but her question remained unanswered. The smell of the ocean filled her nose, and they arrived at a much more disconcerting section of the menagerie. The enclosures were larger, but so were the animals. She stared up in shock at a long-necked creature more than three times her height. Scales covered its silvery body, and at least half of its length was submerged in water.

"I'm not marine life, just so you know," she said as they passed several long, thin creatures slithering through a nearby tank. "Humans don't breathe well underwater. Or, at all."

146

The groundskeeper grunted and continued walking, forcing Taylor to jog in order to keep up. She had no idea how the grumpy old alien was able to move so quickly. At last, he came to a stop and jabbed his bony finger at an empty-looking enclosure. It had grass, several rocks, and a small patch of water in the back corner. She let out a sigh, relief spreading through her. If she had to be trapped in a zoo, this cage wasn't so bad.

"Okay, what now?"

The groundskeeper flipped open a small hatch near one side of the wall and started pressing the buttons behind it. A small section of the purple shield flickered and then vanished. He shoved her toward it. "Strip and get in."

Taylor clutched at her shirt stubbornly and shook her head. "No way. I'll go in, but I'm not leaving my clothes with you."

"Look around," the groundskeeper said. "You see any of the other animals wearing clothes?"

"I'm not an animal," Taylor replied. "Okay, well, technically we're all animals, but I'm an animal with the capacity to be embarrassed naked. The clothes stay on."

The groundskeeper huffed and stopped trying to push her into the enclosure. "Fine. I don't have time to deal with you. The Seekers are almost here."

Once he let go of her, Taylor stepped through the gap. "You really think they'll waste their time coming into the menagerie? Don't they have rebels to look for or something?"

The groundskeeper gave her a twisted grin, needlepoint teeth showing. "Sure, but rebels could hide in here. You're hiding in here, after all."

A few moments later, the gap in the barrier closed with a soft hiss and the groundskeeper disappeared down the path, leaving her alone. Unsure whether to be relieved or worried, she headed toward one of the large grey rocks on top of the vibrantly green grass. Fortunately, it had several uneven rivets in its side, and she had no trouble climbing her way to the top. She inhaled deeply as she rested, enjoying the smell of fresh plants and wildlife. Usually, the station smelled so sterile.

From this height, she had a much better view of the menagerie itself. It was larger than she had anticipated, even bigger than the botanical gardens she and Maia had visited. She sat down on the rock, watching a herd of gazelle-like creatures bound through the enclosure on six springy legs. "I hope she's okay," she sighed, drumming her fingers against her knees. Nerves raced through her. They had discussed the possibility of sending Maia away on a ship, but it was too dangerous with the Seeker squadrons rapidly approaching. They were more likely to seize a rapidly leaving ship than to search every living quarter and safe house on the station.

After several minutes of sitting and watching, Taylor got bored. She slid down from the rock and walked around the enclosure. She ditched her shoes and socks, hiding them in a crevice. She had to admit that a fully clothed human might look suspicious. As much as she hated Sorra's idea, the ikthian knew what she was doing. She had evaded the Dominion for this long while living directly under their noses. Surely she could keep up the ruse a little longer.

* * *

Maia typed quickly at Sorra's office terminal, trying to add one more layer of encryption. It was nearly impossible to delete all data that made reference to rebel activity, but the added layer of protection would deter most attempts to break in to the station's information caches. Hopefully, the Seekers would be more interested in scouring the area for rebels than going through the station's paperwork.

A hand touched her shoulder, and she nearly jumped in surprise. She looked back to see Odelle standing beside her, frowning with worry. "Maia, the Seekers are almost here. We need to move you out."

"Just one moment," Maia muttered. She went back to typing, deleting as many files as she could. There wasn't time to do a thorough job, and she hoped no one would look too closely.

"I haven't spoken with Sorra yet, but she should be taking Taylor to a hiding place right now. We've got to get you out of here."

"All right," she sighed. "This should be enough if one of the Seekers starts poking around in the system. Someone with expertise could recover the files, but hopefully, they won't have cause for suspicion."

"It'll have to do." Maia could hear the tight worry in Odelle's voice.

With a few more keystrokes, she finished her work and shut down the terminal. "Are there any other steps we can take to preserve my research?"

"This is less about preserving your research and more about preserving you," Odelle explained as they headed toward the door. "We've already distributed several seed copies to rebel groups throughout the galaxy. If we lose you, however, there aren't any other rogue evolutionary genetic specialists waiting in line to take your place."

Although she knew Odelle was joking, Maia worried. She clasped her hands together in an attempt to stop herself from going over to the terminal again. "Where am I going to hide while the Seekers are here?"

"In plain sight, we've decided. I'm taking you back to your room. Hopefully, the Seekers won't check the individual quarters at all, but…" Her tone suggested it was wishful thinking. "Our goal is to make you seem as much like a normal civilian as possible."

Maia nodded as they stepped out into the hall and boarded the lift. They rode the elevator to the main floor. When they stepped out into the heart of the station, Maia's eyes widened. People were everywhere, rushing past each other with a clear sense of urgency. Several looked afraid, and the tension stretching through the crowd made her chest constrict. "Where are they all going?"

"To hide, the same as you." She stopped at a nearby transport terminal. "Come on. We'll make quicker time if we grab a ride."

The ride was short, but Maia fidgeted. Her thoughts were torn between the Seekers and Taylor. Their separation had been a blur. One moment, they had been laughing and joking together over lunch, and the next, Joren had interrupted and dragged Taylor away with plenty of apologies but very few explanations. At last, they arrived at her living quarters.

"How much time do we have?" Maia asked Odelle as they left the transport behind.

"There's no way to tell. I just got word the chancellor's ship docked a few minutes before I came to fetch you. She'll be expecting to meet with me soon, probably within the next hour, but I have no idea when or even if the Seekers will check these rooms." Odelle paused as they reached the door to Maia's quarters. "If they do, just try to stay out of the way."

"Perhaps they won't come in here," Maia whispered. Her hands had started shaking, and her fingers slipped when she tried to open a door.

Odelle gently nudged her aside and opened the door that led her back into the bedroom. "Wouldn't that be a stroke of luck? I just want us to be prepared for the worst. You know how the Dominion is. They always do exactly what you'd prefer them not to. I'll see you on the other side."

Odelle left before Maia could ask any more questions. Maia sighed and looked around at her quarters. They felt startlingly empty, more than any other time she had been alone in them. She wandered over to the washroom and looked around. It was clean enough. No evidence of Taylor's lay out for the Seekers to pick up on. Sorra had ordered a sweep of their room first thing.

She caught sight of her reflection in the mirror and paused. She had changed in the past months. Her face was gaunt, the skin stretched tight over cheekbones. She no longer looked the part of a pampered scientist. Dark circles had formed under her eyes. She was inclined not to smile. For the first time in a very long time, Maia took stock of how much had changed for her.

"At least I'm not a prisoner this time," she mumbled, but it did not make her feel much better. She was alone, just as she had been then.

Her hands still shaking, she walked over to an equipment locker and opened it. Weapons were tucked inside, anything that would be standard issue to a paranoid individual living alone. Maia grabbed a pistol. She clutched the grip tightly as her trembling hand rattled it.

"I will no longer be helpless," she said through gritted teeth. "I will no longer be helpless."

She returned to the bedroom with the gun. She sat down on the bed and crossed her legs, fighting the urge to breathe rapidly and lose control. Even though she sat still, her heart beat wildly with worry for Taylor and everyone else aboard the station. The Dominion would not hesitate to eliminate Tarkoht if they saw fit. She could only hope that Sorra and Odelle knew what they were doing. Despite her own words, Maia still felt entirely helpless, a single person against an empire.

***

Sorra risked another glance at Joren while they waited outside the docking bay. He stood with arms behind his back, the very picture of poise and grace—and the complete opposite of how she felt. "How do I look?" she asked. They had been in such a rush to meet the chancellor she had almost forgotten to apply the dramatic makeup her alter ego usually sported.

"As you always do, Dalia," Joren answered without looking at her.

She took the comment to mean she should stop worrying. She cleared her throat and glanced back at the doorway. "Madam

Chancellor must have quite the disembarking procedure to make us wait so unceremoniously."

"Really, Dalia." Despite the chastising tone, she caught a glimmer of a smile on Joren's lips. "The chancellor is just exercising caution like any well-meaning citizen. I know safety is my top concern any time you and I travel somewhere. "

"Joren, how sweet of you."

"It's not your safety I fear for but my own."

Sorra beamed. She managed to muster up some cockiness. When the doors finally hissed open, she walked forward, allowing her extravagant robes to trail behind her. "Madam Chancellor." She greeted the stern ikthian with fairly convincing enthusiasm. "Welcome to our station. I hope your journey here was enjoyable."

The chancellor's expression remained neutral, although the lines of her frown softened ever so slightly. "As enjoyable as any journey can be, I suppose." She offered her hand, and Sorra pressed their palms together in greeting. "Thank you for hosting us on such short notice, Dalia. I know you understand the safety of the Dominion's resources is imperative, but I recognize we have caused you some inconvenience."

Inconvenience was a massive understatement, but Sorra's smile did not falter. "Not at all," she cooed. "It's an honor to serve in any way we can. There have been several improvements to the station since your last visit here. I believe you'll be impressed."

The chancellor gave her an intense, scrutinizing look, and Sorra felt a flicker of nervousness underneath her facade. She had no idea how Odelle managed to work with this woman day in and day out. Although the chancellor had the boring appearance of any other politician— middle aged, bland, and harmless—Sorra could not shake the thought that she had caused countless deaths. This woman's ignorance was the only thing that stood between her and Daashu.

"I'm afraid I won't have time for distractions, however pleasant they might be," the chancellor murmured. There was a hint of steely determination behind her soft veneer of politeness, and Sorra had to tighten her smile. "I need to speak with Odelle as soon as possible. I believe you know where she is?"

"Odelle. I'm afraid I haven't seen her yet today, but Joren met her for lunch. Didn't you, dear?"

Joren stepped forward and nodded politely. "I can take you to see her now, Madam Chancellor. And once again, welcome to Tarkoht."

The chancellor greeted Joren in the same manner as she had Sorra. "Thank you."

The three of them left the docking bay with an entourage of ikthian Seekers following. Sorra tried not to follow the chancellor's gaze as it darted from person to person, her brow furrowing every time she caught sight of some other species. "I've always marveled at your eccentricities, Dalia," she said when a rakash couple darted down a hall. "Being able to live amidst such a...diverse population must be trying."

"Adversity has its own rewards," said Sorra. It was difficult to make the words sound honeyed through clenched teeth. "My partner has always been the more practical one." She gestured at Joren. Probably the most truthful thing she had stated yet. Joren had always been calculating, slow to act, but meaningful when he did. Joren had not been stupid enough to compromise his real name, unlike Sorra had as a young rebel. He had taken Sorra into his protection, and for that he had earned her unwavering trust, something she rarely gave out.

"And how have you fared on the station, Joren?" the chancellor asked.

"Oh, it's manageable. I'm usually too busy arranging trade agreements to interact with the station's population. That's Dalia's territory."

"Well, you certainly do have a flair for...adversity," the chancellor told her, mimicking her earlier word choice. It was not a compliment.

"I believe we arranged to meet Odelle in this conference room," said Joren, pointing down the hall. "Would you like us to accompany you?"

The chancellor frowned. "No. What I have to discuss with Odelle is of the strictest confidentiality." She turned her gaze to Sorra. "I trust we won't have to worry about that being broken?"

Sorra kept her smile frozen in place despite the sickening twist she felt in her stomach. "Chancellor, we would never dream of violating your privacy. Take any precautionary measures you wish."

They reached the conference room door, and the chancellor stepped inside, leaving her Seekers standing in the hall. Joren paused, glancing between them. "Is there anything I can assist you with?"

One of the Seekers nodded. "Yes. You and your partner may leave. This area is restricted. Government business only."

Sorra and Joren backed away. They walked down the hall together, arm in arm. They waited until turning the corner to let their facade drop, if only for a moment.

"Well, I suppose that could have gone worse," Joren said.

Sorra nodded, though she grimaced as she remembered the chancellor's snide comments. "She's not happy with us. She's looking for an excuse to wipe this station off the map."

"Then we shall not give her one."

***

Odelle had to work hard to express the right amount of concern at seeing the chancellor enter the room. "Madame Chancellor," she said, rising from her chair and offering her hands. "I trust you had a safe journey?"

The chancellor did not return the gesture. Instead, she waved one hand dismissively and stood beside the table instead of taking a seat. "Forget the pleasantries. We have larger worries to attend to."

"We do?" Odelle had skimmed the chancellor's brief and concerning messages before her arrival, but there had been very little time to prepare herself for the meeting. "What seems to be our biggest worry, then?"

"An ikthian squad was wiped out on a nearby planet." The chancellor shook her head. "We've even heard reports of humans in the area."

"Humans?" Odelle's stomach dropped. "As in more than one?"

The chancellor nodded. "If our intel is reliable, yes. We don't know where they might be, but if they're out this far, it means the Coalition is making a stronger push than we anticipated. I had to come investigate the matter myself."

Odelle tried to offer a comforting smile, one the chancellor did not return. "Well, there is a human Dalia keeps in her menagerie. It's completely harmless, however, totally cut off from any technology. She treats it more like an exotic pet."

The chancellor gave her a wide-eyed stare, but at last, she blinked and shook her head. "Dalia certainly knows how to make a spectacle. Is her human the only one you've seen?"

"Of course," Odelle said, trying her best to keep her voice neutral. "There are plenty of aliens on Tarkoht, but a human would not go unnoticed here. The Coalition's soldiers wouldn't dare enter Dominion-controlled space."

"They can, and they have," the chancellor snapped. "I know my reports are accurate." Her eyes narrowed, and she folded her hands behind her back and straightened her spine. "Speaking of reports, what have you uncovered so far during your stay here? Have you found any more signs of rebel activity?"

Odelle shrugged. "If I may be honest, there are traces of rebel activity everywhere these days. Tarkoht is no exception. However, I don't think there's any cause for concern about the station. I've already compiled a report on what little I found, and I'll send it with you when you leave."

Unfortunately, her explanation failed to calm the chancellor. She paced, turning in a tight circle each time she reached the edge of the table. "I'm not convinced. Tarkoht is the perfect place for anyone who wants to disappear. Dalia's silly menagerie is only the start. She's turned the entire place into a zoo. The population's always changing, and there's so much money pouring in and out of the station it's impossible to keep track. The Dominion-appointed public security officers are inattentive at best, and it isn't far from Nakonum, either."

Odelle tried to calm her racing heart. She had never seen the chancellor so agitated. There had to be more to this story than she knew, but she was afraid to ask. "What would you like for me to do?"

The chancellor looked at her. "How well do you know Dalia?" she asked, crossing the room one last time and stopping purposefully in front of her. Odelle had to force herself not to break eye contact. "It's obvious her foolishness is just an act, but for what purpose, I have no idea. It wouldn't surprise me if she was connected with them."

This time, Odelle could not hide her shocked expression. She panicked for a good five seconds before throwing herself even further into the reaction. It was her only chance at putting on a convincing lie. "You don't mean that," she said, trying to take on a wounded look. "Dalia and I have been friends for years. We were in school together. It's true she's not as stupid as she pretends to be, but it's only for amusement's sake. I'm positive she isn't working with the rebels. Even if she was, my investigation would have turned up some kind of connection."

"Maybe you weren't looking hard enough." The chancellor activated her communicator, keying in something as she spoke. "Friendship can be blinding. The Seekers and I are going to take a second look. Hopefully, you're right about all this, but just in case..." She turned toward the door, preparing to leave the room. "Come along. I trust you'll know the best places to start?"

Odelle followed reluctantly. "Madam Chancellor, are you sure? I understand the severity of the situation, but, as you said before, Tarkoht is a very valuable asset to the Dominion. A full-scale investigation into the station's activities could very well shrink profits here for months, profits we'll need if we're going to continue our skirmishes with the Coalition."

"I'm not concerned with profits." The chancellor stopped before they entered the hallway, and Odelle found it hard to breathe under her intense gaze. "The only thing I care about is finding these rebels and stomping them out. I'll do whatever is necessary to preserve the Dominion's security. And I'm sure I can trust in you to do the same."

Odelle bowed her head. It was a statement, not a question. "Of course, Madam Chancellor. You can trust me."

Chapter Sixteen

RACHEL FROWNED, DRUMMING HER fingers against the handle of her pistol as she waited outside General Oranthis' office. After their return to Nakonum, Elurin had agreed to speak to the general on her behalf, but the longer she waited, the more she doubted he would allow her to visit Tarkoht unsupervised. The naledai rebels still barely trusted her, and she didn't think they'd be likely to lend her a ship any time soon.

She braced herself against the wall, still keeping her hand close to her gun as she stared down the two surly looking naledai guards who waited with her. They were there to protect Oranthis, not watch her every move, but their presence still made her uncomfortable. They rarely took their eyes off her, and it was obvious the uneasiness she felt around them was mutual.

After another long, tense stretch of unbroken eye contact, the door opened for Elurin. Relief uncoiled the tension in her and shocked Rachel. The squad leader was an ikthian, but at least she didn't constantly look alarmed or wary of Rachel like the rest of the rebellion. She pushed herself off the wall and nodded a greeting. "What'd he say?"

Elurin sighed. "Sorry, Harris. He was happy about the prisoner we brought back, and he was actually going to let you tag along to Tarkoht with a detachment of ours in a week or so, but then a transmission came through. There are Seekers at the station. They're investigating reports of rebel activity and are going to tear the place apart searching for proof. It's not safe anymore."

Rachel narrowed her eyes. If the Seekers headed to Tarkoht, that could mean Taylor and Maia were aboard. With no other choice, she decided to appeal to Elurin one last time. "You remember that friend I was talking about earlier, the one who killed the rest of the prisoner's squad? That's why the Seekers are there. They're hunting her. I can't let them find her."

"I believe you," Elurin said, "but it doesn't make a difference. The only reason the rebels have lasted so long is because we always cut contact as soon as the Seekers find one of our bases. We destroy everything and block all communications. If anyone goes there, it could expose our position here." Her eyes darted to the side, and Rachel thought she caught a shudder running through the ikthian's body. "The Seekers have...ways...of convincing prisoners to talk."

"Look, I know what the Seekers are capable of. I've fought them before with the Coalition. But it doesn't matter. I have to get her out of there before they kill her."

To her surprise, Elurin gave her a small smile. "It's admirable you want to save your friend, but there's no other option. You'll have to wait until Oranthis gives the all clear to go to Tarkoht. None of us are even allowed off-base until this blows over."

Rachel felt a stab of guilt at Elurin's praise. Before Maia, it might have been true. She gladly would have gone to face a whole army of Seekers on Taylor's behalf. But now, Taylor had been tricked into helping the ikthian. Even if Maia was merely a prisoner of war, caught up like Elurin, she could not let Taylor throw away the Coalition, her people, for some stranger's cause.

"Thanks." She nodded toward the exit. "I'm going to head back to my room, if you don't mind."

"Sure. Maybe I'll come find you later. If you don't mind the company of an ikthian, that is."

Rachel wanted to push Elurin away, but she was right. She was alone, mostly because of her own doing, and it hurt. What hurt even more was the realization that not all ikthians were the monstrous creatures she remembered fighting. In fact, the longer she stayed immersed in alien culture, the more obvious the similarities between their species seemed.

"I...that would be nice," she said, unsure of why she gave the answer even as she spoke.

Elurin smiled. "Perhaps I'll bring a strategy set. You look like someone who appreciates mind games."

Rachel cringed at the awkward wording in her translator. All she could think of was her accusation of Maia brainwashing Taylor. "I'd like that."

Elurin walked out to the hallway and disappeared. Rachel exhaled slowly and closed her eyes. She needed to focus. She needed to decide what to do. More than anything, Rachel wanted her old life back. She wanted things to be normal again. But the further she got from normal, the more impossible it seemed. In addition to the improbability of actually finding Taylor, she found it increasingly more difficult to swallow the Coalition's propaganda with each passing day. Elurin had saved her life and proved to be a valuable ally in combat. She could no longer believe the simple mantra that all ikthians were evil. Without that belief, her whole reason to chase Taylor crumbled. *Why, then, do I need to rescue her from the rebels? If anything, I need to keep her from being captured by the Seekers.*

Rachel took a deep breath and opened her eyes. The unfamiliar walls of the rebel base filled her vision. She had wandered too far from home, she realized. She started back toward her quarters. She didn't see a single human face, and that no longer unsettled her the way it used to.

Did Taylor see the Coalition's prejudice all along? The thought came to her as she walked past a naledai and an ikthian laughing together. The idea troubled her. More than anything, she wanted to have someone to talk to. She wanted her siblings, a friend, someone she knew would not try to sway her thought but allow her to just talk it out.

Rachel reached her room and tried to set up a long-range call back to her family, but all access out of the base had been blocked. Even then, the time back on her homeworld was well into the night. No one would answer. Rachel sighed and collapsed on her bed, groaning as she tried to come to a decision. She had to do something. To sit and wait was torture, and Taylor might not be at Tarkoht much longer. If she even was there in the first place. Her thoughts scattered when the intercom to her room went off. She sighed as she remembered Elurin's promise to stop by.

"Who's there?"

"You know." Elurin's now familiar tone lilted through the speaker. "If you don't mind letting me in, I brought refreshments and a playing board. I can teach you some ikthian strategy games." Rachel stood up and entered the command sequence to open the door. Elurin smiled at her as the panel slid aside. She held up a box filled with food, drink, and a gaming tablet. "I hope this is a custom familiar to humans. I don't want to come off rude or intrusive."

Rachel let her in. "Depends on the custom." She should have been in a panic, allowing an ikthian into her room. Instead, she just felt relief from the unending loneliness she suffered since her exile.

"Comforting someone who is upset with company and good food."

"It's considered a good thing. Mostly between friends, though." Rachel cleared the table and pulled over an extra chair from the corner of the room. "It's usually odd when you don't know the other person that well."

Elurin set the box down. "In your situation, I might be the only person acquainted with you for light-years."

Rachel laughed nervously and sat down. Elurin sat across from her and pulled a bottle of amber liquid from the box, followed by two glasses.

"It's a rough spot to be in, yeah." Rachel watched Elurin unscrew the cap from the bottle, pour the sloshing drink into the glasses and push a glass toward Rachel.

"This should be safe for humans, though I don't know what effect alcohol content has on your metabolism."

"A good one." Rachel took up the glass and sipped cautiously. It was sweet, but not sickeningly so. "This tastes expensive." If she were on Earth, she would be concerned about Elurin spending so much on wine for her.

Elurin laughed. "It is, I suppose. It was a gift, but I've neglected to try it for so long, I decided this was as good an occasion as any." She sipped from her own glass. "It's comforting to know that good taste in drink is universal."

"Certainly makes planning for parties easier." Rachel sipped again. "Though it's weird to think of all these different species being so miraculously similar."

"And why is that?" Elurin pushed the box aside so they could more directly see one another. She stirred her drink in her glass and took another slow sip.

"Well, you know. We're separated by light-years, hundreds of them. How did our species develop along such close lines? How did we develop language the same way?" She sighed and set down the half-empty glass. "It was easier to assume humans and ikthians were too different to cooperate."

"Your government tells you that?"

"And yours," Rachel shot back. "The last time I checked, we were at war with the Dominion." She sighed and crossed her arms, leaning back in her chair. "I don't know anymore." She hated to admit it. The words burned worse than the alcohol. But despite her fears, Elurin had been nothing but kind to her.

"I have to admit, you didn't seem too fond of me the first time we met." Elurin dug the game board out of the box and placed it between them. She activated it, and the holo projections flickered to life above the table, drifting into a triangular formation over the crosshatched landscape. "You were swearing up a storm, and I think you called me 'that' until I told you my name."

Guilt kicked Rachel in the gut, and she leaned back, letting go of the tension in her shoulders. "Yeah, I'm sorry. You were decent to me, even when I thought you were just another Seeker out to kill me." Her brow furrowed as she looked at the game board. "How do I play this, anyway? We don't know any ikthian games on Earth."

"Obviously." Elurin brushed the tablet again, highlighting one of the pieces. "It's fairly simple…"

But even as she launched into an explanation, Rachel couldn't bring herself to listen. She was actually enjoying her time with Elurin, contrary to what she expected, but she couldn't stop thinking about Taylor. She had been so invested in the idea her friend had been brainwashed, but she was starting to doubt herself. She had never felt like anyone other than herself while she was in Elurin's presence, which made the whole brainwashing theory hard to swallow. "Sorry," she mumbled when she realized Elurin was staring and waiting for her to respond.

Elurin's brow wrinkled, and the gesture seemed so human Rachel did a double take. She stared into Elurin's face and realized she only saw a person there. Not an ikthian or a threat, but a friend. Shock raced through her. She had never bothered to study Elurin's facial features before. The high cheekbones could have been cut from marble. The purple hue dusting her cheeks and crown barely offset the ivory of her skin. Elurin clearly had a warrior's body, hardened from years out on the field, but she did not show it in her face. Their gazes met for a moment, Elurin's dark irises capturing hers. Rachel glanced back down at her drink.

"So, shall we play?"

Rachel nodded. "I don't quite think I get it, but I'll try."

Elurin laughed and activated one of the figures on her end of the board. "It's all right. The game functions better with active explaining. Here. I'm going to move one of my agents to the center of the board. The goal is to eliminate your major figures while retaining mine." She gestured to a row of larger symbols on her end of the board. "A common gambit is to lure out important figures with your own valuable pieces."

Rachel frowned and examined her pieces. The game appearance made it fairly clear which ones were more important by emphasizing an elegance in design and larger size. "But won't that put your own important figures at risk?" She moved one of her larger pieces into place.

"Sometimes, yes, but you'd want to pair this strategy with a flanking maneuver. Arrange your smaller figures so they can eliminate the larger target. You lose more of the small pieces with this gambit." Elurin moved a small figure to the side of the board.

"But I'll see it coming." Rachel went to move one of her other pieces to the center, but Elurin placed a hand over hers. She had to fight the frightened impulse to pull away. For Ikthians, touch was a weapon. One brush of their fingers could kill. But instead of jerking back, she let Elurin guide her hand to another figure on the board.

"This one would be a better move," she said, removing her hand.

Rachel nodded and moved the other piece into the center. Her skin tingled where Elurin had touched her. Her hand was warm, soft, just like any human's hand would have been. Rachel took a sip from her drink. "So how does this work now that we know each other's strategies?"

Elurin laughed. "Oh, I don't expect this to be a particularly challenging game. The gambit I'm using is an older ikthian move, but one they're still fond of in military tactics. They always love baiting an enemy out with a large prize. It's one reason Maia Kalanis was so important for them to retrieve. They feared the rebels would use her to draw out the ikthian leaders from safety."

"Hasn't she done that already?" Rachel moved another piece, only to have it lost to one of Elurin's. "I mean, those Seekers were drawn out to Tarkhot, weren't they?"

Elurin nodded and moved another piece into place. Rachel did not really understand the game mechanics, but she enjoyed herself. It had been a long time since she had relaxed with someone.

"It's the other way around, actually," Elurin said. She smirked at the move Rachel tried to make, which caused her to double back and make another play. "They've sent the chancellor there, or so we believe. Such an important figure is undoubtedly a ploy to draw out any rebel activity."

Rachel froze in surprise. "The chancellor, as in the universal leader among the empire? Wouldn't that be too dangerous? They could just assassinate her."

Elurin raised her glass and took a long drink from it. "Many people have tried," she said, destroying one of Rachel's key pieces. "None have succeeded. She's calculating and ruthless, and she has spies everywhere. Even on Tarkoht, it would be difficult to kill her."

Rachel frowned as she stared at the board. "So she went to the station to draw out any rebels?" She tried to make a careful move, but no matter how she positioned herself, there was a gaping hole left straight to the larger figures. Elurin had easily outmaneuvered her.

"She went to Tarkhot hoping someone aboard that station would rise to the bait. It only takes one mistake to reveal secrets, one traitor to hand over a rebel cell. If she can apply enough pressure, something or someone will break."

Rachel nodded but did not make any more moves. She stared at the game board, lost in thought. Once again, she was struck by how little she actually knew about other species. The ikthians had a completely different way of thinking, of conducting warfare. If Taylor and Maia were on Tarkhot, the Seekers had probably already devised some method of luring them out.

"Are you okay?" Elurin asked. "The wine isn't too strong, is it?"

She shook her head. "No. It's not that. I'm just worried about Taylor." She found herself studying the contours of Elurin's face.

"That's your friend, isn't it? The one you think is on Tarkoht."

"Yeah, for all the good it does me." She had to drag her eyes away from Elurin again. She didn't want to be caught staring. "I thought she left because she was brainwashed." She hesitated. "They kept Maia Kalanis on our base as a prisoner. Taylor started getting friendly with her."

Elurin nodded. Rachel wasn't sure what she had expected. Disgust, maybe. Righteous indignation. But not calm acceptance.

"You aren't the first alien to think that," Elurin said. "I can't blame you. For most of the galaxy, ikthian is synonymous with Dominion. You can't like one and hate the other. There are all sorts of rumors about us floating around."

"I'm starting to figure that out. But if the ikthian didn't brainwash her that means a lot of other things don't match up. I don't know what I'm saving Taylor from anymore." *If I'm even saving her from anything.*

Elurin gave her a sympathetic look, one that made Rachel shift in her chair. "I don't want to upset you, but if she's on Tarkoht, she might need saving. The ikthians are probably already there looking for her."

Rachel stood up, pushing back her chair. "They can move that fast?" She set her glass aside and hurried over to the dresser where she had left her travel pack. She had thought she would have at least a day, maybe more to figure out a plan. But if the Seekers were already on Tarkoht, it wouldn't take them long to find Taylor. And even though she still wasn't sure what she was going to do when she found her friend, she knew she couldn't just leave her to die. "I need to leave," she said, flinging the pack over her shoulder and reaching for her weapon.

Elurin stood up as well. "You'll never get clearance to leave the station."

"So?" Rachel checked her pistol for ammunition and held the gun aloft. "Maybe I'll just have to get my own clearance."

Elurin stepped toward her. "That's not necessary, you know."

"Oh really? Because from what I understand, my friend is in danger of being captured by the Dominion, and no one is going to do anything about it."

"They're very much aware of what the chancellor is attempting, I assure you. Sorra is a gifted strategist, even if she is a bit reckless." Elurin held her gaze as she took another step closer. "I know you're worried for Taylor. I understand what you must feel right now."

"You don't know a damn thing," Rachel said, picking up her travel pack and turning away. A hand on her shoulder stopped her.

Elurin turned her around. "I'm coming with you, idiot."

Rachel took a step back, eyes wide. "I...you are?"

She nodded. "I can't let a human outsmart the Dominion without me, can I?" Elurin smiled softly. "Besides, I've grown fond of you, Rachel Harris. I'd hate to lose a good soldier to bad tactics."

Chapter Seventeen

TAYLOR CHECKED HER COMMUNICATOR, frowning. It felt like she had been sitting in the menagerie for hours instead of minutes. No one had come to check on her. She was beginning to doubt Sorra's assertion the Seekers were combing through every part of the station. Strange noises drifted over from the other pens. The same stupid rock on the other side of the enclosure caught her gaze once again.

As always, her thoughts returned to Maia. If everything was going according to plan, she should already be in hiding. Somehow, that thought wasn't comforting. "I should be with her," Taylor murmured. She sighed and slumped down against the trunk of a small tree, staring out through the shimmering barrier to the path beyond.

A noise tugged at her ears, different from the other sounds she had grown used to. Footsteps. More than one person, if she had to guess. She looked up just in time to see a squad of ikthians rounding the bend. They all held guns, and Taylor recognized the Dominion's armor. A group of Seekers, just as Sorra had predicted.

The Seekers saw her a few seconds after she saw them. One lifted a finger and pointed at the enclosure, nudging her companion's side with her elbow. "Look! Told you she had one." The other five ikthians turned to stare, and Taylor swallowed. Even though there was a barrier between them, being stared at by six armed Seekers terrified her. She twisted her face into a slack-jawed expression, hoping they wouldn't decide she was a threat.

Fortunately, the second ikthian rolled his eyes. "This is what we're supposed to be fighting? Can that thing even hold a weapon? If this is what they're like, why haven't we taken their planet yet?"

A third ikthian gave the first two a disapproving look. She seemed older than they were, with a silvery scar across one eye. "Don't underestimate them," she said, staring into the enclosure. "Humans are tricky. Not as smart as us, but cunning. They'll kill you the first chance they get. Then you won't think they're so stupid."

"Well, that one isn't much to look at," the first ikthian said.

Taylor continued staring ahead, pretending not to understand their conversation. Hopefully, the opinions of the first two would win out and the squad wouldn't decide to try and lower the barriers between them to neutralize her.

The third ikthian glared at the others. "It doesn't matter how they look. Humans wiped out my first squad. If you know what's good for you, you'll stay well away from that barrier."

"Fine." A fourth ikthian stepped between the two of them. "We're not just hunting humans. A dissenting ikthian is way more dangerous."

"Tell me about it," the first ikthian said. "Did you see the news this morning? They finally made Irana Kalanis step down from her position on Chancellor Corvis' council."

The fourth ikthian shuddered. "Step down? I heard the chancellor had her sent to Daashu." There was a heavy pause, and the rest of the group fell silent.

Taylor frowned. *Daashu.* Where had she heard that word before? Realization struck. Of course. The prison Maia had mentioned. Her mother had been sent there after all.

"You know what they say," the third soldier said. "Talking about Daashu is the fastest way to get sent there. There's nothing for us to find in the menagerie. Let's get out of here and keep looking for the rebels. Hopefully we can find Kalanis and get out of here without blowing the whole place up."

With one more look in her direction, the ikthians left, walking down the path and toward the enclosure exit. As soon as they disappeared, Taylor hopped to her feet. The Seekers weren't just looking for rebel activity. They were looking for her and Maia. She hurried to the edge of the enclosure, only sparing a quick glance down the path before deactivating the shield. *We have to get off the station—fast.*

* * *

"So how do we get out?" Rachel ghosted Elurin's footsteps as they made their way through the base, trying to appear calm as she glanced at each person who passed them. She knew it wasn't a smart way to behave, but she couldn't help feeling jumpy. Everyone seemed to be watching her.

Elurin shot her a glare. "We don't talk about it, for a start. Try to pretend we're having a good time with one another. Like we don't want to be disturbed."

"How good a time are we talking?"

"That depends on how good you want it to be." Elurin smirked then laughed as Rachel looked away, her face reddening.

"Don't be like that," she muttered, clutching the handle of her pistol for a little extra security. "You're going to trip me up."

Elurin laughed harder. "Well, at least you're not acting like a moron anymore. This will be very simple, I promise. Trust me."

They stopped in front of a small doorway, and Elurin placed her hand on the scanner. A green light flashed above the pressure pad, but the door remained sealed and a mechanical voice echoed through the hallway. "Unauthorized personnel detected."

Rachel glanced nervously over her shoulder, afraid that someone had noticed, but Elurin said, "Override code four three five one. Authorization: Elurin." The doors hissed open. "That's better. Shall we?"

"Just how much power do you have?" Rachel asked as they stepped into the abandoned hallway.

"Enough." The hallway emptied out into a hangar, and Elurin raised her hand for them to stop. "Wait here a moment." She stepped out into the open room and looked around. Rachel waited as Elurin walked to a small fighter and lowered the loading ramp. "Come on. You're riding in the storage until we're clear. Once we've broken through the atmosphere, you can come up to the copilot's chair. Don't want the dock officer to see you riding off with me."

Rachel glanced suspiciously at the tiny space. She would be able to fit inside, but only if she pulled her knees up to her chest. "Won't that be dangerous?"

"It would be if I weren't one of the best pilots in the fleet."

Rachel chuckled as she stepped onto the ramp. "Do you know how many soldiers make that same claim?"

Elurin scoffed. "Yeah, but I'm not lying."

Rachel hesitated a moment longer before climbing into the small cargo hold. Since there wouldn't be much room to turn around later, she decided to sit facing the small hatch connecting the storage space with the front of the ship. She turned to look back over her shoulder one last time before Elurin left her alone. "You'll just have to prove it to me, won't you?"

Elurin closed the loading door. "It'll be my pleasure."

Less than a minute later, the fighter's engines began to rumble. Rachel's gut lurched as they took off. She had never gotten sick during a flight before, but she found herself wishing for the anti-nausea meds the Coalition usually provided. She closed her eyes and gritted her teeth, bracing herself against the walls as she waited for the worst to pass. Finally, the shaking eased and her stomach settled. She cracked open one eye, tapping on the small hatch.

"Elurin? Are we stable?"

"That depends. Did you manage to spare your clothes?"

The hatch opened, and Rachel clambered into the cockpit, sighing as she took the empty copilot's seat. "It was a near miss. Not like that," she added as Elurin turned to look at her uniform. "I didn't throw up, but it's a good thing I skipped lunch today, or I might not have been so lucky. Where'd you learn how to fly, anyway?"

"On Korithia. I was a pilot in the Dominion's fleet before I defected. Two more kills, and I'll officially have shot down more ikthians as part of the rebellion than I've shot naledai as part of the Dominion."

Rachel stared at Elurin in surprise as she fastened her harness. "Exactly how many people have you killed, anyway?"

Elurin refused to meet her gaze. "You don't want to know. Anyway, I don't suppose you have some sort of plan for dealing with the Seekers once we land on Tarkoht?"

"I guess not," Rachel admitted. "I've fought Seekers before. They're tough. If they don't shoot you right away, it only takes one touch to poison you."

"At least you don't have to worry about mind control, right?"

Rachel had the decency to feel guilty. "Right," she mumbled. She hadn't known Elurin for long, but it had been long enough to make her feel ashamed of her previous assumptions. And the things she had done to try and 'rescue' Taylor from Maia. "So, you've come with me this far. What do you think we should do when we land?"

"The first thing we need to do is find Sorra," Elurin said. "She's the heart of the station, and the most influential member of the rebellion on this side of the galaxy. If anyone can tell us where your friend is, it's her."

"It's a decent place to start. How are we going to find her?"

"That depends on how far to shit things have gone when we land," Elurin said. "If the Seekers are already tearing up the place, we'll have to fight our way to her. She'll probably be holed up in the middle of the station. She's got a few bunkers down there. If things are really bad, she might be hiding down in the maintenance tunnels. They run beneath the entire station."

"Let's assume the Seekers aren't killing everyone yet. How can we pass them without getting shot?"

Elurin continued staring out at the stars while she steered. "Then things will be a little more complicated. There's only one way a human can walk among the Seekers without getting shot."

Realization dawned, and Rachel swallowed. Her newfound camaraderie had its limits. "You're not suggesting what I think you're suggesting...are you?"

"Unless you have a better idea. If you pretend to be my prisoner, I doubt many people will question us. I remember enough from my time in the Dominion's military to bluff my way through a checkpoint or two."

"And you're willing to stake my life on that?"

Elurin nodded. "And mine. If they catch us, they won't hesitate to kill me. I'm a deserter, remember? My death will be even worse than yours. They'll probably only put a bullet through your head, but I'll be sent to Daashu."

Rachel stared down at her lap. "Then why did you come?" She asked when she couldn't stand the silence any longer. "You didn't have to help me."

Elurin messed with the controls in a way Rachel knew was stalling for time. "I haven't done much good in my lifetime," she said. Rachel did not know if it was the translator or her own instincts, but she heard regret behind Elurin's words. "The small acts I can do to make up for the worst of it have to be enough." She paused and glanced back at Rachel, offering her a small smile. "And I find myself wanting to help you. Can't explain why. Not truly. When I try to verbalize my reasons, they always fall short." Elurin's gaze met hers, and Rachel's stomach dropped. And then she was looking forward again, her eyes lost to the expanse of stars. "So who's the one exercising mind control now?"

Rachel's heart thudded, and she hated it. She tried to think of an adequate response but found nothing suitable, so they sat there with nothing but the hum of the engines to break the silence.

"We should be approaching Tarkoht momentarily. We'll need a cover story for why I'm bringing you in," Elurin said. "Normally, an ikthian soldier wouldn't stop over there."

"Do ikthians have bounty hunters? Or does your oppressive government frown on that?" Rachel meant for it to sound teasing, but the jab fell flat.

"We do, actually." Elurin adjusted the angle of the craft as they entered an asteroid belt. "And it's not a bad idea. A bounty hunter would go to Sorra's station first, though she's known as Dalia to the ikthian Empire. That's something you'll have to watch yourself on. Actually, you probably shouldn't speak. No one will expect you to anyway."

Rachel leaned back in her seat. "So I'm supposed to be a silent, willing captive of yours? Is that what the empire thinks humans are like?"

Elurin glanced at her and grinned. "Not all of them think that. It's just what is expected. And besides, I have a suspicion if you were captured, you'd be the most obstinate, challenging prisoner in the Dominion's history."

"Is that supposed to be a compliment?"

Elurin looked at the controls. "Maybe. We'll be at the station soon enough."

Rachel crossed her arms and allowed herself to enjoy the brief moment of serenity. This would probably be the last she would find in a while. Her stomach had clenched itself into knots, troubling her. She did not usually get nervous like this during a mission, so why now?

Rachel looked at Elurin. She did not like the possible answers her mind offered.

"All right, Rachel. We're in range of the station's scanners. When they hail us on the frequency, don't respond. And put these on." Elurin tossed her back a pair of restraints.

Rachel picked them up. "Do you always have these on you?"

Elurin smirked. "A good soldier is always prepared." She cleared her voice and turned on the ship's incoming comm channel. "Landing is going to be the only trick. If we can get onto the station, we'll be fine. It's so overrun with people of all species that we won't attract much attention."

Rachel caught sight of the large station in the distance. Though it appeared first as a pinprick through the viewer, she watched in awe as it grew in size. Other ships appeared as well, a constant stream of traffic navigating around the station. It seemed an ideal place to lay low for anyone of any species, though she doubted humans ever landed there.

"Craft four eight three one, please transmit your docking codes."

The incoming message made her jump. Elurin glanced back at her and raised a finger to her lips.

"Please transmit your docking codes. Failure to comply will result in your detainment."

"This is craft four eight three one, transferring docking codes now." Elurin pressed a sequence of buttons and waited.

"Thank you. You are cleared for docking. Uploading coordinates to your navigator."

Rachel laughed nervously and leaned back in her chair. Her heart hammered and her palms were sweaty, but they were that much closer to finding Taylor. Then, perhaps, she could find a sense of normalcy in her life once more, away from roguish aliens and political intrigue.

***

"Madam Chancellor, are you sure this is the best use of your time? I've already sent you all of Tarkoht's financial reports. What use is there in looking over them again?" Odelle asked. Her face ached from holding a neutral expression, and the heavy knot in her chest kept tightening.

Although she knew Sorra wasn't foolish enough to keep incriminating evidence in her office, it wasn't much comfort. The chancellor acted strangely. Instead of searching through the lower warehouses near the docking bay or questioning civilians, she had decided to go through Dalia's personal files instead. The deviation from her usual routine was unnerving. *Ancestors, I hope Maia had enough time to clear the terminal earlier...*

The chancellor looked up, and Odelle had to fight a flinch. Her eyes were hard, and the stiff set of her lips was all too familiar. The same face haunted Odelle's nightmares, a face that almost always meant someone was going to disappear. "I'm not reviewing the financial reports. Tell me, Dalia is your friend, isn't she? Would you call her a paranoid person?"

Odelle struggled to show just the right amount of surprise. "Paranoid? Perhaps a little," she lied. "She has a rather eccentric personality."

"Eccentric enough to give herself access to the station's security feeds from her office?"

Odelle cleared her throat. "I'm not sure. Aside from removing the files you requested and confirming they were genuine, I haven't spent any time accessing Dalia's terminal. The assignment you gave me required a subtle touch. If you suspect her of being a rebel sympathizer, I can look more closely into the matter. Perhaps use my proximity with her to an advantage?"

The chancellor's eyes narrowed. "I suspect everyone of being a rebel. You know that. It's the only reason I'm still alive after all these years." She went silent, still swiping through files on the terminal. Odelle bit her lip, hoping Sorra's people had been thorough in cleaning out the security feeds. If they had forgotten to scrub any footage of Maia and Taylor, all their careful planning would fall apart.

"Of course. But maybe if you tell me what you're looking for."

"No need. I've already found it."

The screen flickered, and the bottom dropped out from Odelle's stomach. Maia and Taylor were not on the terminal. Instead, the screen showed her and Sorra, sitting down for a fancy dinner on the first night of her arrival. "Is something the matter? You know Dalia and I are old friends."

"Friends?" the chancellor repeated, a clear note of suspicion in her voice. She continued watching the feed, pausing on one frame. Sorra's hand was clasped tight over hers, and they gazed into each other's eyes. "Are you sure that's all you are?"

Odelle took a deep breath, deciding to reveal one secret in order to preserve another. "Surely my private life isn't of any interest to you. You know Dalia is married. Joren's a good man, but we..."

The chancellor silenced her with a look. She minimized the paused feed and selected another. Odelle clenched her fingers into tight fists as she watched. Every part of her screamed to run, to do something, but she stayed put. There was still some miniscule chance that she could talk her way out of this, and she would cling to it to the very last second. There they were again, in the botanical gardens this time, laughing as they strolled down the path. Even though no sound attached to the images, she sucked in a sharp breath when she saw her own lips curl around the wrong name. *Sorra*.

Odelle whirled away from the terminal to see the chancellor removing one of her long white gloves. "As I said," the chancellor murmured, tossing the fabric aside, "I suspect everyone of being a rebel."

Odelle tried to dart for the door, but the chancellor was too quick. Steel fingers gripped her throat, and she cried out as toxins burned the top layer of her skin. She waited for her mind to fog, but the flood of poison never came. The chancellor simply kept holding her, one touch away from death. "It's a pity. I was very fond of you, Odelle. But make no mistake, I will end the life of every miserable creature on this station, starting with you."

Odelle's arms flailed as she clambered to take hold of Chancellor Corvis. She tried to summon enough strength to use her toxins, but the chancellor grabbed one of her wrists in another bruising grip.

"After that, I'll find a new campaign manager, one that doesn't bed filthy dissenters," the chancellor said. "We will end this rebellion once and for all."

"You're—you're too late," Odelle stammered, blinking tears from her eyes as her flesh continued to sear. Any more poison, and pain would be the least of her problems.

"What?"

"The plan is already in motion. Kalanis' research was distributed to every corner of the galaxy. Kill me now, and you'll never undo the damage."

"You're bluffing," the chancellor hissed, but doubt flickered in her eyes.

The pain stopped growing worse, and Odelle held her gaze. "Care to find out?"

The grip around her neck loosened ever so slightly, but it was enough. She kicked out as hard as she could, landing a blow on the chancellor's stomach. The hand around her throat slipped, and Odelle yanked away, slamming her fist against the chancellor's jaw. Finally, she broke free and made a dash out of Sorra's room, activating her communicator on the way. "Sorra!"

"What?"

Odelle nearly sobbed with relief at the familiar sound. "The chancellor knows. Evacuate the station." She ended the call and continued running, exiting the office to the bewildered look of two Seeker guards.

"Stop her!" the chancellor shouted after her, but it was too late. She already had a head start.

Odelle did not wait to see if the Seekers would give chase. She bolted for the nearest passageway she could find. After ducking down a narrow alley, she slid a false panel out of the way and tucked herself into one of the station's maintenance passages. Emergency evacuation procedures began to blare over the station's intercom, but she ignored them. There wasn't any time.

A loud clang told her the Seekers had found the entrance to the maintenance tunnel, but there was nowhere to go but forward. Her foot snagged on something. She turned to see her ankle tangled in a set of fiber optic cables. Odelle bit her lip and bent over, trying to untangle her foot without making any noise.

"I think there's something ahead," said one of the Seekers.

Odelle swore under her breath and tugged harder. A loud clang echoed through the tunnel, and her heart stopped. She froze then heard it again, coming from the opposite direction.

"This way." She heard the Seekers shuffling to turn around. "Wait. Someone needs to still scout this tunnel."

Damn all of them. Odelle redoubled her effort to get her foot free and finally slipped out of the cables. She stumbled backward.

"She's here!" a Seeker called.

Odelle made one last lunge for freedom, but another clang sent a panel of metal crashing into the corridor. "Fire!" Odelle ducked as the blare of gunshots filled the space. She glanced up just in time to see a Seeker's body collapse next to her, bleeding out onto the twisted cables below.

"Odelle!"

She knew that voice. Odelle looked up to see Sorra striding toward her with a squadron of naledai guards. She clutched a rifle tightly in one hand. "Sorra?"

"Thank goodness you're here!" Sorra ran to her, leaping over the bodies of the Seeker squadron.

"Would you slow down?" Odelle snapped. "You'll give our position away."

Sorra ignored her and swept her into a tight hug. "I was so scared when our security feed showed the Seekers following you."

Odelle glanced over Sorra's shoulder, afraid she would see another squadron bearing down on them, but Sorra's guards stood at the ready. Finally, she allowed herself to return Sorra's hug. "How did you find me so fast?"

"Luck and a lot of firepower."

Odelle laughed as they pulled apart. She smiled at Sorra, who stared at her with shimmering eyes. "We need to evacuate."

Sorra nodded. "There should be an emergency exit to the docks up ahead. But it might be worth it to hunt down Taylor and Maia before we leave. It should be easy enough if those idiots stay put." Sorra glanced back at one of her guards. "Well?"

The naledai shifted his stance and glanced away. "We have no visual confirmation of Taylor. Maia is still in her room."

Sorra leveled her rifle toward the end of the hall. "Well, I guess we know where to start looking."

Chapter Eighteen

TAYLOR'S LUNGS BURNED AS she sprinted through the menagerie. Most of the twisting paths looked the same, and she was fairly certain she was lost, but she ran ahead anyway, praying she could retrace her steps fast enough. Her heart pounded harder with each ragged breath. *Maia.* The Seekers were looking for Maia. At last, she caught a glimpse of the exit off to her right. She changed course abruptly, veering for the door.

"Wait, stop!"

Taylor halted in her tracks. Instinctively, she grasped for her pistol, and a spike of fear pierced her chest when she remembered it was still missing. She whirled around anyway, preparing to face the squad of Seekers unarmed, but found a much more friendly sight. Akton ran along the edge of the path, hurrying to catch up with her.

"Akton!" she panted, hurrying back toward him. "Thank God it's you. We have to get out of here."

"I know. The Seekers are tearing Tarkoht apart. The evacuation orders were just given."

"They're looking for Maia," Taylor said. "They know she's here. We have to go back for her."

Akton reached for a pistol clipped to his waist. "Here, take this. I thought you'd need a spare."

Taylor took the gun gratefully, wrapping her finger around the trigger. Even without armor, she felt much safer with a weapon in her hand. "What's the fastest way out of here?"

"There isn't a fast way out of here," Akton replied. "The Seekers are everywhere. Once the kill order came in—"

"Kill order?"

"I told you. They're purging the station, shooting anyone that gets in their way."

Taylor's stomach sank. She jogged toward what she hoped was the entrance with Akton following a breath behind. Unfortunately, a squad of Seekers waited for them just outside the menagerie gates. Taylor threw herself onto the ground at the first spray of gunfire, ignoring the sparks ricocheting from the metal doors and the ringing in her ears. She dashed to the side, crouching around the corner.

"Shit. How many?" she yelled, firing a few blind shots.

"Just six." Akton's voice was fuzzy because of the ringing in her ears, but she understood when he waved her forward. "Go, I'll cover you."

Taylor gritted her teeth. As soon as Akton started firing, she leapt to her feet. The first Seeker went down with a shot to the head. Her fire pierced his helmet, and he fell to the floor. Once he collapsed, the other five fell back, finding cover of their own. Taylor tried to get in one more shot, but she wasn't quick enough. They all disappeared from sight.

"Damn it. Now what?"

Akton shook his head. "We've got to find another way out of here. With five on two, I don't like our odds, especially if they call for backup." He glanced at a nearby wall. "Though I think I found our exit." He ran toward the monochrome wall, smashing into it with his shoulder.

"Akton!" Taylor shouted as a loud clang rang throughout the station. "What the hell are you doing?"

"Getting us out of here!" He ran at the wall one more time, bashing in a panel. He backed up and kicked it inward, sending the flimsy metal clattering down. "Get in." He pointed with his gun, and Taylor scampered forward, ducking into the new exit as she dodged bullets. "Just keep moving." He jumped in after her, and Taylor pushed forward, brushing aside cables and insulation as they made their way into the station's guts.

"How did you even know this would be here?"

"I guessed." Akton grunted and clawed at a cable caught on his shoulder. "Now keep moving. They'll only wait for so long before realizing we're gone."

"We don't even know what direction we're moving in," Taylor replied.

"The one away from certain death." Akton shoved her down another corridor. "If we head left, we'll get far enough away from the Seekers and closer to Maia's general vicinity. Just trust me, all right?"

Taylor pressed onward. "I do. But..." Maia's name hung unspoken between them.

"We'll find her." Akton glanced back when an echo rang through the tunnels. "We just need to make sure no one else finds us in the process."

They traveled in silence, flinching at every clang. The station had come alive with shouts and gunfire. Taylor glanced at her communicator, but no new messages had shown up on it. "You think I should try and contact her?"

Akton shook his head. "Any communication is a liability. Just turn right up ahead. We can exit at the next hatch we find. This should have given us enough distance."

Taylor nodded and followed his directions. "You know, you're always around to save my ass. I'll have to pay you back one of these days."

Akton chuckled. "Taylor, I'd be a terrible friend if I didn't feel helping to keep you alive was worth my time."

"You're not familiar with the phrase *every man for himself*, are you?"

They ducked down the corridor. "Humans always spend too much time worrying about their own hides." He must have noticed her frown, because he added, "Though, I admit being hunted by the Dominion creates a certain paranoia after a while." He grabbed her shoulder. "Here's the exit hatch."

They pushed their way back out into one of the main halls. It was deserted, thankfully, and Taylor recognized where they were.

"Maia should be this way," she said, nodding to the left.

Akton followed her down the hall. They made their way to her room without running into another ikthian squad, but they passed several terrified people fleeing the station.

"The door's untouched," she said with relief. She keyed in the access code and rushed in. "Maia?" she called. "Maia, where are you?"

She heard a rustling from the bedroom. "Taylor?" Maia ran out into the living room. "I'm so glad you're here! I was about to come looking for you."

Without another word, Taylor pulled Maia into her arms. "You're alive," she breathed, her voice cracking as she held Maia tight against her chest. "I thought..."

"Me too." Maia's breath whispered against her cheek, and tears stung in Taylor's eyes. "I'm here."

They hugged tightly, not letting go until Akton cleared his throat. "I hate to break this up, but we need to get off this station before the Dominion decides to bomb it."

Reluctantly, Taylor and Maia let go of one another. "Of course," Maia said. She glanced around the room. "I suppose there's nothing I really need to take, except...my research!" Her eyes widened. "Oh no. The rebellion already has seeded copies on Nakonum, but they could find Sorra's backups. I ran out of time before I could fully erase them from her terminal earlier. All it would take is someone with a little knowledge to restore the files."

"Maia, there's no time." Taylor grabbed her hand. "We have to leave."

"No." Maia pulled away. "I have to do this. I refuse to let them twist my work to further their own sick agenda any longer."

Even though all her instincts screamed this was a terrible idea, Taylor knew she had no choice. Short of dragging Maia off the station, there was no way she could convince her to leave. Her eyes were unnaturally bright, and her new face was set with determination. With a sigh, Taylor glanced at Akton. "Well, what do you think of all this?"

Akton glanced down at his communicator. "I'd say we have a little bit of time before the station is blown up and its debris harvested. As soon as we start running into Seekers, though, I'm pushing us into the nearest escape pod."

"Fair enough." Taylor turned back to Maia. "Where do we need to go?"

"The local backups are in Sorra's office. It isn't far. I'll destroy the entire terminal if I have to. If the Seekers are already tearing Tarkoht apart, the time for subtlety is over."

"Right. What's the strategy, Akton?"

Akton snorted. "Strategy? There is no strategy. We just have to run as fast as possible and hope no one spots us. We need to keep moving." He waved one of his shaggy arms toward the door, raising his pistol as he headed for the hallway.

Maia moved to follow him, but Taylor reached out one last time, catching the edge of her hand. "Maia, I..." Before she could speak, Maia's lips collided with hers in a quick, hard kiss. It was too rough, too short, and exactly what she needed.

The taste of tears burned against her mouth, but she couldn't bear to pull away until Maia started tugging on her arm. "Come on, Taylor. We have to hurry."

Head spinning, Taylor followed her through the door, blinking to clear her eyes. She wouldn't be any good to Maia at all if she couldn't even shoot straight.

***

Rachel kept her head bowed as Elurin led her through the deserted docking bay, but the quick glances she stole from the corner of her eye unsettled her. Several sleek ikthian ships sat around the hangar, waiting to be used, but no one else was in sight. "I don't like this," she muttered. "Why would the Seekers leave all their ships unguarded? Anyone could escape."

"Oh, they're not unguarded," Elurin said. "There are probably at least three squads just outside the hangar. We'll have to talk our way past them. I don't care how good a shot you are, we can't take eighteen Seekers at once." She continued forward at a steady pace, looking the same as she did while strolling through the rebel base on Nakonum.

Rachel couldn't help but be impressed by Elurin's calm attitude. If it was faked, she couldn't tell the difference. "How are we going to manage that?"

"We'll keep it simple. I was coming in to dock when my squadron ran into an enemy ship leaving Tarkoht. You shot down everyone else, but I managed to disable and board your ship. I took you as my prisoner, and since you're a human, I have to bring you to the chancellor."

"You really think they'll buy that?"

"Do you have a better idea? Ikthian fighter squadrons are just like Seekers. They always travel in groups. The only reason I would have abandoned the others is if they had been shot down and I captured the person responsible."

Rachel took in a deep breath. She offered one of her bound arms, shivering a little as Elurin gripped her elbow. "Right. Well, let's get this over with." Elurin led her toward the hangar exit, but before they even reached the doors, an alarm started blaring. Elurin stopped and Rachel looked around wildly. "What's going on?"

"Again, this is not a drill." An electronic voice filtered through the station's overhead speakers. "All persons are to continue evacuation immediately. There is a life-threatening situation in progress."

"Shit," Rachel muttered. "What do we do now?"

"I don't suppose you'd agree to leaving the station?"

Rachel shook her head. "I came here for a reason. I need to try and find Taylor."

Elurin glared at her for several seconds, her head raised and pointed nose upturned. Rachel did not like how perfect she could look even when judging people. "Fine." She walked toward the hangar exit, gun raised and cocked.

"Really?" Rachel followed.

Elurin glanced back at her. "People are going to tear one another apart to get off this station. I'd like to help the civilians while we look for your friend."

Rachel felt her face grow hot, probably from embarrassment. She cleared her throat and caught up to Elurin. "So, how long are you going to keep this 'decent person' act up?"

Elurin stopped at the door to the hallway and began messing with the control panel. "Only long enough to seduce you." She smirked when Rachel took a step back and looked away. "Or until you realize I can be a decent person."

Rachel tried to will the heat from her cheeks. "You've already managed that. The 'decent person' thing, that is. You're not my type for seduction."

"You certainly don't respond well to the jokes." The door slid open and Elurin glanced outside. "Well, it looks like the patrols have gone into a panic and scattered."

"Or they had more important things to do." Rachel stepped out into the empty hallway. She glanced down the side and saw a naledai corpse, blood spilled everywhere. "Like gun down the station residents. Where do you think everyone is?"

Elurin shrugged. "You know your friend. What do you think she would do?"

Rachel shrugged. "If she wasn't with everyone she cares about, she would have left to find them. Otherwise, she'd be smart enough to get the hell out of here."

Elurin nodded and pulled up her communicator.

"What are you doing?" Rachel asked.

"Looking up the different departure points on this station. The Seekers will have the largest ones heavily defended. We're lucky they weren't here, but no one has the authorization codes to take off with Seeker ships anyway." She scrolled through a few different images on the small screen. "We should head left. It's most likely where everyone is convening to get off this station."

Rachel nodded and moved to follow Elurin, but before she could take a step, a squad of Seekers marched past the end of the wide hallway. All of them were in full body armor, and they held their weapons up, ready to fire. Rachel's heart hammered as they caught sight of her, and she jerked to grab her gun, only to have the fake restraints keep her arms together.

Elurin took on an aggressive stance beside her, shoulders forward and weapon raised. "Move," she barked, shoving hard in the middle of her back.

They met the Seekers half way down the hall. Rachel kept her eyes fixed on the floor, praying they wouldn't look too closely. Fortunately, the leader of the group focused her attention on Elurin. "What the hell are you doing down here? Where's the rest of your squad? We've got orders from the chancellor."

Elurin rolled her eyes. "Look, I don't know who the hell you are, but you aren't the only one with orders. My squadron crashed and burned just outside the station. We were supposed to look for departing ships and evac shuttles, and we found one. This human," Elurin paused to give her another convincing shove, "was trying to escape in a naledai fighter. She shot down everyone else before I finally managed to board her."

The leader reached out and grabbed Rachel's chin in a tight grip. She held her breath, staring up into the ikthian's eyes and trying not to think about the calloused fingertips against her face. Any second, the ikthian might choose to poison her and end her life. Her pulse throbbed in her throat.

Finally, the Seeker shoved her away. "Was anyone else with her?" she asked, looking over at Elurin. "An ikthian, maybe?"

Rachel's eyes widened. *These Seekers think I am Taylor.*

Elurin shook her head. "Didn't see anyone else. The fighter was too small to hide another person. Even the storage compartment was empty."

The Seeker gave her a suspicious look. "What was the name of your squadron again?"

"Laniakea. I didn't mention it."

For one terrifying moment, Rachel was certain the Seeker wouldn't believe Elurin. She ran her thumb over the release on the cuffs, preparing to throw them off and run. She wouldn't make it more than a few feet, but she wasn't just going to stand still and wait to die. After what felt like ages, the ikthian nodded. "If you caught her trying to escape, Kalanis must be trying to do the same." She activated her communicator and spoke in a sharp, clipped tone. "All available units report to the nearest docking bay. The target might be trying to leave the station."

Rachel frowned. She had just made it that much more difficult for Taylor to escape the station alive.

"What now?" Elurin asked, nudging her with the barrel of her pistol. "My squad's gone. I want to make sure this human pays for it. Are you going to let me pass?"

"Better. We'll escort you. If this human knows where Kalanis is, I'm going to make damn sure she talks."

*　*　*

Odelle ran after Sorra down the hall. The heart of the station was in utter chaos, with ships departing left and right. Sorra barked orders into her communicator.

"Sorra!" Odelle grabbed her by the arm and stopped. "Where are we going?"

Sorra paused then finished relaying an order into her communicator before answering her. "We need to get to the control tower and do what we can to stop the Seekers from tearing this place apart."

"Are you insane? We need to leave." Odelle tugged in the direction of the escape pods, but Sorra remained unmoved. She glared at Odelle and tugged her arm away. Odelle narrowed her eyes. "What is your problem?"

"My problem is that this station is falling apart, and you want to jump ship just to save your own skin," Sorra spat. She turned and walked down the hallway. "I thought you had changed."

Odelle chased after her again. "Damn it, Sorra, I have changed! Did it ever occur to you I said we should leave because you're going to throw your life away doing this?" She tried to grab Sorra's hand and missed, snatching at air. "The rebellion needs you alive. You're worth more to them while still breathing, even if your cover is blown." Odelle could feel tears brimming in her eyes. It was all too much. She was going to lose everything. She could not handle losing Sorra, too. "You're one of the few people keeping this whole effort together. I don't know what we'd do without you."

"Well, start learning. I'm just one person." Sorra turned down a hall and punched in her access codes to the first door. When it opened, she turned to Odelle. "Now are you going to come help me or run away?"

Odelle could see the threat in Sorra's eyes, the promise she would do everything in her power to save the people aboard the station, even if it meant sacrificing herself. This drive to put others first had always been something Odelle loved about Sorra. Now, she realized it was her defining characteristic. Sorra was a better person than her, and Odelle could not decide if she loved or hated her for it. With a frustrated groan, she grabbed Sorra by the shoulder and pulled her down for a kiss. Their lips met quickly, and Sorra yanked away.

"Are you staying?"

Odelle nodded. "You're such a fool, but you're my fool."

Sorra grinned. "Let's get to work."

The control tower had been abandoned, from what Odelle could tell. Sorra jumped on a terminal and typed in the override codes. Odelle watched for a moment before asking, "What are you doing?"

"Activating a firewall to block any incoming Seeker signals. They'll be attempting to gain control of the station remotely. Their top priority right now is keeping people on the station. Mine is getting everyone out. If they take over, they'll shut down all the docking bays and prevent people from escaping." She nodded at another terminal. "Can you verify Taylor left the menagerie and then release the locks on the cages?"

"I'm sorry, what?" Odelle asked.

"Release the locks on the cages. We could use a little more chaos." Sorra paused in her typing and glanced at her. "It's not like I keep anything dangerous on board this station. I just want the Seekers to have one more annoyance to deal with."

Odelle walked over to the terminal. She started it up and found the camera access. "No intelligent life remaining in the zoo," she muttered. "Unlocking cages." Even as she entered the command, Odelle could not help but feel they were making a mistake. This whole effort was a mistake. "Any other ridiculous demands?" she asked, turning to Sorra.

"Nope." Sorra had dropped to her knees, rummaging through wires beneath the main terminal. Sparks flew, and she came up grinning. The terminal's glowing screen blinked out, leaving only the blank space of the wall behind. The wailing of the sirens grew louder, and she threw her hands up to cover her ears.

"What did you just do?" Odelle shouted as the lights above them flickered.

"Low-tech solution to a high-tech problem. I fried the inside of the terminal. They can't shut down the docking bays if it won't turn on. Now I just need to—" The sound of someone pounding on the door made her look over. "Are they serious?"

Another deafening thump clattered through the room, and Odelle recognized the sound of a pulse rifle firing. "They going to be in here soon. Is there another way out?"

Sorra stooped and pried up a plate in the floor, revealing a narrow ladder that descended into the bowels of the station. "Just this way," she said, then gestured toward the entrance. "After you."

Odelle clambered into the hole. "We are going to die. I hope you know that."

Sorra chuckled and waited for her to descend far enough before joining her. "Don't count on it yet." She lowered the panel back into place, enclosing them in darkness.

Chapter Nineteen

"HOW MUCH FURTHER?" TAYLOR panted as they whipped around another corner. The station halls and buildings were mostly deserted, unless she counted corpses. Several bodies lay sprawled across the ground, and she splashed through pools of blood as they ran.

"Not far." Maia pointed toward a large suite of rooms. "Sorra's office is up there. I just hope the elevator's working with all the..." The lights above them flickered again, and a low rumble shook the deck plating. "Power surges."

Taylor swallowed. "Hope this place has a good backup generator. If the Seekers cut off life support, we're all dead."

"No," Akton said. "That isn't how the Dominion operates. The Seekers want you two alive. They won't risk killing you unless they can't see any other options."

Taylor's throat constricted. "Of course." So far, they hadn't run in to any more Seekers, but their luck wouldn't last. Sooner or later, they would have to fight their way to the escape pods. Hopefully, going back to destroy Maia's research wouldn't cost them too much time.

They arrived at the office entrance. After one last check over her shoulder, she motioned Akton and Maia through the door. The wail of the warning sirens was softer inside, but the lights kept flickering as they made their way to the elevator. Maia slammed her palm into the pressure plate to summon the lift, but nothing happened. A second attempt only sent a low groan echoing down the shaft. "That doesn't sound promising," Maia whispered. "Perhaps the stairs are a better option."

Taylor held up her hand. "No, hold on. Let's wait and see if it comes down."

After several agonizing moments, the lights around the lift flashed green and the doors hissed open. The floor of the elevator was tilted at a strange angle, and Akton gave her a skeptical look. "You sure about this, Taylor? I don't want to get stuck. Or, you know...fall." His lips peeled back over his teeth in what Taylor recognized as a nervous gesture.

"I don't want to risk the stairs. It's an easy place for an ambush, and they'll hear us coming. Let's give it a try." She stepped into the elevator, trying to ignore the treacherous way it rocked beneath her feet. Maia followed, and Taylor wrapped a hand around her waist to offer some extra support. Finally, Akton took a deep breath and joined them. The elevator creaked and groaned but remained in place. The doors closed, and Taylor pressed the button for the top floor.

The sharp, high-pitched squeal of metal scraping metal echoed through the lift, but at last, it started moving up. Taylor braced herself against the wall just in case, pulling Maia a little closer. Of all the things that could kill them, an elevator was definitely the stupidest.

"What should we do once we're up there?" Taylor watched the floors climb.

"We have to physically destroy Sorra's terminal. It's a little drastic, but I don't think she'll mind. Tarkoht is already dead, for lack of a better word, and my data can't be the only incriminating information she has hidden away. We can't risk letting the Dominion take it."

Taylor nodded, and her stomach lurched as the elevator came to a halt at the top of the offices. The door hissed open and she raised her gun as she scanned the empty floor. "No one's here. Come on." They ran into the room, but Taylor had no idea what to do. "So, what next?"

"Just give me a moment to dig out the hard drive." Maia walked over to the main terminal and knelt down, prying off the protective panel and digging through the mass of wires.

After a few minutes, Taylor began to worry. "What's taking so long?"

"I can't…" Maia panted and pushed aside more wires, looking deeper into the console. "I can't find it. The space where it should be is normally right…"

Her words died. Taylor glanced over at Akton, but he shrugged. "What's wrong?"

Maia extracted herself from the wires. Her silvery skin had turned a white. "It's gone. The hard drive is missing."

Taylor's eyes narrowed. "What? Who took it?"

"We have no way of knowing!" Maia stood up and crossed the room. Taylor drew her close. Maia sighed into her shoulder, "I wasted our time for nothing."

"No, don't say that. We're still going to get out of here. We just need to keep moving."

"That might be a problem," Akton said. She let go of Maia and looked for Akton, but he was nowhere in sight. She rushed back for the hallway, clasping Maia's hand in her own. Akton stood in front of the elevator, slamming his fist into the pressure pad. The lights remained dim. "Looks like we broke it. I'm amazed it took us up this far. We'll need to use the stairs."

"Damn," Taylor said. The stairwell still seemed like a prime place for an ambush, but unless they wanted to take their chances and break into the air ducts, they didn't have any other options. "Guess we'll have to risk it. Maia, stay behind us until we can find you a gun. I don't want you in the line of fire when you can't shoot back."

Maia looked like she would object, but she didn't say anything. Taylor wanted to offer comfort, but there was nothing to say—not when they still needed to escape from Tarkoht with their lives. Fortunately, Maia seemed to shrug it off a few moments later. She removed her gloves and stuffed them in her pocket. "I doubt you'll let them get close to us, but if they do..."

Taylor gave her a slow nod. "All right. Let's move."

Together, she and Akton opened the door to the stairwell. She listened at first, but no voices or footsteps floated upward. She crept onto the stairs, trying to move as quickly and silently as possible. Akton stayed close by her side, yellow eyes narrowed and ears pricked. His nose twitched every time they turned a corner. "I think we're clear," he whispered as they moved down to the next floor. "I don't hear or smell any..."

A loud crash came from somewhere beneath them, echoing up through the stairwell, and they froze. Moments later, voices followed. "I don't know why you're taking us up here," a female voice said. Even with her translator, she could tell that it belonged to an ikthian. "Everyone outside was already dead."

"Last I heard, this is where the chancellor was. She'll want to see your human, soldier."

Taylor shared a terrified glance with Maia and Akton. If the Seekers below them had taken a human hostage, that made the situation even more complicated.

"She's not mine," the ikthian said. "I don't even know who she is, or if she has any information about..."

"Don't be stupid. She knows where Kalanis is. How many humans do you think we've got running around this station?"

The sound of Maia's name made Taylor's heart thud, but she motioned forward with her arm, creeping down the stairs. They might have a chance to fight their way through if they got in a few surprise shots first. When they reached the bottom of the stairwell, she stopped. She glanced toward the opening, trying to see their enemy. She met Akton's gaze and nodded. He raised his weapon.

They ran from the stairwell, aiming at the two nearest ikthians in full uniform. Taylor caught a brief glimpse of another human standing between them, but she ducked away immediately, dragging one of her captors with her. She didn't have time to stop them before they disappeared from sight. She aimed at another Seeker instead, taking him down with a shot to the head. Akton's gun fired beside her, and a third Seeker fell, but neither of them would be fast enough to stop the rest of the squad before they were in arm's reach.

They launched forward, hands outstretched. Taylor panicked and jumped backward. Someone fired. The sound ricocheted around the small space, causing a moment of confusion. An ikthian ran right into the one charging Taylor, shoving the Seeker to the ground. Taylor looked around for the final Seeker, but the fifth one was dead. She saw the human standing with her weapon drawn, her frown set deep as she took aim at the Seeker pinned by the other ikthian. "Take the shot!" the ikthian screamed.

She did, blasting a hole in the Seeker's head. The final ikthian stood up, and Taylor trained her gun on her. "Don't move."

The ikthian raised her hands. "I won't if you don't shoot, but we don't have long to talk. More squads are bound to be on their way."

"Are you with the rebellion?" Maia asked, pushing Taylor aside.

"She was talking to the soldiers like she was one of them," Akton said, keeping his own gun pointed at the ikthian. "We can't be sure."

"She's not with them!"

Taylor glanced at the human walking toward them. The dark skin tone and even darker hair looked so familiar, but it was not until Taylor got a closer look at her face that she recognized her. "Rachel?" The grip on her gun faltering. She wanted to lower the weapon, but she was all too aware of the fact the last time she and Rachel had been in the same room, Rachel tried to kill her.

"Yeah. What other human would be crazy enough to chase you out here? Put the gun away. We all need to get out of here alive, so I can chew you out for leaving me with your mess to clean up."

Taylor finally lowered her gun. "Rachel, I—"

"I said we'd talk about it later." She nodded toward the exit. "Come on, we have a ship ready to go."

"But the data," Maia said, grabbing Taylor by the arm. "If the chancellor has it..."

Taylor met Maia's gaze and wished she hadn't. "We can't."

Maia stepped away from her. "We have to. The chancellor will corrupt everything I've built again. I can't let her do it."

"We don't know where the copy is. There's nothing we can do." Taylor didn't care that she saw tears brimming in Maia's eyes. She didn't care that every second standing there was a second wasted. She was going to be heard. "Maybe the chancellor will use your research against us. It doesn't matter. The entire time I've been on this station, everyone has plotted endlessly about how to use this data to make people see reason. Why the hell wouldn't they see reason anyway? Why aren't we out there, talking to these oppressed worlds, convincing them to join in our fight? If the chancellor is really so terrible, then why do we need this data? Why do we need a set of numbers to convince people to do the right thing when they can plainly see what's so wrong with this universe?" When she stopped, no one spoke up. Everyone was staring, she knew it, but it still felt good to finally have her say, even in the middle of an all-out assault.

"Hearts and minds are won differently than yours, human," said the remaining ikthian. She offered a half-smile to her and then Maia. "If the chancellor got her hands on this data you're talking about, there's nothing to be done about it." She extended her hand. "Maia Kalanis, I assure you we will not waste your talents if you come with us today. The rebellion needs you, needs all three of you, alive."

Taylor glanced from Maia to the new ikthian.

Finally, Maia spoke. "Who are you?"

"Elurin. Someone who's done a lot of harm and will always pay for it. I understand the fear of the Dominion turning you into a weapon. We won't let that happen." She bent down, taking one of the guns abandoned by the Seekers, and offered it to her with an outstretched arm. "Just come with us."

Maia nodded and took the weapon. "Very well." Together, they hurried back down the stairwell, leaving the bodies of the Seekers behind.

***

Odelle ducked her head to avoid another overhanging pipe. Everything around them was dark, and it smelled like sewage, but at least no one appeared to be following them. The rush of water beneath the grated floor drifted to her. She clutched Sorra's hand, following her lead since she couldn't see more than a few feet at a time. "Please tell me you know where we're going," she whispered.

"Of course I know where we're going. Who do you think had this escape route built?"

This didn't shock Odelle. Of course Sorra had built a secret tunnel near the control tower. If the station ever did fall under attack, she would need a way in and out to make sure the docking bays remained active. "You've been planning this for years, haven't you? You knew Tarkoht wouldn't be able to sustain a rebel base forever."

She could just make out Sorra nodding in the darkness. "I'm impressed we lasted as long as we did. And...thank you. For staying to help me."

"I didn't really help. I would have left if it weren't for..."

"But you're here, aren't you? You're crawling through who knows what with me instead of flying out of here on an escape pod. Why is that?"

Odelle sighed. It didn't feel like an appropriate time, but for all she knew, there could be another squad of Seekers waiting for them at the exit. She might not get another chance. "If you haven't figured it out by now, you're more dense than I thought."

Sorra froze, and Odelle waited for her to say something. But instead of turning toward her, she peered forward into the shadows. "Quiet," she mouthed. After a moment, Odelle heard footsteps coming toward them. It only sounded like one person instead of a squad, but that didn't mean they were friendly.

Finally, she made out the shape of a figure coming toward them. Sorra let out a sigh and let go of her hand, rushing forward to greet the intruder. "Joren! You made it down here. I wasn't sure if..."

"It wasn't hard. Most of the station is empty," Joren said. "Everyone is either dead or flying away."

Sorra smiled. "So they didn't manage to shut us down completely. Hopefully more of them will make it out. Any word on Kalanis and her friends?"

Joren didn't answer, and Odelle's heart sank. "Hopefully if you haven't found them, that means Taylor managed to get Maia off the station in time. We should do the same before the Dominion shuts down life support. Are there any escape pods left?"

"More than enough," Joren said. "The problem is getting there. The Seekers are still sweeping the station, searching for survivors. Most of them are probably near the exits."

"Well, we can't stay here and get caught," Sorra said. "If everyone else is dead or gone, we need to take our chances. The nearest exit is right up ahead."

"Get moving." Joren ushered them past him. "Most of the station is evacuated. I doubt the chancellor will wait much longer before scrapping us." They moved more quickly through the tunnel, stopping as the hall ended in a ladder. Odelle glanced up at the hatch and frowned.

"There's no way to defend ourselves if we head up this way," she said.

"Then I'll go first," Sorra said, grabbing a rung.

"Nonsense, I'll go." Joren grabbed the rung as well, trying to push Sorra out of the way.

"Dear heart, your sacrifice is too noble," Sorra growled, shoving back.

"Would you both stop it?" Odelle hissed. "You're wasting time." She shoved them both aside and clambered up the ladder, lifting the hatch at the top and peering down both ends of an empty hallway before clambering out. "Come on," she called down.

Sorra climbed out next, accepting Odelle's offered hand to hoist her out. She turned and lowered an arm to help Joren up. As he climbed the ladder, Odelle heard footsteps approaching from down the hall. Odelle, eyes widened in fear, met Sorra's gaze.

"Get out of here," Joren said. They both glanced at him as he retreated back down the ladder. "Close the hatch and get out of here! I'll find my way later."

"Joren, wait, you—" Sorra reached down to grab him but missed. In response, Odelle pulled her to her feet and kicked the hatch shut.

"We're leaving," she said, ignoring the glare Sorra shot her. "And no amount of your desire for self-sacrifice is going to stop that."

"Self-sacrifice? You think a squad of Seekers is going to destroy me?"

"Yes!" Odelle yanked her down another hall. "I think they're going to lose about half their squad, but ultimately, you'll die." She continued dragging Sorra along, relying on pure instinct to get to an escape pod. A sharp yell came from behind them, followed by the crisp, shattering sound of gunfire. Both of them shared a terrified look, but neither stopped running. A look of determination crossed Sorra's face, and Odelle knew she wouldn't turn back, however much she wanted to.

At last, they reached the escape pods. Sorra leaned against the wall and peered around the final corner. "Is it clear?" Odelle asked.

Sorra looked back and nodded. "Yes."

They made a dash for the escape pods just as an armored squad appeared at the other end of the hallway. The Seekers raised their weapons, but they were out of range. Odelle shoved Sorra into one of the last remaining escape pods and dragged the door shut behind her. The shouts and gunfire disappeared all at once, and everything became eerily silent.

"I can't believe we left him," Sorra said as they strapped themselves into their seats. Her soft, trembling voice seemed loud in the quiet pod. "I can't believe they..."

"Sorra, we don't have time," Odelle pleaded. "I don't know how to fly this thing. We need to get out."

"Right." Sorra slammed her hand on the eject button. The engine fired, and they blasted away from the station in a shudder of metal. As they launched into the darkness of space, Odelle saw a shimmering line trailing down the side of Sorra's cheek. Her breath hitched, and she had to swallow down a sob of her own when she realized it was one of the only times she had seen Sorra cry.

Chapter Twenty

"HOW MUCH FARTHER TO the docking bay?" Maia gasped as they sprinted down the hallway.

"Hundred yards," Akton huffed behind her. He ran abreast with Taylor, shooting glances back over his shoulder to make sure they weren't being followed. So far, they hadn't run into any more Seekers, but the lights above them flashed more urgently, and Maia was certain the soldiers would not be far behind. "We'll have to steal a ship if there are any left. There won't be enough pods for all of us."

"There were several abandoned ships when we came through," Elurin said. "They only fit two, but we could take—" They whirled around another corner and almost slammed into a fresh squad of Seekers.

The soldiers fired. Maia tried to throw herself to the ground, but a firm hand yanked her back. Elurin stood in front of her, absorbing a few of the rounds with her armor. Her body jolted backward, and Maia nearly fell to the floor in an effort to dodge as both of them stumbled backward. The hand on her shoulder squeezed tighter, dragging her around the corner. Taylor stood beside her, staring at her with terrified eyes. "Maia, run. Please, you have to."

"I'll hold them," Rachel said, aiming her weapon around the corner as Elurin crouched beside her. A shout came from the squad, and sparks ricocheted off the metal as the ikthians returned fire. After a moment, the noise faded as both groups ran for cover. "Taylor, get out of here. I'll keep the position and—"

"Take her," Taylor said. "Please, Rachel. She has to make it out."

"I'm not leaving without you," Maia said.

Taylor shook her head. "We're the only two they won't kill on sight. The Seekers will shoot the rest of them. I'll buy you time, then surrender."

Maia reached out, hand fumbling for Taylor's. She grasped it tightly, searching Taylor's eyes for some strand of hope, some reason to make her come with them. "Taylor, I..."

"You don't have to say it." She squeezed Maia's hand once and brought it to her lips. "I'll see you soon. You can tell me then. I promise." Taylor dropped her hand and looked to the others. "Get out of here, now." She ran around the corner, and Maia heard the sound of gunfire along with shouts to stop shooting. She swallowed a rising lump in her throat and forced tears back.

"Come on," said Akton, pulling her along. Maia tried to block out the fading sounds of the ikthians fighting Taylor. She kept hoping to hear the sound of footsteps. Hoping to see Taylor running after them, because she had somehow managed to beat an entire squadron. That never happened.

They arrived at a hangar, but only the smallest fighters were left. "We'll have to split up," said Elurin. She nodded toward the nearest ship. "Rachel and I will take off and provide a distraction. Akton, focus on getting out of here and to the secondary base. We'll rendezvous there."

They split up, Akton helping Maia into the nearest fighter. As she settled into the pilot's seat, he asked, "You know how to handle one of these?"

"Better than most," Maia said. She buckled her safety harness but felt nothing. Numb to all around her, her emotions especially. She started the engines as Akton scrambled to pull the cockpit doors shut. Sounds were muted. Her heart thudded but no pain came, just a quiet, seething anger. "Are you ready?"

Akton settled into his seat. She heard the click of his safety harness and saw Rachel and Elurin's ship take off. She followed after them, darting out of the hangar as fast as she dared. Akton yelled, his claws digging into the headrest of her own seat as he sought for something stable to grip. "Slow down, will you? We're going to attract attention."

Maia ignored him, sending the ship into a hard dive away from the space station, pulling up the navigation panel and passing it off to Akton. "Do something useful and give the coordinates for the warp drive."

As Akton fumbled with the navigation controls, Maia banked the ship away from an approaching squadron of fighters. They took a shot at their ship, and she pushed them into a sharp turn. She launched a volley of spitfire, catching the wings of half the fighters as they zoomed past.

"That will slow them down," said Akton.

Maia chose not to respond. She pushed the ship around to take another pass at the fighters. She opened fire, catching them by surprise. One ship lit the darkness with flame then was snuffed out in the vacuum of space. Another followed soon after. Their own ship rocked as a hit landed on their side.

"I think we need to get out of here," said Akton.

"Are the coordinates in?" Maia asked.

"Well, almost!"

"Keep working, then." Maia shot one of the passing ships down. Only two remained from the attacking squadron.

"How do you even do that?" Akton typed a way at the navigation panel.

"Calculations. Quick ones."

The navigation panel flickered in the cockpit. "Well, never let me get on your bad side while you're flying." She heard the confirmation sequence for the coordinates. "We're good to leave."

No. She veered to the right, aiming just above the station they had left behind. *No, we're not.* Taylor was still trapped on Tarkoht.

Maia's heart clenched. Part of her almost wished her lover was dead. A much worse fate awaited her if the Seekers succeeded in taking her to Daashu. She wasn't ready to let go. She found it difficult to imagine the future on most days. But without Taylor a bleak chasm loomed in her mind, a night sky with no stars to navigate by.

She clenched her teeth, biting back the words she had been too scared to tell Taylor. The words she should have said. The words she might now take to her grave. She flipped the last switch. The fighter blasted forward, and the cockpit settled into eerie stillness as the windows beside them blanked out.

***

"Where are we?"

Sorra picked her way across what little remained of their escape pod, gazing up at the sky. She saw no stars, no way to mark their location. "I'm not sure."

"What do you mean, you're not sure?" Odelle followed her, barely avoiding a pile of twisted, smoking metal. "Don't you know the planets near your own station?"

"Hey, I didn't pick where we landed." Sorra lifted her head, scanning the horizon. A clump of trees stood in the distance, but a high mountain range loomed over them. It didn't look familiar at first glance, but at least the planet supported life. "I'm just grateful the atmosphere is breathable and the crash didn't kill us. Getting lost is the least of our problems."

Odelle came forward to stand at her shoulder, and Sorra caught a glimpse of her hand reaching out. It withdrew before making contact. "I'm sorry about Joren. I know you didn't want to leave him."

"Don't apologize for things that aren't your fault," Sorra said flatly. Thinking about Joren made her sick to her stomach. Best-case scenario, the Seekers had given him a clean death. She couldn't bear to imagine the alternative. "So, what now? I'm thinking we salvage what we can from the ship, try to get communications up and running. The Seekers are out in full force around Tarkoht right now, but maybe we can get a message through to Nakonum. We're probably close enough."

"Probably?" Odelle asked. "Isn't there a way to know for sure?"

Sorra shook her head. Until they got part of the ship working for power or found someone to help them, they were stranded without any kind of map. She took a deep breath and clenched her hands into fists, attempting to hide her shaking. "Let's focus on the basics first. All the escape pods come with emergency rations. Maybe we can dig them out."

"In a second." Odelle's warm hand grabbed hers, and Sorra turned to look at her. But when she did, Odelle's expression wasn't anything like she imagined. She had expected fear, anger, and maybe hurt. Instead, she found something tender in Odelle's eyes. The rest of her plans faded. Suddenly, she remembered how grateful she was to be alive. Alive and still with Odelle. An hour before, those things hadn't been certainties. It was a miracle they had escaped unharmed. "You are the most stubborn ikthian in existence."

Sorra tried to offer a cocky grin, but the gesture felt forced. "Well, we both knew that already."

Odelle reached a hand to her face, cupping her cheek and rubbing her thumb over the skin in slow strokes. Sorra closed her eyes and breathed in. Some of the tension eased from her shoulders. "You are also kind beyond measure, a person with unquestionable morals, and someone I am very grateful to know." Odelle leaned up and placed a soft kiss on her lips, and she couldn't find it in herself to pull back.

***

Rachel groaned and slumped back in the navigator's seat. There wasn't much left to do while they waited for the warp to get them back to Nakonum, and she was beginning to feel restless. After checking the dash for what had to be the fiftieth time, she finally risked a glance over at Elurin. Grooves had formed in her normally smooth brow, and Rachel wondered if ikthians displayed stress the same way humans did. The more time she spent with Elurin, the more uncanny their similarities became.

"Are we in the clear yet?"

Elurin glanced over. "Now that's an interesting phrase. 'In the clear,'" she repeated with a small smile. "I suppose we are clear of more threats, at least for the moment." They sat together in silence for another minute. "So, was it worth finding Taylor?"

The question struck Rachel like a punch to the gut. "I..." She drew in a breath, trying to find her equilibrium again. "I'm still thinking about that. I came all this way to kill her. Then, I came to save her. And now, she's gone anyway."

Elurin nodded. "That is a fair answer." She stared out of the cockpit, watching the streaks of starlight blur into lines. "Do you know what will become of Taylor? Has your Coalition told you what happens to humans who are taken by the Dominion?"

"I don't really want to know." Rachel tried not to think about what effect her actions might have had on Taylor's capture.

"Then don't dwell on it," Elurin said. "You won't be any good if your thoughts stay with her."

"How can they not? She's my friend. I spent so long trying to hunt her down and drag her back to Earth. When I do find her, she gives up everything so I can live." Rachel shook her head. Tears threatened to spill over, but she fought to contain them. She did not want Elurin to see her this vulnerable. "I'm a horrible person."

In the soft light of the cockpit, Elurin reached out. If it had been a week ago, she might have flinched, certain she would be poisoned, bewitched, or worse. Instead, she allowed Elurin to grip her hand tightly.

"You are not horrible."

Their gazes met, and for a moment, Rachel forgot that she was looking at an ikthian. She was just Elurin, someone who had saved her life as much as Taylor had. She shook her head and sniffed, fighting to get herself under control. "I appreciate that, but I am. I need to make this right, though I can't ask you to come with me this time."

"You don't need to." Elurin released Rachel's hand. "We'll need resources, but Oranthis has those. I'm sure we can manage a small search and rescue. Maybe we can get to her before they take her to Daashu."

Rachel frowned at the strange word, but she didn't ask questions. The way Elurin had voiced the word both times made it clear it wasn't a pleasant place. Another question rose in her mind instead. "But why help me?"

Elurin gave her another small grin. "Gunning people down gets tiring, whether they're naledai or ikthian. It might be nice to save a life instead of taking one. And I've grown quite fond of you. I would hate to see you worry yourself into danger over this."

Rachel settled back in her seat. "Well, I think I've grown fond of you, too." The words sounded so natural. She shook her head again. When Hunt and the brass had exiled her, she had been certain she would end up dead. But here she was, alive, and even more unbelievably, she could now count an ikthian as her friend. Perhaps it wasn't such a wild stretch of the imagination, then, to think that they had a chance at rescuing Taylor.

"I'll find her again," she promised, turning to gaze back out through the viewport. "And then I'll tell the generals back on Earth to shove it. I've seen the galaxy, and it's nothing like what they told me."

***

Cold. Cold floors. Cold air. Cold everything. Taylor trembled as the pair of ikthian Seekers dragged her through what she assumed was the belly of a frigate. They had blindfolded her before bringing her on board, but she remembered walking up a gangplank. Her heart pounded despite her resolve to hide her fear from her captors. *I did it. I saved Maia.* That thought alone brought a smile to her lips.

Suddenly, pain split across the side of her face. She staggered at the blow, slamming her shoulder into a metal wall. "Quit smirking, human!" one of the ikthians growled beside her. But she couldn't help it, despite the pain. She had overheard her captors' ceaseless chatter about how the others had escaped. Maia and her friends were safe, so they had nothing to threaten her with.

Taylor fought the urge to smile again as they shoved her through yet another door. She landed hard on the ground, grunting from the impact. Her shoulder throbbed along with her face, but nothing else hurt too much. She did not bother to move as the minutes ticked by. Instead, she stayed in the dark, blindfolded and bound. The room sounded empty, but she did not trust the ikthians. They were probably waiting for her to try and stand. They would punish her swiftly for it, she knew. They had already developed a habit of kicking her in their brief time together.

Finally, someone spoke. "So, you're the alien that captured Doctor Kalanis' attention." Taylor wanted to turn toward the sound, but she controlled the impulse. She couldn't see through her blindfold anyway. "I must admit, there is something fascinating about lesser creatures. They always make such interesting cases for study." The voice was female, cold like everything else. "I know you can talk. We aren't that ignorant about your species." Rough hands gripped her shoulders and pulled her up into a kneeling position. "Well, human? Don't you have anything to say?"

Taylor refused to answer. She tried to keep her mind blank, her face neutral. She felt a hand on her face, and the blindfold was tugged away. She blinked against the harsh flood of light, and when her eyes adjusted, she saw the ikthian standing before her. She was tall, her silvery skin stretched over the severe lines that made up her face. Despite her formal dress and lack of armor, Taylor was certain this woman could kill her just as easily as the Seekers if she chose to do so.

"Who are you?"

The ikthian smiled. She seemed to like the fact she had provoked a response. "You may address me as Madam Chancellor, Taylor Morgan. We are going to get to know one another very well."

Without another word, she walked past Taylor and out of the room. She heard more footsteps. The door clanged shut, and Taylor finally looked around. She was alone in a windowless cell. Taylor closed her eyes and took a deep breath. Carefully, she settled back down on the hard floor. The Dominion could do whatever it wanted to her. Maia was safe. Nothing else mattered.

The End

About the Authors

Michelle Magly

Michelle Magly is a writer living in Alaska with her wife and fellow writer, Sy Itha. She has discovered that the frozen tundra makes excellent inspiration. Michelle has a short story, "Heart," featured in the 2012 Understory anthology from the University of Alaska, Anchorage.

Michelle co-authored her first novel with Rae D. Magdon, *All the Pretty Things* in 2013. Their second novel, *Dark Horizons* was released February 2014.

Chronicles of Osota - Warrior was released in July 2014. She is now working on the second book of the series *Thief. Chronicles of Osota – Warrior and Dark Horizons* were finalists in the 2014 Rainbow Award SciFi/Fantasy category.

When not writing, Michelle hikes, snowboards, skis, and plays a lot of video games.

Connect With Michelle Online
Facebook
Twitter
E-mail: mmagly@desertpalmpress.com

Rae D. Magdon

Rae D. Magdon is a writer living and working in the state of Alaska. She has coauthored three books with Michelle Magly, *All the Pretty Things* and *Dark Horizons*. *Starless Nights* marks their third collaboration.

The first book in the Amendyr series *The Second Sister*, was published in March 2014 and was soon followed with *Wolf's Eyes* published in August 2014. The third book of the series, *The Witch's Daughter* was released in April 2015. *Wolf's Eyes* and *Dark Horizons* were finalists in the 2014 Rainbow Awards SciFi/Fantasy category.

She enjoys writing fantasy and science fiction, in addition to modern-day romances. When she is not writing original fiction, she~~wastes~~ spends her time dabbling in ~~unapologetically smutty~~ romantic lesbian fanfiction. Her favorite fandoms are Law & Order: SVU and Mass Effect. In her free moments, which are few and far between, she enjoys spending time with Tory, her wonderful spouse, and their two cats.

Connect with Rae online
Website
Facebook (https://www.facebook.com/RaeDMagdon?fref=ts)
Tumblr
Email

Other Books by Rae D. Magdon

Amendyr Series

The Second Sister
ISBN: 9781311262042

ELEANOR OF SANDLEFORD'S entire world is shaken when her father marries the mysterious, reclusive Lady Kingsclere to gain her noble title. Ripped away from the only home she has ever known, Ellie is forced to live at Baxstresse Manor with her two new stepsisters, Luciana and Belladonna. Luciana is sadistic, but Belladonna is the woman who truly haunts her. When her father dies and her new stepmother goes suddenly mad, Ellie is cheated out of her inheritance and forced to become a servant. With the help of a shy maid, a friendly cook, a talking cat, and her mysterious second stepsister, Ellie must stop Luciana from using an ancient sorcerer's chain to bewitch the handsome Prince Brendan and take over the entire kingdom of Seria.

Wolf's Eyes
ISBN: 9781311755872

CATHELIN RAYBROOK has always been different. She Knows things without being told and Sees things before they happen. When her visions urge her to leave her friends in Seria and return to Amendyr, the magical kingdom of her birth, she travels across the border in search of her grandmother to learn more about her visions. But before she can find her family, she is captured by a witch, rescued by a handsome stranger, and forced to join a strange group of forest-dwellers with even stranger magical abilities. With the help of her new lover, her new family, and her eccentric new teacher, she must learn to gain control of her powers and do some rescuing of her own before they take control of her instead.

The Witch's Daughter
ISBN: 978131672643

Ailynn Gothel has always been the perfect daughter. Thanks to her mother's teachings, she knows how to heal the sick, conjure the elements, and take care of Raisa, her closest and dearest friend. But when Ailynn's feelings for Raisa grow deeper, her simple life falls apart. Her mother hides Raisa deep in a cave to shield her from the world, and Ailynn must leave home in search of a spell to free her. While the kingdom beyond the forest is full of dangers, Ailynn's greatest fear is that Raisa will no longer want her when she returns. She is a witch's daughter, after all—and witches never get their happily ever after.

Desert Palm Press

Written with Michelle Magly

Dark Horizons
ISBN: 9781310892646

Lieutenant Taylor Morgan has never met an ikthian that wasn't trying to kill her, but when she accidentally takes one of the aliens hostage, she finds herself with an entirely new set of responsibilities. Her captive, Maia Kalanis, is no normal ikthian, and the encroaching Dominion is willing to do just about anything to get her back. Her superiors want to use Maia as a bargaining chip, but the more time Taylor spends alone with her, the more conflicted she becomes. Torn between Maia and her duty to her home-world, Taylor must decide where her loyalties lie.

Desert Palm Press

All The Pretty Things (Revised Edition)
ISBN: 9781311061393

With the launch of her political campaign, the last thing Tess needed was a distraction. She had enough to deal with running as a Republican and a closeted lesbian. But when Special Agent Robin Hart from the FBI arrives in Cincinnati to investigate a corruption case, Tess finds herself spending more time than she should with the attractive woman. Things get a little more complicated when Robin begins to display signs of affection, and Tess fears her own outing might erupt in political scandal and sink all chances of pursuing her dreams.

Desert Palm Press

Other Books by Michelle Magly

Chronicles of Osota - Warrior
ISBN: 9781311834324

Alina knew that one day she would return to the heartland of Osota, even after eleven years of isolation. But how could she know her return to the capital would coincide with the arrival of young Warrior-in-training Senri? Beautiful and strong, Senri makes for a pleasant distraction from Alina's troubles. But as the prospective ruler of a nation, Alina can hardly devote time to pursuing a romance. As a new threat looms over the kingdom of Osota, she is left with little choice but to turn to Senri for help.

Cover Design By : Rachel George
www.rachelgeorgeillustration.com

Note to Readers: We have made every effort to edit this book. However, typos do slip in. If you find an error in the text, please email: lee@desertpalmpress.com so the issue can be corrected. We appreciate you as a reader and want to ensure you enjoy the reading process. Bright blessing.

Manufactured by Amazon.ca
Acheson, AB